The Twilight of the Souls

by

Louis Couperus

The Echo Library 2011

Published by

The Echo Library

Echo Library
Unit 22
Horcott Industrial Estate
Horcott Rd
Fairford
Glos. GL7 4BX

www.echo-library.com

Please report serious faults in the text to complaints@echo-library.com

ISBN 978-1-40689-691-6

THE TWILIGHT OF THE SOULS

by

LOUIS COUPERUS

Author of "Small Souls," "The Later Life," etc.

Translated by Alexander Teixeira de Mattos

New York

Dodd, Mead and Company

1917

THE BOOKS OF THE SMALL SOULS

By LOUIS COUPERUS

Translated by

ALEXANDER TEIXEIRA DE MATTOS

TRANSLATOR'S NOTE

This is the third of the novels known as *The Book of the Small Souls* and is by some considered the greatest of the series. Be this as it may—and I confess that personally I like *Small Souls* the best—it is, beyond dispute, one of the most masterly and striking stories that this generation has produced. It can be read separately and independently, but will be enjoyed more fully by those who are familiar with *Small Souls* and *The Later Life*. The series will conclude with the next volume, which, in the English version, will be entitled *Dr. Adriaan*.

ALEXANDER TEIXEIRA DE MATTOS

HARROGATE,

10 *August,* 1917

THE TWILIGHT OF THE SOULS

CHAPTER I

When Gerrit woke that morning, his head felt misty and tired, as though weighed down by a mountain landscape, by a whole stack of mist-mountains that bore heavily upon his brain. His eyes remained closed; and, though he was waking, his nightmare still seemed to cast an after-shadow: a nightmare that he was being crushed by great rocky avalanches, which he felt pressing deep down inside his head, though he was conscious that the red daylight was already dawning through his closed eyelids. He lay there, big and burly, sprawling in his bed, beside Adeline's empty bed: he felt that her bed was empty, that there was no one in the room. The curtains had been drawn back, but the blinds were still down. And, though he was awake, his eyelids remained closed and through them he saw only the red of the daylight as through two pink shells: it seemed as if he would never be able to lift those two leaden lids from his eyes.

This after-weariness flowed slowly through his great, burly body. He felt physically rotten and did not quite know why. The day before, he had merely dined with some brother-officers at the restaurant of the Scheveningen Kurhaus: a farewell dinner to one of their number who was being transferred to Venlo; and the dinner had been a long one; there was a good deal of champagne drunk afterwards; and they had gone on gaily to make a night of it. One or two of the married ones had refused, good-naturedly, but had come along all the same, so as not to spoil sport; Gerrit had come too, in his genial way. At last, he had decided that that was about enough and that the road which the others were taking was not his road: he was one of your sensible, moderate people, who never went to extremes; he was very fond of his little wife; indeed, he already felt some compunction at the idea of perhaps waking her at that time of night, when he went into the bedroom, after undressing. As a matter of fact, she did wake; but he had at once reassured her with his gruff, good-natured voice and she had gone to sleep again. He had stayed awake a long time, lying there with wide-open eyes angry at not being able to sleep, at having forgotten how to take a glass of wine with the rest. At last, in the small hours, when it was quite light, he had slowly dozed off into a misty dreamland; and gradually the mists had turned into solid landscapes, had become a stack of heavy mountains, which pressed heavily upon his brain until they crumbled down in rocky avalanches.

Now, at last, he shook off the strange heaviness, took his bath; and, when he saw himself naked—that expanse of clean, white skin, the great body built on heavy, sinewy lines, a good-looking, fair-haired chap still, despite his eight-and-forty years— he wondered that he sometimes had those queer moody fits, like a lady's lap-dog. And now, as he squeezed the streaming water over himself out of the great sponge, he tried to pooh-pooh those moody fits, shrugged his shoulders at them, muttering to himself as he kept on squeezing the sponge, squeezing out the water until it splashed and spattered all around him. He had the sensation of washing the inertia from him; he drew a deep breath, flung out his chest, felt his strength returning and, still naked, took his dumb-bells and worked away with them, proud of a pair of biceps that were like two rolling cannon-balls. His eyes recovered their usual jovial expression, which also played around his fair moustache with a roguish sparkle, as of inward mockery; the wrinkles vanished from his forehead, which was gradually acquiring a loftier arch as the crop of fair hair on his head diminished; and the blood seemed to be flowing normally through his big body, after the bath and the five minutes' exercise, for his cheeks, now shaved, became tinged with an almost pink flush. And he simply could not make up his mind to dress: he looked at himself, at his big, strong, clean body, which he kneaded yet once more, as proud of his muscles as a woman of her graceful figure.

Then he quickly put on his uniform and went downstairs to breakfast. The children surrounded him instantly; and he at once felt himself the father, full of a father's affection, passionately fond as he was of his children. He was only just in time to see Alex and Guy go off with their satchels: the school was close by and they went by themselves, two sturdy little fellows of nine and seven; but the other children, all except the eldest, Marietje, who was also at school, were eating their bread-and-butter at the round table, while Adeline sat in front of her tea-tray. And Gerrit, in the little dining-room, at the round table, felt himself become normal again, quite normal, because of his wife and his children.

The dining-room was small and very simply furnished, containing only what was strictly necessary. Adeline, now thirty-two, looked older: a plump little mother, with not much to say for herself, full of little cares for her little brood; and Gerrit, noisy and clamorous, filling the whole little room with the gay thunder of his drill-sergeant's voice, was full of incessant jokes and fun. There were half-a-dozen younger ones round the table: two girls, Adèletje and Gerdy; three boys: Constant, Jan and Piet; and the latest baby, a girl, Klaasje. Gerrit had given the youngest three their names, in his annoyance at the high-sounding names of the others: Alexander, Guy, Geraldine, christened after Adeline's family, while Marie and Constant were called after Mamma and Papa van Lowe.

"Look here, not so many of those grand names," Gerrit had said, when Jan was coming.

And, after Klaasje[1]—a name which the whole family considered hideous—Gerrit said:

"If we have another, it shall be called after me, Gerrit,[2] whether it's a boy or a girl."

"Gertrude, surely, if it's a girl?" Adeline had suggested.

"No," said Gerrit, "she shall be Gerrit all the same."

---

[1] Nicolette.

[2] Gerard.

Gerrit's manias were Mamma van Lowe's despair; but so far there had been no question of a grand-daughter Gerrit.

Gerrit had no favourites. His long arms swung round as many children as he could get hold of and he drew them on his knees, between his knees, almost under his feet; and by some miraculous chance he had never broken an arm or leg of any of them, so that Adeline and the children themselves were never afraid and only Mamma van Lowe, when she witnessed Gerrit's embraces, went through a thousand terrors. And to the children the joy of life seemed to be embodied in their father, a joy which they soon came to picture instinctively as a tall man, an hussar, with a loud voice and any number of jokes, a pair of high riding-boots and a clanking sword.

Gerdy was a tiny child of seven, who loved being petted; and, as soon as she saw Gerrit, she hung on to him, nestled on his knees, rubbed her head against the braid of his uniform, tugged at his moustache, dug her little fists into his eyes. Or else she would throw her arms round his neck and stay like that, quietly looking at the others, because she had taken possession of Papa.

This time too she left her chair, crept under the table, climbed on Gerrit's knees and ate out of his plate, although Adeline tried to prevent her. Gerrit ate his breakfast, with Gerdy on his lap; and the childish voices twittered all around him, like the voices of so many little birds. And this twittering produced a brightness in his heart, so that he began to smile and then to poke fun at Klaasje, the baby in her baby-chair, sitting beside him rather stupidly. Klaasje, who did not talk much yet, was still a little backward and just fretted and whimpered.

Latterly, he had felt a strange pitying tenderness when he looked at his children, as though surprised at all this dainty, flaxen life which he had created, he who had always said:

"Children are what you want; without children you have no life; without children nothing remains of you; children carry you on."

He had married, fairly late, a very young wife; and that had been the reason of his marriage, the root-idea: to beget children, as many children as possible, because it seemed to him a dismal thought that nothing of him should survive. And now, when he looked around him, now that Marietje, Adèletje and Alex were twelve and ten and nine, he sometimes had, deep down in his heart, a strange feeling of wonder and pity, even of sadness, as though the thought had suddenly come to him:

"Where do they all come from and why are they all round me?"

A strange, wondering astonishment, as though at the riddle of childbirth, the secret of human life, which suddenly became impenetrable to him, the father and husband. Then he would give a furtive glance to see if he could discover that same wondering astonishment in Adeline; but no, she quietly went her way, the gentle, fair-haired little mother, the domesticated little wife, very simple in soul and limited in mind, who had quietly, as a duty, borne her husband her fair-haired children and was bringing them up as she thought was right. No, he noticed nothing in her and he was the more surprised, because, after all, she was the mother and therefore ought really to have felt that strange thrill of wonder even more than he did.

"And all these are my children," he thought.

And, while he boisterously tickled Gerdy and pretended to eat up Klaasje's bread-and-butter, like the great tease that he was, he thought:

"Now these are all my children and Adeline's children."

And he was filled with wonder as he saw them around him, the pretty, flaxen-haired children: the wonder of an artist at his work, wonder such as a sculptor might feel on contemplating his statue, or a writer reading his book, or a composer listening to his melodies, a simple, wondering astonishment that he should have made all that, a wondering astonishment at his own power and strength.

And then, in the midst of his astonishment, he suddenly grew frightened, frightened at having heedless begotten so much life simply because he had been depressed by the thought that, if he had no children, nothing of him would survive after his death. Yes, they would survive him now, his children, his flaxen-haired little tribe, his nine; life would scatter them, the little brothers and sisters who were now all there together like little birds in the nest of the parental house, sheltered by father and mother; and what would they be like, what would their life be, what their sorrow, what their joy, when he himself, their father, was old or dead? He was afraid; a terror shot through him strangely enough at that breakfast-table where he sat eating with Gerdy out of one plate and teasing little Jan with his jokes, which made the boy crow aloud. And the strangest thing to him was that no one should suspect what he was thinking, that it was hidden from them all, from Adeline, from his mother, his brothers and sisters, because in appearance he was a great robust fellow, a sort of Goth, a civilized barbarian, with his flaxen head and his white, sinewy body, devoted to sport and racing, revelling in his work as an officer; outwardly almost commonplace, with his solid, healthy normality; loud of voice, a little vulgar in his jests, even exaggerating his noisiness and vulgarity out of a sort of bravado, an instinctive desire to hide his real self. Yes, that was it: he hid himself, he was invisible; nobody saw him, nobody knew him: not his wife, nor his family, nor his friends; nobody knew him in those strange fits of giddiness and faintness which suddenly seemed to empty his brain, as though all the blood were flowing out of it; nobody knew the secret of his temperateness, the hidden weakness that would not even allow him to take two glasses of champagne without that horrible congestion at his temples which made him feel as if his head were bursting; nobody, not even the wife at his side, knew of that heavy, oppressive nightmare which came to him when, after lying awake for hours, he dozed off, that nightmare of piled-up mountains and rocky avalanches weighing upon his brain; nobody knew of his fears and anxieties about his children, while outwardly he was the gay, jovial father, "a healthy brute," as some of his brother-officers had called him.

Sometimes, he had silently thought of the designation and smiled at it, because he knew himself to be neither a brute nor healthy. Gradually, almost mechanically, he had gone on showing that unreal side, posing successfully as the strong man, with cast-iron muscles and a simple, cast-iron conception of life: to be a good husband, a good father and a good officer; while inwardly he was gnawed by a queer monster that devoured his marrow: he sometimes pictured it as a worm with legs. A great, fat worm, you know; a beastly crawling thing, which rooted with its legs in his carcase, which lived in his back and slowly ate him up, year by year, the damned rotten thing! Of course, it wasn't a worm: he knew that, he knew it wasn't a worm, a worm with legs; but it was just like it, you know, just like a worm, a centipede, rooting away in his back. Then he felt himself all over, proud notwithstanding of his sound limbs, his well-trained, supple muscles, his youthful appearance, though he was no longer so very young; and then it seemed to him incomprehensible that it could be as it was, that that confounded centipede could keep worrying through those limbs, at those muscles, right into the marrow of his strong body. Nothing on earth would ever have induced him to see a doctor about it: he took walking-exercise, horse-exercise, rode at the head of his squadron; and the brazen blare of the trumpets, the dull thud of the horses' hoofs, the sight of his hussars—his lads—would make him really happy, would make him forget the confounded centipede for a morning. As he sat his horse, with head erect, twisting his fair moustache above his curved lip, a burly, straight-backed figure, he would say to himself:

"Come, get rid of all those tom-fool ideas and be a man—d'ye hear?—not a nervy, hypochondriacal girl. You and your centipede! Rot! I just had a peg yesterday; and that, damn it, is what I mustn't do: no peg at all, not one!... Perhaps not even any wine at all ... and then not more than one cigar after dinner.... But, you see, giving up drinking, giving up smoking: that's the difficulty...."

Gerrit had just finished his breakfast and was putting little Gerdy down, when there was a violent ring at the front-door bell. Adeline gave a start; the children shouted and laughed:

"Ting a-ling, ting-a-ling, ting-a-ling!" cried little Piet, mimicking the sound with his mug against his plate.

"Hush!" said Adeline, turning pale. She had seen Dorine through the window, walking up and down outside the door excitedly, waiting for it to be opened. "Hush, it's Auntie Dorine.... I do hope there's nothing wrong at Grand-mamma's!..."

But now the maid had opened the door and Dorine rushed into the room excitedly, perspiring under her straw hat, with a face as red as fire. She was in a furious temper; and it was impossible at first to make out what she said:

"Just think ... just think...."

She could not get her words out; the passion of rage seething inside her made her incapable of speaking; moreover, she was out of breath, because she had been walking very fast. Her hair, which was beginning early to turn grey, stuck out in rat-tails from under her sailor-hat, which bobbed up and down on her head; her clothes looked even more carelessly flung on than usual; and her eyes blinked with a look of angry malevolence, a look of spite and discontent gleaming through tears of annoyance.

"Just think ... just think...."

"Come, Sissy, calm yourself and tell us what's the matter!" said Gerrit, admonishing her in a good-natured, paternal, jovial fashion.

"Well then—just think—that horrible creature came to Mamma first thing this morning ... and made a scene...."

"What horrible creature?"

"Why, are you all deaf? I'm *telling* you, I began by telling you: Miss Velders, the creature who keeps the rooms where Ernst lives ... came and made a frightful scene ... and upset Mamma awfully ... and Mamma sent for me. Why me? Why always me? What can I do? I'm not a man! Why not Karel? Why not you? ... Oh *dear* no: Mamma of course sent for *me!*... Off I went to Mamma's, found Mamma quite ill, that horrible creature there.... Then I went off with Miss Velders ... first to Karel's ... but Karel was absolutely indifferent ... a selfish pig, a selfish pig: that's what Karel is.... Miss Velders had to go home.... Then I went off to Ernst ... and, when I had seen him, I came on to you.... Gerrit, you're a man ... you know about things, you know what to do; I'm a woman ... and I do *not* know what's to be done!"

Her voice was now a wail and she burst into tears.

"But, Sissy, I don't yet know what's happened!" said Gerrit, quietly.

"Why, Ernst, I'm telling you ... Ernst, I'm telling you...."

"What about him?"

"He's mad!"

"He's mad?"

"Yes, he's mad!... He wanted to go out into the street last night: he's mad!..."

Adeline had rung for the nurse, who took the children away.

"He's mad?" Gerrit repeated, passing his hand over his forehead.

"He's mad," Dorine repeated. "He's mad. He's mad."

"Oh, well," said Gerrit, in a vague, conciliatory tone, "Ernst is always queer!"

"But now he's mad, I tell you!" Dorine screamed, in a shrill voice. "If you don't believe me, go and see him. Don't you see, something's *got* to be done! I, I don't know what. I'm a woman, do you hear, and I'm utterly unnerved myself. Why didn't Mamma send for you at once? Why me? Why *me?* And Karel ... Karel is a nincompoop. Karel at once said that he had a cold, that he couldn't go out. Karel? Karel's a nincompoop.... A cold, indeed! A cold, when your brother's gone mad all of a sudden!..."

"But, when you say mad ... is he really mad?" asked Gerrit, doubtfully.

"Well, go and see him for yourself," said Dorine, fixing her irritated gaze full on Gerrit. "You go and see him for yourself; and, when *you've* seen him as *I've* seen him ... then you won't ask me if he's mad...."

"All right," said Gerrit. "I'll go at once. I must look in at barracks first and then...."

"Oh, you must look in at barracks first," said Dorine, angrily. "Of course you must look in at barracks first. And then, if you have a moment to spare...."

"I can go from here," said Gerrit, dejectedly. "Are you coming?"

"I?" screamed Dorine. "Do you think *I'm* going back with you? No, thank you. I've told Mamma, I've told you and now I'm going home to bed. For, if I'm not careful and go trotting about wherever you send me, I shall go off my head myself.... I? I'm going to bed...."

She rose, walked round the table, sat down again; and suddenly her voice changed, tears of pity came into her eyes and she wailed:

"Poor Mamma! She's quite ill.... What an idea of that horrible creature's, to go running straight to Mamma. Why frighten her like that? Why not first have told one of us?... I'll just go round to Constance ... and to Adolphine: then they can console Mamma a bit.... You call in at Paul's on your way: he may be able to help you, if there's anything to be done.... But, after that, I'm going home to bed."

"Yes," said Gerrit, "I'll go now."

And then at once he began to hesitate: ought he not to go to barracks first? Should he go first to Paul ... or straight to Ernst? He went into the passage, strapped on his sword, put on his cap. Dorine followed him out:

"So you're going to him? Well, when you've seen him ... you won't ask me again if he's mad."

And she made a rush for the front-door.

"Dorine...."

"No, thank you," she said, excitedly. "I'm going to Constance; to Adolphine ... and then ... then I shall go home to bed."

She had opened the door and, in another moment, she was gone. Gerrit saw Adeline weeping, wringing her hands in terror:

"Oh, Gerrit!"

"Come, come, I don't expect it's so bad. Ernst has always been queer."

"I shall go to Mamma, Gerrit."

"Yes, darling, but don't make her nervous. Tell her that I'm on my way to Ernst and that I don't believe he's so bad as all that. Dorine always exaggerates and she hasn't told us what Ernst is like.... There, good-bye, darling, and don't cry. Ernst has always been queer."

He flung his great-coat over his shoulders, for the weather was like November, cold and wet. Outside, the pelting rain beat against his face; and he saw Dorine ahead of him, wobbling down the street under her umbrella, with that angry, straddling walk of hers. She turned out of the Bankastraat on the left, into the Kerkhoflaan, on her way to Constance. He took the tram and, in spite of the rain, stood on the platform, with his military great-coat flapping round his burly figure, because he was stifling, as with a painful congestion, and felt his veins, surfeited with blood, hammering at his temples:

"That confounded champagne last night!" he thought. "I don't feel clear in my head.... I'd better go to Paul first.... Yes, I'd better go to Paul first.... Or ... or shall I go straight to Ernst?..."

He did not know what to decide and yet he had to make up his mind while his tram was going along the Dennenweg, for Ernst lived in the Nieuwe Uitleg. But, because he did not know, he remained on the tram, on the platform, with his back bent under the pelting rain; and it was not until he reached the Houtstraat that he jumped down, his sword clanking between his legs.

Paul lived in rooms above a hosier's shop. Gerrit found his brother still in bed:

"Ernst is mad," he said, at once.

"He's always been that," replied Paul, yawning.

"Yes, but ... it appears that he's absolutely mad now," said Gerrit.

He felt so seedy and heavy-witted that he could hardly speak: his swollen tongue lolled between his teeth. However, he told Paul about Dorine's visit:

"We must go on to Ernst, Paul, and see how much there is in it."

Paul was listening now:

"Ye-es," he drawled. "But I must dress myself first. You see, the curious thing about this world is that, whatever happens, we have first to dress ourselves...."

"I was dressed," laughed Gerrit.

"Oh, really!" said Paul, amiably. "Well, that was lucky."

There was a note of sarcasm in his tone which escaped Gerrit, in his dull condition.

Paul, stretching himself, decided to get up. And for a moment he remained standing in front of Gerrit, in his pink pyjamas:

"Do you think Ernst is really mad?" he asked.

"Perhaps it's not so bad as that," Gerrit ventured.

"Everybody is a little mad," said Paul.

"Oh, I say!" said Gerrit, in an offended voice.

"No, not you," said Paul, genially. "Not you or I. But everybody else has a tile loose. I'm going to have my bath."

"Don't be long."

"All right."

Paul disappeared in his little bathroom; and Gerrit, who was suffocating, flung open the windows, so that the bedroom suddenly became filled with the patter of the summer rain. And Gerrit looked around him. He had hardly ever been here, at Paul's; and he was now struck by the exquisite tidiness of the rooms. Paul had a bedroom, a sitting-room and a dressing-room in which he had installed his tub.

"What a tidy beggar he is!" thought Gerrit and looked around him.

The bedroom was small and contained nothing but a brass bedstead, a walnut looking-glass wardrobe, a walnut table and two chairs. There was not a single object lying about. The pillows on the bed showed just the faintest impress of Paul's head; the bed-clothes he had thrown well back, when he got up, very neatly, as though to avoid creasing them.

Gerrit heard the ripple of water in the dressing-room. It was as if Paul were squeezing out the sponge with exquisite precaution, so as not to splash a single drop outside his tub. The bath lasted a long time. Then all was silence.

"Can't you hurry a bit?" cried Gerrit, impatiently.

"All right," Paul called back, in placid tones.

"What are you up to? I don't hear you moving."

"I'm doing my feet."

"My dear fellow, can't you get on a bit faster? Or shall I go on?"

"No, no, I wouldn't miss going with you. But I must get dressed first, mustn't I?"

"But can't you make haste about it?"

"Very well, I'll hurry."

There came a few sharp, ticking sounds as of scissors and nail-files that were being put down on the ringing marble. Gerrit breathed again. But, when everything became silent once more, Gerrit, after an interval, cried:

"Paul!"

"Yes?"

"Will you soon be ready now?"

"Yes, yes, but don't be impatient. I'm shaving. You wouldn't have me cut myself?"

"No, of course not. But we must look sharp: you don't know what sort of state Ernst may be in."

Paul did not answer; and Gerrit heard nothing more, except the swish of the rain. He heaved a deep sigh, moved about restlessly, stretching out his long legs. After some minutes, which seemed hours to Gerrit, Paul opened the door, but closed it again at once:

"Gerrit, will you please shut the window!" he cried, angrily.

Gerrit fastened the window; the rain no longer pattered into the room. Paul now came in: he was in a sleeveless flannel vest and knitted-silk drawers; a pair of striped socks clung tightly to his ankles; his feet were in slippers.

"Good Lord, my dear chap, have you only got as far as that?" asked Gerrit, irritably.

Paul looked at him, a little superciliously:

"No doubt you fling yourself into your uniform in three minutes; but I can't do that. Since one *has* to dress one's self and can't just shake one's feathers like a bird, I at least want to dress myself with care ... for otherwise I feel disgusting."

"But do remember ... if Ernst...."

"Ernst won't go any madder than he is because I dress myself properly and keep you waiting a quarter of an hour longer. I can't dress any quicker."

"Because you don't choose to!"

"Because 'I don't choose to?'" retorted Paul, pale with indignation. "Because I don't choose to? Because I *can't*. I can't do it. Do you want me to go as I am? In my drawers? Very well; then send for a cab. I'll go like this, just as I am. But, if you want me to dress myself, you must have a little patience."

"Oh, all right!" Gerrit sighed, wearily. "Oof! Get on with your dressing."

Paul opened a door of his wardrobe. Gerrit saw his shirts lying very neatly arranged, coloured shirts and white shirts. Paul stood hesitating for a moment, looked out of the window at the rain and at last selected from the coloured stack a shirt with black stripes. He put the stack straight and hunted for his studs in his jewel-case.

"How much longer will you be?" asked Gerrit.

"Ten minutes," said Paul, lying angrily, though he was inwardly delighted to make Gerrit lose his temper.

He found a set of niello studs and links that went well with the black-striped shirt and deliberately and neatly put them into the front and cuffs.

Gerrit rose impatiently and walked up and down the room. Through the open partition-door, he saw the bathroom and was surprised to find everything tidied up, with not a drop of water anywhere.

"Do you do your wash-hand-stand yourself?" asked Gerrit, in amazement.

"Of course," said Paul, who was now getting into his shirt. "Did you think I left that to the servant? Never! She has nothing to do but empty my slop-pail. I do my tub, my basin, my soap-trays, everything myself. I have separate cloths for everything: there they are, hanging on a rail. The world is dirty enough as it is, however tidy one may be."

"In that case," said Gerrit, astounded, "you haven't been so long after all!"

"It's method," replied Paul, airily, though secretly flattered by Gerrit's remark. "When you have method, nothing takes long."

And, basking in Gerrit's praise, he rang, while pulling on his trousers, and told the maid to bring his breakfast:

"I'll only take a hurried bite," he said, amiably, just bending the points of his stand-up collar at the tips.

Then he picked out a tie, in a large Japanese box.

"By Jove, what a number of ties you have!"

"Yes, I have a lot of them," said Paul, proudly. "They're my only luxury."

And in fact, when the maid pushed back the folding-doors, revealing the sitting-room, which Paul, loathing other people's furniture, had furnished himself, in addition to his other two rooms, Gerrit was struck with the plainness of it: comfortable, but exceedingly simple.

"I adore pretty things," said Paul, "just as much as our mad Ernst. But I can't afford them: I haven't the money."

"Why, you have the same income that he has."

"Yes, but he doesn't dress. To dress yourself well is expensive."

Paul's dressing was now finished; and he had turned up the bottoms of his trousers very high, showing nearly the whole of his well-cut button-boots. He merely drank a cup of tea, ate a piece of dry bread.

"Butter's so greasy," he said, "when you've just brushed your teeth."

And he went back to his bathroom to rinse his mouth once more.

He was ready now, took his umbrella and followed Gerrit down the stairs. Gerrit opened the door.

"What beastly weather!" growled Paul, furiously, in the passage.

He drew his umbrella carefully out of its case, while Gerrit was already outside, with his blue military coat flapping round his shoulders, because he had not put his arms through the sleeves.

"What a filthy mess!" raved Paul. "This damned, rotten mud!" he cursed, pale with rage.

He had folded up the umbrella-case and slipped it into his pocket and was now opening his umbrella: he seemed to fear that it would get wet.

"Come on!" he said, seething with inward rage.

And, taking a desperate resolve, he stepped aside, fiercely slammed the front-door and carefully placed his feet upon the pavement:

"We'll wait for the tram," he said.

He glared at the rain from under his umbrella:

"What a dirty sky!" he grumbled, while Gerrit paced up and down, only half-listening to what Paul said. "What a damned dirty sky! Dirty rain, filthy streets, mud, nothing but mud. The whole world is mud. Properly speaking, everything is mud. Heavens, will the world ever be clean and the people in it clean: towns with clean streets, people with clean bodies? At present, they're mud, nothing but mud: their streets, their bodies and their filthy souls!..."

The tram came and they had to get in; and Paul, in his heart of hearts, regretted this for, as long as he had stood muttering under his umbrella, he could still yield to his desire to go on raving, even though Gerrit was not listening. They got out in the Dennenweg; but by this time he had lost the thread of his argument and moreover he had to be careful not to step in the puddles:

"Don't walk so fast!" he said, crossly, to Gerrit. "And mind where you walk: it's all splashing around me."

They were now in the Nieuwe Uitleg. That ancient quarter was quite dark, soaked in the everlasting rain that fell perpendicularly between the trees, like curtains of violet beads, and clattered into the canal.

"Do you think he's really mad?" asked Gerrit, nervously, as he rang the bell.

Paul shrugged his shoulders and looked down at his trousers and boots. He was satisfied with himself; he had walked very carefully: he had hardly a single splash. A fat landlady opened the door:

"Ah!... I'm glad you've come, gentlemen.... Meneer is quite calm now.... And have you been to a doctor?"

"A doctor?" said Gerrit, startled.

"A doctor," thought Paul. "Just so: we've been practical, as usual."

But he didn't say it.

They went upstairs. They found Ernst in his dressing-gown; his black hair, which he wore long, lay in tangled masses over his forehead. He did not get up; he gazed at his two brothers with a look of intense melancholy. He was now a man of forty-three, but seemed older, his hair turning grey, his appearance neglected, as though his shoulders had sunk in, as though something were broken in his spinal system. He did not appear very much surprised at seeing the two of them; only his sad eyes wandered from one to the other, scrutinizing them suspiciously.

And all at once the two brothers did not know what to say. Gerrit filled the room with his restless movements and nearly knocked down a couple of Delft jars with the skirts of his wet great-coat.

Paul was the first to speak:

"Aren't you well, Ernst?"

"I'm quite well."

"Then what is it?"

"What do you mean?"

"What was the matter with you last night?"

"Nothing. I was suffocating."

"Are you better now?"

"Yes."

He seemed to be speaking mechanically, under the influence of the last glimmer of intelligence, for his voice sounded uncertain and unreal, as though he were not quite conscious of what he was saying.

"Come, old chap," said Gerrit, with good-natured bluntness, laying his hand on Ernst's shoulder.

As he did so, Ernst's expression changed; his eyes lost their look of intense melancholy and became hard, staring hard and black from their sockets, like two black marbles. He had turned his head in a stiff quarter-circle towards Gerrit; and the hard gleam of those black marbles bored into Gerrit's blue Norse eyes with such strange fierceness that Gerrit started. And, under his brother's big hand, which still lay on his shoulder, Ernst's limp body seemed to be turned to stone, to become rigid, hard as a rock. He stiffened his lips, his arms, his legs and feet and remained like that, motionless, evidently suffering physical and moral torture, shrinking under the pressure of Gerrit's hand, without knowing how to get rid of that pressure. He remained motionless, stark; every muscle was tense, every nerve quivered; Ernst seemed to shrink and harden under Gerrit's touch just as a caterpillar shrinks and becomes hard when it feels itself touched. As soon as Gerrit removed his hand, the tension relaxed and Ernst's body huddled together again, as though something had given way in the spinal system.

"Ernst," said Paul, "wouldn't you do well to get some sleep?"

"No," he said, "I won't go to bed again. There are three of them under the bed."

"Three what?"

"Three. They're chained up."

"Chained up? Who's chained up?"

"Three. Three souls."

"Three souls?"

"Yes. The room's full of them. They are all fastened to my soul. They are all riveted to my soul. With chains. Sometimes they break loose. But I was dragging two of them with me for ever so long yesterday, in the street, over the cobble-stones. They were in pain, they were crying. I can hear them now in my ears, crying, crying.... There are three under the bed. They're asleep. When I go to bed, they wake up and rattle their chains. Let them sleep. They are tired, they are unhappy. As long as they're asleep, they don't know about it.... I ... I can't sleep. I haven't slept for weeks. They only sleep when I'm awake. They're fastened to me.... Don't you hear them? The room is full of them. They belong to every age and period. I've gathered them around me, collected them from every age and period. They were hiding in the jars, in the old books, in the old charts. I have some belonging to the fourteenth century. They used to hide in the family-papers. The first moment I saw them, they rose up, the poor souls ... with all their sins upon them, all their past. They are suffering ... they are in purgatory. They chained themselves on to me, because they know that I shall be kind to them ... and now they refuse to leave me. I drag them with me wherever I go, wherever I stand, wherever I sit. Their chains pull at my body. They hurt me sometimes, but they can't help it.... Last night ... last night, the room was so full of souls that there was a cloud of them all round me; and I was suffocating. I wanted to go out, but the landlady and her brother prevented me. They are a miserable pair: they would have let me die of suffocation. They are a pair of brutes too: they tread on the poor souls. Do you hear ... on the stairs? Do you hear their feet? They are treading on the souls...."

Paul's face was white; and he said, nervously trying to change the subject:

"Have you seen Dorine this morning, Ernst?"

Ernst looked at his brother suspiciously:

"No," he said, "I have not seen her."

"She was here, wasn't she?"

"No, I haven't seen her," he said, suspiciously; and his eyes wandered round, as though he were looking for something in the room.

The two brothers followed his gaze mechanically. Everything about the large, comfortable sitting-room suggested the man of taste and culture, of quiet and introspective temperament, but acutely sensitive to line and form. The sombreness of the ceiling, wall-paper and carpet stood out against the yet greater sombreness of old oak and old books; and a very strange note of blue and other colours was struck in the midst of it all by the pottery, which was not all old, but included some examples of more recent art. The modern harmonies of line and the very latest discoveries in earthenware suddenly appeared with their weird flourishes in vases, jars, pots, like enamelled flowers, from modern conservatories, that had sprung up in the shadows of some old, dark forest. On the book-shelves too, the brown leather bindings of the ancient folios were relieved by the direct contact of the yellow wrappers of the latest French literature or the *art-nouveau* covers of the most modern Dutch novels. This lonely, silent man, who walked shyly through the streets, gliding along the walls of the houses; who had no friends, no acquaintances; who only on Sunday evenings— because he dared not stay away, from a last remnant of respect for maternal authority—consented to suffer martyrdom among the assembled members of his family, even to the extent of taking a hand at bridge: this man seemed, hidden from every one of them, to lead a rich, abundant life, a secret, inner life, a life not of one age but of many. Because he never spoke, they looked upon him as a crank; but he had lived his years abundantly. Had he filled his silent, uncompanioned loneliness too full with the ghosts of literature, history and art? Had the ghosts loomed up and come to life around him, in that dark and gloomy room, where the old and modern porcelain and earthenware glowed and rioted around him with the haunting brilliancy of their colours and glazes, of their tortured, gorgeous curves and outlines?

The two brothers, who had come because they thought their brother mad, looked round the room; and to both of them the room also seemed mad. To the captain of hussars, whose earlier depression had passed off, who suddenly felt himself becoming healthy and normal again as he listened to his eccentric brother's ravings, the room became a demented room, because it lacked a trophy of arms, riding-whips, prints of horses and dogs and the oleograph of a naked woman, bending backwards and laughing. To the other brother the room also seemed demented because here the vase was no longer an ornament, because the vase had become a morbid thing, like a many-coloured weed, growing in rank profusion among the dark shadows of the curtains and oak book-cases. To Paul the room seemed demented because there was dust on the books and because the basket full of torn paper had not been emptied. But to both of them the man Ernst himself seemed more demented than the room: the man Ernst, their brother, an eccentric fellow whom for years they had been compelled to think "queer" because he was different from any of them. When he confessed to them that his room was full of souls, souls that hovered round him like a cloud until he was on the point of suffocating, souls that chained themselves to him and rattled their chains, they thought that he was raving, that he was stammering insane words. It was the view of both of them, the view of normal, healthy men, outwardly sane in their senses, in their gestures, expression and language, because their gestures, expression and language did not clash with those of the people about them, whatever they might sometimes feel deep down in themselves. But to the man himself, to Ernst, his own view was the normal, the very ordinary view; and he thought his two brothers Gerrit and Paul queer and eccentric because he was able, in his furtive way, to see that neither of them noticed anything of the innumerable souls, though these writhed so pitifully and thronged so closely around him, as though he were in purgatory. To him there was nothing mad or insane in his room, in his words, or in any part of him. He looked upon them as mad, he looked upon himself as sensible. When, last night, he tried to go out in his nightshirt, because the souls pressed upon him until he felt as if he were suffocating in the throng, he had simply wanted air, nothing but air, had wanted to breathe without the discomfort of clothes, coat or waistcoat, upon his chest; and he had thought it quite natural that he should go downstairs with a candle and try to open the door with his key. Then the fat landlady and her lout of a brother had heard him and had come upon him, making a great to-do with their silly hands and their loud voices; and the two, the fat landlady and her lout of a brother, had stood there shouting and gesticulating like a pair of lunatics while he had already loosened the chain from the front-door and felt the draught doing him so much good, because it blew upon his bare flesh under his flapping shirt. Then Ernst had become angry, because the fat landlady and her lout of a brother did not listen to what he said: he had a soft voice, which could not cope with the rough, loud, vulgar voices of people without feeling, of people without soul, knowledge or understanding. He had become angry, because the brother, the coarse brute, had locked the door again, dragged him away, hauled him up the stairs; and he had struck the brother. But the brother, who was stronger than he was, had hit him, hit him on the chest, which had been bursting before and at that had become still worse, because all the souls had thronged against him in terror, beseeching him to protect them. And, roughly, rudely, like the unfeeling brutes that they were, the fat landlady and her lout of a brother had dragged him upstairs between them; and, as they dragged him, they had trodden not only on his bare feet but also on the poor souls! Their vulgar slippers, their clumsy, caddish feet had trodden on the poor, poor tender souls, trodden on them in the passage and along the stairs; and he heard them panting and sobbing, so loudly, so loudly, in their mortal anguish, that he could not understand why the whole town had not come running up in sheer alarm, to see the poor souls and help them. Oh, how they had moaned and gnashed their teeth, oh, how they had sobbed and lamented, most terribly!

And nobody had come. Nobody would hear. They had refused to hear, those townsfolk; no rescue had arrived; and the two brutes, that fat landlady and that wretched cad of a fellow, her brother, had hauled him along, up the stairs, into his room, had flung him in, locked the door behind him and barricaded the door on the outside. And in the passage, caught in the front-door, on the landing, caught in the door of his room, lay the poor panting, sobbing souls; they lay trodden and trampled, as if a rough crowd had danced on those tender gossamer beings, on their frail bodies; and he had spent the whole night sitting on a chair in a corner of his room, shivering in his nightshirt, in the dark, listening to the lamentations of the souls, hearing them wring their hands, hearing them pray for his pity, for his commiseration, for they knew that he loved them, that he would not hurt them, the poor souls.... He understood, yes, he understood that those two brutes, the woman and her brother, thought that he was mad. But he had only wanted to breathe the cool night-air, to feel the cool night-air blowing over his hot limbs, which were all aglow because, in bed, the souls pressed so close upon him, though he tried to push them softly from him. It wasn't mad, surely, to want a breath of fresh air, to want to feel the cool air blowing over one's self. That was all he wanted.... And, in the morning ... yes, he had seen her at the door, opening it very carefully. He had seen the face of his sister Dorine that morning, seen her grimacing and laughing and cackling, with a devilish grin, glad, she too, at the sight of the frail bodies of the poor souls lying trampled on the stairs and in the passage; but he had been clever: he had remained sitting in his shirt, in the corner of his room, and pretended not to see her and taken no notice of her devilish grin, so as not to satisfy her evil pleasure.... Then at last the poor souls that still lived had settled down: he had lulled their fears with gentle words of consolation. Then they had fallen asleep around him; and he had been able to get up softly, without rattling their chains, and wash his face, put on his trousers, his socks, his dressing-gown.... What were his brothers doing now? He knew, he knew: no doubt they were also thinking, like the landlady and her beast of a brother, that he was mad, mad, bereft of his senses. But it was they who had lost their senses: they had no eyes, not to see the slumbering souls that filled the house; they had no ears, not to hear the plaint of the souls last night ringing through the universe. They, they were mad: they knew nothing and felt nothing; they lived like brute beasts; and he hated them both: that big, burly officer and the other, that fine gentleman, with his smooth face and his moustache like a cat's whiskers, which he couldn't stand, which he simply could not stand. Somehow, he had had to tell them about the poor souls; but, now that he saw that they were mad, he would never mention the souls to them again: otherwise they would be sure to want to beat him too and pull him about and tread on the poor souls, as those two horrible brutes had done.

So he remained sitting quietly, waiting for them to go and leave him to himself, in the peaceful solitude to which he was accustomed. For he was tired now; and, sitting straight up in his chair, he closed his eyes, partly to shut out the sight of his brothers' faces. Around him lay the souls, countless numbers of them, but they were still and silent, slumbering around him like children, though their faces were wrung with all the grief and pain that they had been made to suffer the night before.

Gerrit and Paul had stood up, were pretending to look at the vases, talking in whispers:

"He is pretty calm," said Gerrit.

"Yes, but what he said was utter nonsense."

"We must go to a doctor."

"Yes, we must go to Dr. van der Ouwe first. Perhaps to Dr. Reeuws afterwards, or any other nerve-specialist whom Van der Ouwe recommends."

"What do you think of him? Is he absolutely mad?"

"Yes, mad. He never used to talk in that incoherent way. Up to now, he was only queer, dreamy, eccentric. Now he is absolutely...."

"Mad," Gerrit completed, in a low voice.

"Look, he's shut his eyes...."

"He seems calm."

"Yes, he's calm enough."

"Shall we go?"

"Yes, let's go."

They went up to Ernst:

"Ernst...."

"Ernst!"

He slowly raised his heavy eyelids.

"We're off, Ernst, old chap," said Gerrit.

Ernst nodded his head.

"We shall be back soon."

But Ernst closed his eyes again, yearning for them to go, driving them out of the room with his longing....

They went. He heard them shut the door softly, carefully. Then he nodded his head with satisfaction: they were not so bad, they had not waked the souls.... He heard them whispering on the landing, with those two beasts, the landlady and her brother. He got up, crept to the door, tried to listen. But he could not make out what they said.

Then he laughed contemptuously, because he thought them stupid, devoid of eyes, ears, heart or feeling:

"Wretched brutes, infernal brutes!" he muttered fiercely, clenching his fists.

A mortal weariness stole over him. He went to his bedroom, let down the blinds and got into bed, feeling that he would sleep.

All around him lay the souls: the whole room was full of them.

CHAPTER II

Old Mrs. van Lowe's neighbours thought it a funny thing that, after dinner that evening, the whole family arrived, one after the other, rang the bell and went in, though it was not Sunday. Except on those "family-group" Sundays, there was never much of a run on Mrs. van Lowe's door. And they wondered what could be the matter; and, as it was very warm, an August day, they opened all the windows, kept looking across the street and even sent their maids to enquire of Mrs. van Lowe's maids. But the maids did not know anything: they only thought it must be something to do with the young mevrouw, the one in Paris—Mrs. Emilie, as they called her—who had gone off with her brother.

"It's very queer about the Van Lowes," said the neighbours, looking out of window at the old lady's front-door, at which somebody was ringing again for the hundredth time.

"There come the Van Saetzemas."

"And here are those fat Ruyvenaers."

"What's up?"

"Yes, what can be up?"

"The servants say it's something to do with Emilie."

"A nice thing for the Van Ravens!"

"They say that Bertha has become quite childish, don't they?"

"I don't know about that: she just sits staring in front of her. They never come now: they're living at Baarn."

"Here are the Van der Welckes."

"Like aunt, like niece."

"Now they're all there."

"All?"

"Yes, I've seen them all. Captain van Lowe and his wife, Paul, Dorine and Karel."

"And Ernst?"

"He hasn't come yet."

"But then he doesn't always come."

"I wonder what's up."

"Yes, I wonder."

"There must be some scandal with Emilie."

"And, when you think of what the Van Naghels used to be.... Such big people!"

"And now...."

"Absolute nobodies...."

"Oh, I think they're rather nice people!..."

"Yes, but they're all a bit touched, you know."

"Well, suppose we go to Scheveningen?..."

"Yes, let's go to Scheveningen. We may hear there what's happened...."

"Yes ... about Emilie, you know...."

And Mrs. van Lowe's neighbours went off to Scheveningen, with the express object of hearing what had happened about Emilie....

Old Mrs. van Lowe was sitting in the conservatory, with the windows open, and crying gently, like one who was too old to cry violently, whatever the sorrow might be. Uncle Herman, Aunt Lot, all the children had come in gradually, their faces blank with utter dismay; and they were moving like ghosts about the large, dark rooms, where no one had thought of having the gas lit.

"Herman!" the old lady cried, plaintively.

Uncle Ruyvenaer and Aunt Lot approached.

"Have you seen him, Herman?" asked the old lady, wringing her old, knotted hands.

"No-o, Marie. But I ... I shall go to him to-morrow ... with Dr. van der Ouwe."

"And who is with him now?"

"A male nurse, Mamma," said Gerrit. "We've seen to everything. He's quite calm, Mamma dear, he's quite calm. It won't be very bad. It's only temporary: it'll pass, the doctor said."

Cateau's bosom suddenly loomed through the open doorway of the conservatory:

"Oh, Mam-ma," she said, "how *sad* ... about Ernst! Who would ever have im-a-gined ... that Ernst would become ... like *this*!"

And she bent over her mother-in-law and gave her a formal kiss, like the kiss of a stranger paying a visit of condolence.

"And how are you, Mamma?" asked Karel, as though there were nothing the matter. "I hope you're not suffering from the heat."

The old woman nodded dully, pressed his hand.

"All that I ask," said Adolphine, addressing her husband, Paul, Dorine and Adeline, "is that you will not talk about it. Don't talk about it to outsiders. The less it's talked about, the better pleased I shall be.... We have that Indian lack of reserve in our family, that habit of at once going and telling everybody everything.... If people ask, we can say that Ernst has had a nervous break-down; yes, that's it: let's arrange to say that Ernst has had a nervous break-down...."

She asked them to give her their word; and they promised, in order to keep her quiet.

"You'll see," she said, "this business with Ernst will mean that Van Saetzema will once more fail to get elected to the town council."

Paul looked at her in stupefaction, failing to grasp the logic of her remark. Then he said, calmly:

"Yes, you see funny things happen sometimes."

"Yes," said Adolphine, nodding her head to show how much she appreciated the fact that Paul understood her. "It's horrid for *me*: you'll see, Van Saetzema won't get in...."

"I believe that Ernst ... is the sanest of the lot of us!" thought Paul.

And, as he moved to a seat, he first looked to make sure that there were no bits of fluff on the chair.

But Constance had come in; and, when the old lady saw her, she half-rose, threw herself into her daughter's arms and began to sob more violently than she had done. It was strange how she had gradually come to look upon Constance once more as the nearest to her of her children, this daughter whom she had not seen for years and years, until at last Constance had returned to Holland and the family. As a mother, she had never had a favourite; yet she would often, for months at a time, feel drawn now more towards the one, then again towards the other. She was growing old, she was getting the broken look which a mother's face begins to wear as she sees sorrow coming into her children's lives: a sorrow which, in her case, arrived so late that by degrees the illusion had come to her that there would never be any sorrow. The sudden break-up of Bertha's house—that house which she was so fond of visiting, because she found in it the continuation of her own life, the reflection of her own past grandeur—had fallen on her as a painful blow: Van Naghel's sudden death; the sort of apathy into which Bertha had sunk; the divorce between Van Raven and Emilie after Emilie had refused to come back from abroad, preferring to stay in Paris with her brother Henri, who had been sent down from Leiden: a divorce obtained in the face of all the persuasion which Uncle van Naghel, the Queen's Commissary in Overijssel, had brought to bear upon them; Louise living with Otto and Frances, in order to help Frances, who was always ailing, with the children, so that Bertha was living alone with Marianne in her little villa at Baarn, now that Frans had taken his degree and gone to India, while Karel and Marietje were at boarding-school. The big household had broken up, in a few months, in a few days almost; and the old grandmother, whose dearest illusion it had always been to keep everything and everybody close together, had been seized with an innocent wonder that things could happen so, that things had happened so.... She no longer went about, finding a difficulty in walking; and, because Bertha had become so apathetic and had also ceased to go about, she had as it were lost Bertha and all who belonged to her. It had produced a void around her which nothing was able to fill, even though she saw Constance every day. A void, because with none of her other children did the old lady find the same atmosphere of rank and position which she had loved in the Van Naghels' ministerial household. She would often complain now, a thing which she never used to do: she would complain that Karel and Cateau were so selfish, so stiff and Dutch, that they were getting worse every year; she would complain that at Gerrit's the children were always so noisy, that Adeline was unable to manage them, that both Gerrit and Adeline were much too weak to bring up so many children—nine of them—with proper strictness; she would complain that Adolphine was growing more and more envious and discontented, because her husband did not make his way, because Carolientje was not married, because the three boys were so troublesome; she would complain of Dorine and Paul and had all sorts of little grievances against both of them. Then, on the Sunday evenings, when the children and grandchildren came to her, she felt the void which Van Naghel and Bertha had left behind them, missed the sound of a few aristocratic names, missed any reference to the Russian minister in her children's conversation; and, with a little half-bitter laugh, she would say to the Ruyvenaers that the family was no longer what it had been, called it a *grandeur déchue* and took a melancholy pleasure in the phrase, which she would repeat again and again, as though finding consolation in its gentle irony. And Constance had become the child towards whom she felt most drawn in these dreary days, because Constance devoted herself regularly to her old mother and also because she, Mamma, in her secret heart, loved to talk with Constance about Rome, about De Staffelaer even, about the Pallavicinis, the Odescalchis, whom Constance had known in the old days; because Constance, whatever might be said against her, was connected with the best Dutch families; because Constance had a title; because Addie was the only one of her grandchildren who bore a title, good family though the Van Naghels were. Oh, those grandchildren, whom she now saw so seldom! And, now that the terrible thing had befallen Ernst, the terrible thing which the children had at first wished to conceal from her, but which she had guessed nevertheless, because she had so long feared it, feared it indeed from the time when Ernst was a tiny child—oh, what frightful convulsions he used to have as a child!—now that the terrible thing had befallen Ernst, it was Constance in whose arms she was first able to sob out her grief, in whose arms she first felt how sorely she had been stricken in her declining days:

"Connie," she cried, her voice broken with sobs, "Connie darling, it's true!... Ernst ... Ernst is *mad*!"

And the word which no one had yet uttered to her, though she had guessed what they meant, rang shrill through the fast-darkening room, in which every whisper was suddenly hushed in terror at the shrill sound of the old woman's high-pitched voice. Silence fell upon everything; and the word sent a shudder through the room. The children looked at one another, because Mamma had uttered the word which none of them had spoken, though they had thought it silently. The word which Mamma uttered so shrilly, almost screaming it at Constance, in the intolerable pain of her sorrow, struck them all with a sudden dismay, because, coming from Mamma's lips, it sounded like an open acknowledgment of what they all knew but did not wish to acknowledge except among one another, in great secrecy. They would merely say that Ernst was suffering from a nervous break-down, nothing more. A nervous break-down was such a comprehensive term! Anybody could go to a home for nervous patients for a rest-cure. But the word uttered by Mamma to Constance in shrill acknowledgment of the truth had cut through the dim room, where no one had even thought of lighting the gas. Adolphine, Cateau, Karel, Uncle Ruyvenaer, Floortje and Dijkerhof exchanged sudden glances, terrified, struck with dismay, because they would never have been willing to utter the word aloud, in open acknowledgment of the truth.

Aunt Lot's loud "Ah, *kassian!*"[3] now came from a corner of the dark room; and Toetie was so much upset that she suddenly burst into sobs. That was your Indian lack of self-restraint again, thought the Van Saetzemas and Cateau; and it did not seem to them decent to let yourself go like that, it made them feel that the business was a hopeless one. But the door opened and the two doctors entered, groping their way in the darkness: the old family-doctor, a retired army-surgeon, Van der Ouwe; and Reeuws, a young nerve-specialist. At their entrance, Toetie, abashed, ceased her sobbing. The doctors had come from the Nieuwe Uitleg, where they had left Ernst reading peacefully, with the male nurse, a stolid, powerful fellow, in an adjoining room. And, when the brothers and sisters crowded round the two doctors, the older began, quietly:

"Our poor Ernst can't stay where he is, all by himself. We must see and get him to Nunspeet, at Dr. van der Heuvel's: that will do him good ... the country, change of environment, nice, quiet people, who will look after him...."

"Nunspeet?" asked Adolphine. "That's not...?"

"No," said the old doctor, decisively, understanding what she meant. "It's not."

And he did not speak the word, left it to be implied, the word that must not be uttered, the terrible word that denoted the house of shame, the family-disgrace.

"It's a nice, pleasant villa, where Dr. van der Heuvel minds a few nervous patients," he said, calmly and kindly, casting a glance round at the brothers and sisters; and his grey head nodded reassuringly to all of them.

They admired his tact; and they the more readily condemned Mamma's shrill word, which had cut through the darkness and made them shudder, they the more readily condemned Aunt Lot's exclamation and Toetie's outbreak of sobbing.

And, breathing again, they lit the gas, suddenly noticing that the room was pitch-dark now that the two doctors had gone to Mamma and were telling her quietly that it would be all right and that Ernst was just a little overstrained from being too much alone and poring too long over his dusty books.

---

[3] Malay: "Poor dear!"

CHAPTER III

Constance went to the Nieuwe Uitleg next morning; the landlady, shaking her head, let her in; Dr. van der Ouwe met her in the passage:

"I thank you for coming, mevrouw. It won't do for Ernst to remain here any longer; I should like to take him down to Nunspeet, with one of you, as soon as possible, to-morrow. But it won't be an easy matter ... poor fellow!"

"I'll do my best," said Constance, doubtfully.

"Then I'll leave you alone with him. You won't be nervous? No, you're not nervous. He's quite quiet, poor fellow. Don't be afraid: I shall be near."

Constance went upstairs, with her heart thumping in her breast. She tapped softly at the door and received no answer:

"Ernst!" she called; and her voice was not very steady. "Ernst...."

But there was no reply.

She slowly opened the door. The door-handle grated into her very soul; and before entering she asked once more:

"Ernst.... May I come in?"

He still did not answer and she walked into the room. She had made up her mind to smile at once, to come up to him with a smile, so that the expression of her face might put her poor brother at his ease. And so she smiled as she entered, looking for him with kindly eyes, as though there were nothing at all out of the common.

But her smile seemed to freeze on her lips when she saw him sitting huddled in a corner of the room, in a flannel shirt and an old pair of trousers, with his long hair hanging unkempt. Nevertheless she controlled herself and said, in as natural a tone as she could command:

"Good-morning, Ernst. I've come to see how you are."

He looked at her suspiciously from his corner and asked:

"Why?"

"Because I heard that you were not well. So I thought I would see how you were getting on."

"I'm not ill," he said, in a low voice.

"Why are you sitting in that corner, Ernst? Are you comfortable there?"

"Ssh!" he said. "They're asleep. Don't speak too loud."

"No. But I may talk quietly, mayn't I, Ernst?... Can't you get up from your chair? For there's no room there to sit beside you. Come, dear, won't you get up?"

And she smiled and held out both her hands to him.

He smiled back and said:

"Ssh! Don't wake them."

"No, no. But do get up."

He gave way at last and, grasping her hands warily, allowed her to pull him up, out of his corner, and once more said, earnestly:

"You must promise me not to wake them. All my visitors wake them, the brutes! The doctor woke them too."

"No, Ernst, we'll let them sleep. There, it's nice of you to have got up. Shall we sit down here?"

"Yes. Why have you come? You never come to see me...."

There was in his words an unconscious reproach that startled her. It was quite true: she never came to see him. Since that first time, eighteen months ago, when he had asked her to his rooms on her return to Holland, the day when she had lunched here with him, when he had toasted her with two fingers of champagne out of a quaint old glass, she had never once been back. She reproached herself for it now: she, who did feel all that affection for her family, why had she left that brother to himself, as all the others did, just because he was queer? If she had overcome that vague feeling of distaste, almost of repugnance; if she had felt for him always as she suddenly felt for him now, perhaps he would not have been so self-centred, perhaps he would have retained his sanity.

"No, Ernst," she confessed, "I never came to see you. It wasn't nice of me, was it?"

"No, it wasn't nice of you," he said. "For I'm very fond of you, Constance."

Her heart began to fail her. Her breath came in gasps; her eyes filled with tears. She put her arm over his shoulder and, without restraining her emotion, she cried:

"Did we all leave you so much alone, Ernst?"

"No," he said, quietly, "I am never alone. They are all of them around me, always. There are some of every century. Sometimes they are magnificently dressed and sing with exquisite voices. But latterly," mournfully shaking his head, "latterly they have not been like that. They are all grey, like ghosts; they no longer sing their beautiful tunes; they weep and wail and gnash their teeth. They used to come out into the middle of the room ... and laugh and sing and glitter. But now, oh, Constance, I don't know what they suffer, but they suffer something terrible ... a purgatory! They crowd round me, they suffocate me, till I can't draw my breath.... Hush, there they are, waking again!..."

"No, Ernst, no, Ernst, they're asleep!"

He turned to her with a knowing laugh:

"Yes," he whispered, "you are kind, you love them, you are sorry for them ... you let them sleep ... you don't wake them...."

And they sat quietly together for a moment, without speaking, she with her arm round his shoulder.

"What a lot of pretty things you have, Ernst!" she said, looking round the room.

"Yes," he said, "I collected them ... gradually, very gradually. There was one in every piece."

"Ernst," she said, gently, "perhaps it would be a good thing if you went to the country this summer."

At once he seemed to stiffen and shrink under her touch, as though all his limbs were becoming tense and stark:

"I won't leave here," he said.

"Ernst, it would be so good for you. Do you know Nunspeet?"

She felt him go rigid; and he looked at her angrily and harshly:

"The doctor wants to get me to Nunspeet," he answered, craftily. He laughed scornfully: "I know all about it. You people think I'm mad. But I'm not mad," he went on, haughtily. "You people are stupid: stupid and mad is what you are. You see nothing and hear nothing, you with your dull brute senses; and then you just think, because some one else sees and hears and feels, that he's mad ... whereas it's you yourselves who are mad. I shall stay here; I won't go to Nunspeet."

But suddenly he grew alarmed and asked:

"I say, Constance, you won't force me, surely? You won't beat me? That beastly cad down below, that fellow, that cad: he hit me ... and woke them ... and trod on them! He stood treading on them, the great fool, the blockhead!... Tell me, Constance, you will leave me here, won't you?"

"No, Ernst, no one wants to force you. But it would be a good thing if you went to Nunspeet."

"But why? I'm all right here."

"You would be among kind people ... who will be fond of you."

"No one has ever been fond of me," he said.

"Ernst!" she cried, with a sob.

"No one has ever been fond of me," he repeated, bluntly. "Not Mamma ... nor any of you ... not one. If I had not had all of them ... oh, if I had not had all of them! My darlings, my darlings! Oh, what can be the matter with them? Now they're waking up! Now they're awake! Oh, listen to them moaning! Oh dear, listen to them screaming! They're screaming, they're yelling! ... *Is* it purgatory? Oh, dear, how they're crowding round me! They're stifling me, they're stifling me!... Oh dear, it's more than I can bear!"

He rushed to the open window; and she was afraid that he wanted to throw himself out, so that she caught him round the body with both her arms. The old doctor came in. He shut the window.

"I can do nothing," she murmured to the old man, in despair.

"Yes, you can," said the doctor, calmly. "Yes, you can, mevrouw."

"You are all of you my enemies," said Ernst. "My enemies and theirs."

And he went and sat in his corner, huddled up, with his arms round his knees.

"Go away," he said, addressing both of them.

"I'm going, Ernst," said the old doctor. "But Constance may as well stay."

He sometimes called her by her Christian name, the old doctor who had brought them into the world in India; and to Constance it was touching, to hear that name from under his grey moustache; it called up those old, old days.

"Constance can stay?"

"Very well," said Ernst.

The doctor left them alone: the nurse would be on his guard.

"Ernst," said Constance, "suppose we went together ... to Nunspeet?"

"Why? Why?" he asked, vehemently. "I'm all right here.... And we can't take them with us there," he whispered, more gently. "Ssh! You're waking them."

"It will be quieter for them, perhaps, if you leave them here, dear," she said, kneeling on the floor beside him, feeling for his hand, with her eyes full of tears.

"No, no ... that woman's brother down there ... that cad...."

"But, Ernst," she said, more firmly, with her eyes on his, "dear Ernst, do let me tell you: they don't exist. They exist only in your imagination. You must really get rid of the idea: then you will be well again, quite well.... Ernst, dear Ernst, they don't exist. Do look round you: there's nothing to see but the room, your furniture, your books, your vases. There's nothing else, except our two selves.... Oh, Ernst, do try to see it: there's nothing.... That you feel as if you were suffocating comes from always being so much alone, never going out, never walking. At Nunspeet, we will walk ... on the heath, over the dunes ... and then you will get quite well again, Ernst.... For, honestly, you are ill.... There's nothing here, nothing. Look for yourself: there's only you and I ... and your furniture and books...."

He quietly let her talk; an ironical smile curled round his lips; and at last he gave her a glance of pitying contempt, gave a little shrug of his shoulders. Then he softly stroked her hand, patted it gently, in a fatherly manner:

"You are kind and nice, Constance, but," shaking his head, "you have no sense! I believe you mean what you say, but that's just it: you're narrow, you're limited. You don't see, you don't hear," putting his hand to his eyes and ears, "what I see, what I hear with my eyes and my ears...."

"But, Ernst, you must surely understand that those are all illusions. The doctor says that they are hallucinations."

He continued to smile, looked at her with his contemptuous pity, looked hard out of his black Van Lowe eyes.

"They are hallucinations, Ernst."

"And you?"

"No, I'm not."

"And the room, the books, the vases?..."

"No, they are not. They are all around you, they exist."

"Well ... and why not all of them, the souls?"

"They don't exist, Ernst. They are hallucinations."

He just closed his eyelids, smiled, shrugged his shoulders, to convey that he was utterly at a loss to understand such exceedingly limited perceptions. Then he said, gently and kindly:

"No, Constance dear, you're not clever ... if you mean all you say. I believe you do mean it, but that's just it: you live like a blind person; you don't see, you don't hear. That's the way you all of you live and exist, in a dream, with closed eyes and deaf ears. You none of you see, hear or understand anything. You know nothing. You are as unfeeling as stones. You can't help it, Constance, but it's a pity, for you are so nice. There might have been something to be made of you, if you had learnt to see and hear and feel. It's too late now, Constance. You are stupid now, like all the rest; but I'm sorry, for you are very nice. Your hand is soft, your voice is soft; and you did your best not to tread on my poor darlings ... and not to drag them away on their chains, which are riveted so fast to my heart that they hurt me sometimes, here!"

He put his hand to his heart. A weariness came over her brain, as though she were exhausting herself in the effort to speak and to give understanding to an intelligence and a soul which remained very far away, miles away, and which her words could only reach through a dense cloud of darkness. And suddenly that sense of weariness and impotence became crueller and harder within her: it was as though she were talking to a stone, to a wall; she felt her own words beating back against her forehead like tennis-balls striking the wall.

"But, Ernst," she tried once more, "won't you come to Nunspeet with me ... to please *me*, to walk on the heath with *me*? You would be giving me such immense pleasure. It would be good for *me*...."

"And all of them, here, around me?..."

He pointed round the room, cautiously.

"We will leave them to sleep here."

"And that cad, downstairs?..."

"He sha'n't interfere with them, I promise you.... We'll lock up the room, Ernst, and they shall sleep peacefully."

She humoured him, not knowing if she was doing right, but feeling too tired to convince him.

"You promise?" he asked, suddenly. "You promise that they shall sleep peacefully?"

"Yes."

"That the cad downstairs won't wake them and tread on them?"

"Yes, yes."

"You promise that?"

"Yes."

"We'll lock up the room very quietly?"

"Yes."

"And nobody at all will come in?"

"No."

"You promise that?"

"Yes."

"Will you swear it?"

"Yes, Ernst."

"All right, then."

"Will you come?" she cried, rejoicing and unable to believe her ears.

"Yes. Because you would so much like to go for walks ... on the heath. You're nice...."

He spoke gently, pityingly; and his contempt was not as great as it had been, for he looked upon her as a nice but stupid child that needed his help and his protection.

She smiled at him in return, stood up where she had been kneeling beside him, put out her hands to him, inviting him to get up from his corner also. He let her pull him up; he was a heavy weight: she drew him out of his corner like a lump of lead.

"Then we start to-morrow, Ernst?"

He nodded yes, good-naturedly: she was very nice ... and she was longing for those walks ... and she was so weak, so stupid, she knew nothing, saw, heard and felt nothing, absolutely nothing. He must help her and guide her and support her.

"And shall we pack a trunk now, while I am here?"

He did not understand that a trunk was necessary: he looked at her blankly; but he wanted to please her and said:

"All right. But don't make a noise."

The doctor returned.

"He's coming," she whispered. "We're going to pack his trunk."

The doctor pressed her hand. Ernst looked down upon them both, smiling, as upon poor, unfortunate people who cannot help being so stupid ... so slow of understanding ... so limited in their knowledge ... so dull of perception....

And, while Constance and the doctor opened the clothes-press in his bedroom, he warned them, quietly, but with dignity:

"Ssh! Be careful, you know. Don't let the door of the wardrobe creak. Don't wake them!..."

CHAPTER IV

It was a sultry summer morning and old Mrs. van Lowe sat at the conservatory-window, crying very quietly. She had been crying incessantly now for two long days. After her first sob in Constance' arms, she had sobbed no more; but since then her tears had flowed continually, salt, stinging tears that burned her wrinkled cheeks. She sat with her hands folded in her lap; and from time to time she nodded her head up and down, while she stared at the leafy garden, over which the stormy sky hung dark and heavy as lead. Now and then she cleared her throat, now and then heaved a deep sigh; and her handkerchief was soaked with the tears that kept on flowing, quietly, out of her smarting eyes. Constant fretting had drawn down the corners of her mouth into two long, sad wrinkles. Oh yes, it was very hard! Trouble ... always trouble ... her life had been full of trouble: trouble when Louis and Gertrude had died at Buitenzorg, poor children; what had they not suffered from fever and cholera? Money troubles: an expensive household to be kept up on limited means. Trouble again, terrible trouble with dear Constance; and the heavy trouble of her husband's illness and death: he had never recovered from Constance' disgrace; more trouble over Van Naghel's death, the great change in Bertha and the break-up of the whole household; and now there was this last sore trouble with her son, her poor son, who had gone mad! Oh, if it had only happened a little earlier, when she was younger, she could have borne it, as she had borne the rest, could have accepted it as her natural share, a mother's share of trouble. But she was so old now; and it seemed to her that the supreme trouble was drawing near, a trouble which was coming very late in her life, too late for her to bear it with strength and patience, now that she was growing older and feebler daily; and her only wish had been to see her big family happy together, that great family of children, grandchildren and great-grandchildren, amongst which she had always rejoiced to live, thankful as she had been for that great blessing. It was as though a presentiment were coming to her from very far, from very far out of those heavy, lowering skies, a presentiment which her nerves, sharpened by age, suddenly not only felt but saw coming like a menace, as old people will suddenly see the truth very clearly, the future: a waning lamp which suddenly flickers up brightly, before dying out in darkness; a bright flicker which suddenly reveals the shadows in the room and in which the portraits grin, with faces that seem to speak ... before the lamp dies out, before everything is swallowed up in the black darkness! Oh, the awful presentiment which suddenly approached like a spectre out of the leaden clouds, that filled the whole vista before her eyes with grey terrors; the presentiment that this trouble, the greatest of all, was going to strike her most, now, in her old, old age, when she no longer had the strength to endure it, when she would sink under the weight of it!... O God, why should it now, why now, fall with such pitiless, crushing weight? Why now? Was it not enough that one of her children ... had gone mad, surely the most terrible thing that can happen? Was not that enough? What more could be threatening, looming before her, now that she was growing so feeble? See, did not her old hands tremble at the mere thought, was not her whole helpless body shaking, were not the tears flowing until they smarted in the furrows of her wrinkles and until her handkerchief was just a wet rag? What more could there be coming?

"O God, no more, no more!" she prayed, automatically, believing, in her feeble despair, in the great, infinite Omnipotence which is so very, very far removed from us ... and which she had always worshipped decently, once a week, in church ... formerly ... when she still went out. "O God, no more, no more!"

It was greater, the infinite Omnipotence, than what they worshipped in church; it filled everything far and wide, to the utmost limits of her thought; and it terrified and dismayed her: she saw it threatening from afar; and why, why now? Oh, why had it not all come earlier, when she would have had more fortitude, when she would have borne everything as her natural share, a mother's share, of trouble?... She would have been so glad just now to grow old peacefully, amongst her wide circle of children, grandchildren and great-grandchildren. But, alas, there was so much to bear and ... perhaps there was still more coming!

"O God, no more, no more!" she implored: was it not enough that one of her children ... had gone mad, surely the most terrible thing that can happen?

She moaned in spirit, then felt a little eased as the rain began to patter heavily on the expectant leaves and the lightning flashed and the thunder rolled and the sky was rent asunder. But the tears kept flowing in spite of her relief that the rain had come at last; and, because of the thunder which filled her fast-aging ears, she did not hear the door open softly, did not hear some one come through the drawing-room and approach the conservatory, did not at once see the slender little figure that stood quietly before her, solicitous not to intrude upon the grief of the weeping old woman.

"Granny," the younger woman said, gently.

The old woman looked up in surprise, blinked her eyes, tried to see through the flowing tears, did not recognize the one who called her granny:

"Eh?" she said, plaintively. "Who is it?"

And the girl did not answer at once, because it had given her a shock to see those silent tears flowing down the cheeks of that lonely old woman. She remained standing quietly, a pretty, almost fragile little figure, like a Dresden-china doll, but a very up-to-date doll, like a sketch by one of the ultra-modern French draughtsmen, with the pointed little face below the elaborately-waved hair under the very large hat, a hat which, in the shape of its crown and the sweep of its feathers represented the very latest extreme of fashion and consequently attracted immediate attention in Holland, in these dignified rooms, while the light tailor-made costume looked too dressy for a summer morning at the Hague and a touch in every accessory—the sunshade, the tulle boa—proclaimed that the young woman was no longer of the Hague and of Holland, short though the time was since she had run away.

The old woman, still sensitive in all social matters, remained looking at Emilie a little suspiciously, failing to recognize her and at once noticing, just by those touches—the large hat, the tulle boa—the exaggeration that displeased her.

"But who is it?" she repeated, wiping her eyes to see better.

And now the pretty little doll knelt down beside her and said:

"Don't you know me, Granny? It's I ... Emilie."

"Oh, my child!" cried the old woman, brightening up, glad, delighted. "Is it you, Emilietje? And Granny who didn't know you again!... But then you've got such a big hat on, child. And Eduard: how is he and where is he?"

"But, Granny!..."

Under the arm which she had at once put round Emilie, the old woman felt a shudder pass through the dainty little doll, who had knelt down beside her so impulsively and affectionately; but she did not understand:

"Well, where is Eduard?"

"Why, Granny," cried Emilie, "you know that we're divorced!"

The old woman now shuddered in her turn and closed her eyes and sat rigid. What was this? Was she becoming old, like her old sisters Christine and Dorine, who always muddled up all the children, who never knew anything correctly about their big family? What was this? Was she getting confused? And was this the first time that she had utterly forgotten things ... or had it happened before, that she had doted like an old, old woman?

She opened her eyes sadly and the tears ran down her cheeks:

"Ah, Emilietje, my child, my child ... don't be cross with Granny! She's growing old, dear. She had forgotten it for a moment. Yes, yes, she had forgotten all about it.... Of course, child, you got a divorce. Oh, it's very sad! You oughtn't to have done it so soon, you should have gone on being patient. You see, child, a divorce in a family is always a very sad thing. You know, there was Aunt Constance.... Well, she had had a lot of trouble. You had plenty of trouble too. He used to strike you: yes, Granny knows. But you ought not to have let the world know about it. You were quite right not to let him strike you. But you should have shown him, by remaining gentle and dignified, that he was doing wrong.... No man strikes a woman, my child, if she preserves her dignity. But you used to lose your temper, child, and stamp your foot and call him names and invite scenes. Yes, yes, Granny knows all about it, Granny remembers everything. Mamma used to say it was all right, but Granny knew, Granny saw that it was far from right.... If you had not lost your dignity, child, he would never have dared to strike you. And who knows: you might gradually have made him gentler, have made him respect you ... and you might still have had a very tolerable life. You see, dear, there's always something, in marriage. It's not as young girls imagine, when they are in love. There are always difficulties: you have to get used to each other, to fall into each other's ways. Do you think that Grandmamma never had any differences with Grandpapa? Oh, there were ever so many ... and later on even, after years of marriage! How often didn't Grandmamma and Grandpapa differ about poor Aunt Constance!... And Mamma and Papa: do you think they always agreed?... Temper, Emilie, is a thing we all have in our family, but one has to keep it under. A woman must preserve her dignity towards her husband. What a pity, what a pity it was!... Well, child, and where are you living now? Not with Mamma at Baarn, I know."

"I'm living in Paris, Granny, with Henri."

"What do you say? In Paris? Are you living in Paris? With Henri? Well, you see, Henri too—yes, Granny isn't quite in her dotage yet—leaving Leiden like that! For shame! Why not have finished his college course and gone to India?... And what do you do there, in Paris? It's very nice, for the two of you to be together; but it's not natural, Emilietje. Yes, I remember now: they told me you were living in Paris. I had heard it before. But that's no sort of life: to go running through the bit of money which your poor father left you, in Paris! What will people say! For shame!... No, Grandmamma isn't pleased with you. Instead of remaining quietly with your husband ... instead of Henri's quietly finishing his time at the university! What does it all mean, what you and he have done?"

The old woman rejected Emilie's caresses:

"No, child, don't kiss me; Granny is vexed; she doesn't want to be kissed.... The family isn't what it was. It is a *grandeur déchue*, child, a regular *grandeur déchue*. The Van Lowes were something once. There was never much money, but we didn't care about money and we always managed. But the family used to count ... in India, at the Hague. Which of you will ever have a career like your Grandpapa's, like your Papa's? No, we shall never see another governor-general in the family, nor yet a cabinet-minister. It's a *grandeur déchue*, a *grandeur déchue*.... Ah, child, Granny has too much trouble to bear, too much trouble in her old age! Your Papa's death was a great blow to Granny; Mamma has changed so much since, changed so much. And Granny never sees Mamma now, never. Otto and Frances, once in a way, and dear Louise; but the rest of you are all scattered, you are all independent of one another. Oh, it is so nice to keep together, one big family together! Why need Mamma have gone to Baarn? There's nothing but rich tradespeople there, not our class at all.... And now—have you heard, dear?—poor Uncle Ernst.... Yes, child ... it's quite true: isn't it sad, poor fellow? And hasn't Granny really too much to bear in her old age?... Dear Aunt Constance is taking him to Nunspeet to-day: ah, where should we have been without Aunt Constance?... Addie now is a great consolation to Granny. *He* is a dear, clever boy; and he works hard; and he will enter the diplomatic service: he is the hope of the family. Yes, yes, I know, Frans is doing well; but Henri, Emilietje, has done the wrong thing, going to Paris ... with you.... No, child, don't kiss Granny; she's vexed.... And Karel isn't behaving at all well, so Uncle van Naghel says. They don't always tell Granny; but Granny hears, when they think she's deaf and whisper things to one another. Ah, child, it would be better if Granny died! She's getting too old, dear, she's getting too old.... She could have borne all this trouble once, but she can't do it now, Emilietje, she can't bear it now...."

And the old woman sobbed quietly; the tears flowed without ceasing. She now let Emilietje embrace her passionately; and she listened to all the caressing words with which her grand-daughter overwhelmed her.

Constance entered; and Mamma knew her at once:

"Connie! Connie! Have you taken him there? Have you come back?"

Constance, surprised at seeing Emilie, first kissed her and then said:

"Yes, Mamma, I've taken Ernst down, with Dr. van der Ouwe and Dr. Reeuws. He was quite quiet. We had reserved a *coupé*-compartment; and he travelled down with us very nicely. He did not speak; and he held my hand the whole time. He pities me, I don't know why.... Mamma, don't cry: he's really quiet; and he is very comfortable there. He has a pleasant room, with a bright outlook; Dr. van der Heuvel and his wife are kind, homely people. He will not be by himself: he has his meals with the other patients. It is hard on him to have to do without his books and curios. He misses his books particularly; but the doctor does not want him to read. And he must walk...."

"But walk, Connie, walk? Alone? How can he walk? All alone, on that enormous heath? He'll lose his way, he's not responsible, he'll step into a ditch and be drowned!"

"No, Mamma, we shall look after him."

"How do you mean, child?"

"It will soon be Addie's holidays: Addie and I are going to Nunspeet and we shall be with Ernst."

"Oh, how kind of you, Connie!... But I shall miss you."

"I shall come and see you regularly, Mamma: Nunspeet is not far."

"Oh, child, child, what should I do without you? Thank God, dear, that you returned to us at last!... And what will your husband do without his boy?"

"He will come down occasionally. And he is going away for a holiday with Van Vreeswijck.... I only came back to tell you that Ernst is all right. I'm going back to Nunspeet this afternoon. And from there I shall look Bertha up, at Baarn."

"I'm going to Mamma's too," said Emilie, softly.

When they saw that the old woman was tired, Constance and Emilie rose:

"We must go, Mamma...."

"Yes, child. But don't leave me too long alone. When shall I see you again?"

"In three days."

"So long?"

"The others will come and see you: Aunt Lot, Dorine, Adolphine...."

"Yes, but I am too much alone. I can't understand it: I never used to be alone. I don't like being alone. I'm not accustomed to it. What do all of you do?..."

"Suppose you took Dorine to live with you, Mamma?..."

"No, no ... not to live with me, not to live with me. Every one should be free. But they might come and see me sometimes. I never see Adeline's children now...."

"Why, Mamma, I know they were here two days ago!"

"No, no, it's longer ... it's longer than that. I never see your boy either."

"I'll send him this afternoon."

"Yes, do. Why are we all so separated now? It never used to be like that, never.... Well, good-bye, dear. Will you send Addie? Will you come yourself soon?"

"You must wait a day or two."

"Yes, very well, stay with poor Ernst. You are doing a good work. And tell Adeline too that she is neglecting me and that I *never* see the children now, *never*...."

They both kissed the old woman. When their mother and grandmother was alone, she nodded her head up and down, looked out at the rain; and the tears ran down her cheeks, without stopping ... without stopping....

Emilie had a cab waiting:

"I'll drive you home, Auntie."

They stepped in.

"It's months since we saw you, child."

"Yes, Auntie. I've come straight from Paris. I'm going to see Mamma at Baarn."

"And then?"

"I shall go back to Paris. I'm living there now ... I intended to come and see you too, Auntie."

"Come in then, dear, and stay to lunch."

"I should like to, Auntie."

They got out at the villa in the Kerkhoflaan. Emilie dismissed the fly. Indoors, she removed her hat, took off the tulle boa, lost something of her exaggerated smartness....

"We have an hour left before lunch, Emilie," said Constance. "Come up to my bedroom. I want to talk to you."

They went upstairs; Constance shut the door:

"Tell me, Emilie ... how are you living, in Paris?..."

"With Henri, Auntie."

"With Henri ... but why, Emilie? Why keep your brother from his work?..."

"I don't, Auntie. He doesn't want to do that sort of work. He wants to be free; and so do I."

"Free ... in what way?"

"We don't feel ourselves suited ... to Dutch life...."

"But why not?"

"I don't know: an exotic drop of blood in our veins, perhaps. Try to understand, Auntie ... you have lived abroad a long time yourself. Holland is so narrow ... and I ... I have suffered too much in Holland."

"Dear, I suffered ... away from my country; and I longed for my country when I had not seen it for years."

"You will understand all the same. Auntie, do understand. I can't possibly live in Holland again; nor Henri either."

"How do you live there? Tell me."

"We are both living on the money we had left us."

"I know how much that is. There were heavy debts. You did not receive much: not enough to dress as you are dressed.... Emilie, if you care for me at all, tell me everything frankly. I am not inquisitive, but I am fond of you, fond of all of you; and I take an interest in all of you. You *can't* live on the money you came into from your father."

"I work, Auntie."

"In Paris? What at? What do you do?"

"I paint. I paint fans ... and screens. You know I have a bit of a gift that way. I paint them with a good deal of *chic*. People in Holland wouldn't care for the way I do them. But in Paris I sell them for twenty francs, fifty francs: my screens fetch a hundred francs. I turn them out in half an hour. They have something about them, I don't know what: *chic*, I suppose, that's all. But I sell them: they are quite nice."

"I see nothing against that, child."

"I've been very lucky with them, Auntie. I've brought a screen with me for Granny ... one for you too ... and a fan for Aunt Lot.... They're presents: I knock them off in a moment. It's not art exactly, but *chic* rather, actual *chic*...."

And her delicate little fingers outlined a delicate gesture of sheer twentieth-century artisticity. Constance had to laugh in spite of herself.

"And Henri?" asked Constance.

Emilie suddenly turned very red:

"What do you mean?"

"What does Henri do?"

"He does...."

"Nothing?..."

"No. He does something. But don't ask me to tell you."

"Why can't you tell me?"

"You wouldn't understand. Henri is making money, a lot of money."

"What at?"

"I can't tell you, Auntie. It's not my secret, you see: it's his."

"Is it a secret?"

"Yes, it's a secret."

"Then I won't ask."

"It's a secret ... to the others. Perhaps not ... to you."

She was burning to let it out.

"I don't ask you to tell me, Emilie."

"I'll tell you ... if you promise me not to tell anybody else ... not a soul! Henri is ... a clown!"

"Emilie! No!"

"Yes, he's a clown."

"No!... No!"

Emilie gave a loud, shrill laugh:

"You see, you refuse to believe it! I should have done better not to tell you. You can't understand it. If you saw him as a clown, you would. He is splendid, he is unique. He is not a vulgar clown, not a *dummer August*. He is simply magnificent. He has turned the art of the clown into something really artistic, something all his own. He makes the audience laugh and cry as he pleases. He invents his own scenes, designs his own dresses, or else I design them for him. He has a way of making up.... He has discovered the melancholy side of the clown: he's sublime in that.... He has one turn in the circus with quite fifty butterflies flitting on wires all round him ... he tries to catch them and can't ... and, when he does that turn, the people begin by laughing and end by crying. You see, it's symbolical.... Really, you ought to go to Paris to see him. He's so good, so artistic.... He does a lot of exercises, to keep himself supple. He looks much better than when he was racketing about at Leiden. He's very good-looking and he knows it: he never makes up ugly. A modern sculptor wants to make a statue of him: very fanciful, you know; something *art-nouveau*; in that part, with the butterflies all round him. He is always being asked to sit to artists.... You would never have thought it of him, Auntie. Here, he was just the ordinary undergraduate, racketing about, blowing his money.... I was always fond of him. The moment he got to Paris, he understood that he must do something, show what he was made of, strike out a line for himself; and it came to him with a flash: he would be a clown! But a very, very fine clown, something quite new, not one of your vulgar clowns! He makes heaps of money, I don't know how much.... And that's how we live, Auntie: free and independent of everything and everybody. ... Auntie, you look shocked. But you *mustn't* blame us! Here, I was unhappy, so was he; there, we are happy, happy together. I am fond of him and he of me. I don't know what it is, but we can't live without each other. In Paris, the people think that we are lovers; they won't believe that we are brother and sister. And there you are: we're happy and we don't care what horrible things they say about us in Holland. Do you think I've come back to Holland for any other reason than to see Grandmother, you, Mamma, Otto? I longed to see you; I have no feeling for the others. I am sorry for Uncle Ernst. But I want to lead a free life, independent of Holland, of the family ... and I had to make it independent of my husband, whom I married in mistake ... and who beat me and ill-treated me! We want to *live*, Auntie, and not merely exist!"

But Constance did not know what to say and shut her eyes as if she had been struck in the face. She turned pale. They wanted to live, not merely to exist! Was it for her to blame them, for her, who herself, very late, when she was quite old—too late and too old—had felt the need to live and not merely to exist? But ... had they really found their life in what they now considered their life? Did she not now know that the real life is not for one's self, but for others? Did she not know it even though she had never reached the radiant cities of the new life which had shone far off on those unattainable horizons? Had she not guessed that it was there; and had she herself not seemed very small when she had had to leave out of her reckoning the man who had become so dear to her that she was able to forget everything for his sake, even her son, the comfort of her existence, if not of her life? Was not she herself small and had she the right to condemn, merely because she was older and therefore saw the purest truths gleam at times out of some shimmering mist of self-deception? No, she did not condemn ... but that did not prevent her from being shocked. She could understand now ... and yet the rooted prejudice was there. She was willing to accept their new, fresh, free happiness in a life without conventional bonds; and yet those bonds bound herself, despite her new powers of understanding. She understood; and yet she felt a shudder at those who did not tread the beaten path, the smooth track of their decent respectability. Did not a vague suggestion of tragedy show dimly at the far ends of the new roads? Could they possibly persevere? And what would be the result of so unconventional a view of life? Was anything but convention possible for people such as all of them? Were they not born for it, trained for it? She herself had found new roads that led up to cities of light, but she had not trodden those roads. These ... were these new roads leading up to cities of light? Or was it merely wantonness, youthful levity, turning aside from the smooth tracks, the beaten paths?...

"Emilie," she said, "if what you tell me is true, don't tell any one else, don't talk about it! If Grandmamma heard, it would hurt her so much! And Mamma too!"

"No, Auntie, I won't; besides, it is a great secret ... a secret from the family, from all our friends. I have mentioned it to nobody but you; and I shall mention it to nobody. But come, Auntie, it's not so bad as all that: you look quite upset! We have different ideas from our parents. We can't help it. Who's to blame?"

"When I think, dear, of your house, as it used to be!"

"And now Henri is a clown ... and I paint fans for my living!"

She gave a loud, shrill, almost triumphant laugh, followed by a laugh that sounded sadder:

"Poor Grandmamma!" she said. "Poor, Grandmother! She called our family a _grandeur déchue_. And she is right, from her point of view. I am very sorry for her. I found her sitting there so melancholy, so forlorn; and the tears were running down her cheeks.... Auntie, you're a darling; I feel that you are better than I. But I can't live here. Your trouble made you want to come back. Mine made me want to get away. You felt that there were bonds that drew you here. I felt, on the contrary, that I must throw off every bond. My life began with a mistake."

"So did mine."

"Is it always like that?"

"Often ... often...."

"Don't we know ourselves, then ... when we begin to live?..."

"No, every truth comes to us later, much later...."

"Then you don't think that I know *my* truth?"

"No, Emilie."

"You are not pleased with me?"

"Pleased, child? It is not for me to judge you. All I say is, take care. Don't play with your life. Don't waste it. Our life is a very serious thing; and you treat it as...."

"As what, Auntie?"

"An artistic caprice."

"How well you have put it, Auntie! I never thought of that, never said it. An artistic caprice! Henri too: an *art-nouveau* caprice? Why not?"

"Oh, no, Emilie ... take care!"

"Auntie, we are so small. We don't make any difference. What do people like us matter, women like us, girls such as I was? Nothing. Nothing. Why make tragedies of our lives? Why not rather make them into something fanciful, something fanciful and artistic?" And she made a painter's gesture with her fore-finger and thumb. "When we are dead, it's finished.... What do we matter, that we should be tragic? That is all very well for heroes and heroines ... but not for us. I will not have my life a tragedy. I started with a mistake. Since then, I have conquered my life and given it a definite aim. Do try and see, Auntie...."

"I see, Emilie. But you forget...."

"What?"

"The bonds...."

"Which I unloose...."

"Which you cannot unloose."

"Yes, I can."

"No."

"Yes."

"No. You'll see, later, when you're older."

"I sha'n't grow old, Auntie."

"Oh, child, what do you know, what do you know? How can you tell what you will become, how tragic your life may easily become, if you don't think of it more seriously ... more *seriously*?"

She rose: an irresistible impulse made her embrace the girl passionately.

Emilie gave a start:

"What are you thinking of, Auntie?... What do you mean?..."

But what was the use of saying anything now of her presentiment, when presentiments always deceive? Constance said nothing more; she did not know indeed what more to say; she merely stared in front of her, strangely, vaguely; and what had shone for a moment was gone.

And she looked deep into Emilie's eyes and saw there only a vision: Paris, a circus, a clown, butterflies, quite fifty or more....

The front-door downstairs was opened; there were sounds of footsteps and voices. Ordinary life was beginning again.

"There are Uncle and Addie," said Constance. "Emilie, I'm going to Nunspeet this afternoon."

"I'm going to Otto and Frances after lunch. Let us meet at the station; and I'll go to Nunspeet with you. I want to see Uncle Ernst. And then we'll go to Baarn together."

"Very well, dear. But will you do one thing, to please me?"

"Yes, Auntie."

"Dress a little more simply. Remember that we're in Holland."

Emilie gave a shrill laugh:

"Yes, Auntie. I'll go and buy myself a sailor-hat. All my hats are too exciting for the Hague. The butcher-boys were shouting after me: 'Hat! ... Hat!' And, at Nunspeet and Baarn, I know the whole village would turn out to look at me!"

CHAPTER V

Marietje sat in Marianne's room staring out at the road. The road, white with dust and sunlight, gleamed through the green of the trees, described a curve and wound round the creeper-clad station, which stood in the shade close by. A train came thundering in, making all the walls of the little villa shake. Each time that a train rumbled past, whether it stopped or steamed through almost without slackening speed, it shook the little villa....

Marietje was bored. She was home for the holidays from her Brussels boarding-school, spending a few weeks at Baarn with Mamma and Marianne, and she was bored. She would rather have stayed at school. Of course *madame* was a beast, but Brussels at any rate was better fun than Baarn, even for a schoolgirl.... She wondered how she would be able to stand a month of it. She had reckoned on an invitation from Uncle and Aunt van Naghel to their beautiful country-place in Overijssel, where she would have cycled and played tennis with her boy cousins; but Uncle had not said a word about it: Uncle wanted her to put in her month with Mamma, at Baarn. Lord, how *could* Mamma go and live here, in such a house! It would come tumbling down on her head one day, with that everlasting rumble of the trains. She simply could not get away from the rumble of the trains.... Marianne said that Mamma did not mind it and that she herself had become so used to the noise that once, when there was an accident at Hilversum and the something p.m. train did not arrive at Baarn, she had woke up because of the unwonted silence! Well, that was a bit stiff, thought Marietje. Still, perhaps the rumble of the trains did keep Mamma and Marianne from going to sleep. For what a life it was, in this little villa at Baarn! Neither Mamma nor Marianne knew anybody; and they saw nobody. They had no carriage; and how *can* one live in the country without keeping a carriage? Even if it was only a dog-cart, or a governess-car, with a pony; but you must have *something*.... It was a rotten way of living. A brilliant idea of Uncle Adolf's, wasn't it, to insist that she should come and bury herself here for a whole mortal month and bore herself to death with Mamma and Marianne!... Karel hadn't come, the brute! Oh no, he had gone to Uncle's. Marietje knew why: because Uncle wanted to keep an eye on him! So she didn't even see her brother.... Oh, how dull it all was!... Silly little walks to the Beukenkom, to Soestdijk: once in a way, there'd be the excitement of seeing the Queen drive past. But that was over in a flash—whoosh!—and then there was nothing more to see. Well, if she had been the Queen, she would never have come and spent the summer at Soestdijk!... A month! She would never live through it. She counted the days. She simply longed to go back to Brussels. *Madame* had a young nephew who used to make love to her in great secrecy, even leaving notes under her napkin. It was risky, but it was great fun. He wrote so thrillingly.... Ah, when you compared the life that awaited her, when she came home for good in eighteen months, with what Emilie and Marianne had had: parties at Court; dances at the Casino, with all the smartest people in the Hague; the grand dinners at home: her sisters had had all that.... Pretty frocks too.... And she, what would she have? Nothing at all. She'd just go to Baarn, for you might be sure that Uncle and Aunt would never, never ask her to stay with them! And at the Hague ... who was going to invite her to the Hague? The whole winter at Baarn ... good Heavens! No, she must absolutely get herself invited to the Hague, once she had left school! Granny had a big house ... but Granny didn't like people staying with her; Aunt Adolphine: bah, such a crew, she wouldn't go there if she could; Uncle Gerrit: no, he had too many children, she wouldn't care about that and they hadn't a spare-room either; Uncle Karel was no use thinking about.... No, there was only Aunt Constance, who never saw anybody, and Uncle and Aunt Ruyvenaer, who had no smart friends, nothing but East-Indian people.... Yes, it was an awful nuisance, but she saw no prospect of an invitation. But one thing she did promise herself, to get married as soon as she could ... and to make a good match while she was about it, some one with lots of money! A nice thing she called it: Papa and Mamma brought you up in luxury and, the moment you began to grow up, they let you eat your heart out at Baarn! She was decent-looking, thank goodness, and her figure was going to be all right ... and then she would marry a lot of money! You had to be practical: that was the great thing. There *were* a few rich men left. But she ... she would show some sense and not behave like Emilie, who had got married by mistake or by accident, so it seemed, and accepted Eduard just as you accept a partner for a waltz.... Nor like Marianne either, who had fallen in love with her uncle! No, mark her words, she promised herself that much: since she had been brought up in luxury, now that the luxury was gone, she would see that she married money ... for money was everything. She wasn't going to trouble about a title or a name: if a rich bounder came and proposed, he'd do. But a fine house, fine clothes ... and a carriage ... and jewellery: all that she must have and all that she meant to have; for, without it, life wasn't worth living. To go on vegetating at Baarn, with that incessant rumbling of the trains, which made the walls of the villa shake as if the whole house were going to tumble down on her head: never! She had made up her mind to that: never!

Marianne came into the room, which was her own boudoir, with a conservatory leading into the garden: it was the pleasantest room in the house; the only others on the ground-floor were a small drawing-room and a gloomy dining-room. Marietje, lost in thought, was staring out at the sunny, dusty white road.

"Shall we go for a walk, Marietje?" asked Marianne.

"Beukenkom?" asked Marietje, languidly.

"No, farther than that...."

"Soestdijk?"

"No, farther still, through the Overbosch and across the moor, if you like."

"No, thank you: it's too hot and there's too much dust and glare. Can't we hire the pony-cart? Then I'll drive you."

"That mounts up, you know, Marietje; we can't take it every morning."

"Every morning!" growled Marietje. "Listen to you: every morning!... Well, then let's stay and look out of the window."

"Why don't you play the piano or do some painting?"

"Thank you for nothing. I can do that at school. I have no accomplishments."

"Then take a book and read."

"Oh, rot! The books that amuse me I'm not allowed to read; and the books I'm allowed to read don't amuse me. It's one of the drawbacks of my awkward age! Why haven't you joined a tennis-club?"

"Yes, I'm sorry I didn't. I'll see that I do next year."

"Next year ... that's a long way off. You ought to have thought of it before: you knew that you were expecting your sister and that there wouldn't be much for her to do here. But you can't think of anything here, you can't take your eyes off that horrible white road. It hurts your eyes too.... My poor child, how can you stand this place ... after the Hague! Don't you long for the Hague?"

"Not a bit."

"But what do you do here all the winter?"

"Nothing, Marietje."

"Oh, I know! You've grown pi. You go in for good works. Sewing for the poor."

"There are two poor families for whom I make things sometimes."

"There, what did I tell you? I knew it! Well, give us some nighties, in Heaven's name!"

"Oh no, Marietje, never mind about that!"

"Yes, yes, yes, hand over your nighties and let's sew them!"

Marianne had sat down at her work basket and Marietje, out of sheer boredom, also took up a "nightie." But she did no sewing:

"Just imagine if we wore this sort of thing, Marianne! It would tear my skin.... Oh Lord, there's another train! What a row, what an awful row! Aren't you afraid the house will fall in?"

"No."

"Do you like that noise?"

"Yes, one gets used to it."

"You could sleep to it, eh?"

"Yes, it lulls one."

Marietje shrieked with laughter:

"Oh, Marianne, how sentimental ... you ... have ... be-come, as Aunt Cateau would say...."

And, to herself, she thought:

"No, I'm not like that, you know. You won't catch me falling in love with my uncle for nothing. I mean to marry money, lots of money...."

But she said nothing, just stared out at the sunny, dusty road. A few people came along from the station.

"There's the rank and fashion of Baarn!" sneered Marietje. "The great sight of the day: three tradesmen and a hunch-backed shop-girl. Uncle Paul would say, three and a half atoms of human wretchedness.... Another tradesman and another shop-girl.... Two ladies.... Look, as I live, two ladies!... Goodness me, it's Aunt Constance and ... and Emilie!"

"Nonsense!"

"Yes, yes, it's Aunt Constance and Emilie! Hurrah!"

And Marietje, in sheer wild ecstasy at the unexpected distraction, threw the "nightie" right up to the ceiling, where it caught in the chandelier, and rushed through the garden down the road. She flung one leg up in the air with delight.

"Auntie! Emilie!" Marianne heard her yelling, quite beside herself.

Marietje embraced her aunt and her sister madly at the gate of the villa, conducted them indoors, thanked them personally for the surprise which they were giving her, for the welcome distraction which their arrival provided....

"And Uncle Ernst?" asked Marianne. "Poor Uncle Ernst! We had a letter from Frances...."

Constance told her how he was getting on at Nunspeet, that he was still rather restless, because he would look all over the house for fettered souls that moaned and implored him to help them.

"Will the delusion never leave him?" asked Marianne, with tears in her eyes. "Auntie, will he never get better?"

"The doctor has every hope that it will not be permanent...."

Marietje had taken possession of Emilie:

"And so you're living in Paris? With Henri? What do you do there, the two of you? Come, let's hear! Aren't you going to ask me to stay? Haven't you a spare-room? Look out: I shall come tearing in from Brussels, suddenly! Just imagine if I did!"

But by this time they had passed through the dining-room into the drawing-room, where they found Bertha. She was sitting at the window; she looked up.

"Here's Aunt Constance, Mamma. And Emilie."

Bertha merely stood up, kissed her sister and her daughter and at once dropped into her chair again. She scarcely seemed surprised at seeing them so unexpectedly. She barely asked after Mamma, after Ernst, after Henri. She seemed rooted to her seat at that window, through which she gazed at the shadows of the trees. She had grown thin, her eyes stared blankly and miserably in front of her and, in her black dress, she gave an impression of weary, listless resignation. She spoke scarcely more than a word or two, as if it were quite natural that Constance and Emilie should be sitting there.

"Henri sends you his best love, Mamma," said Emilie.

Bertha gave a faint smile, just blinked her eyes, as though to say yes, it was very nice of Henri. But she asked no questions.

"I have just come from Ernst, Bertha," said Constance. "I took him to Nunspeet with the doctor. I went down again yesterday, to see him; and, once I had started, I thought I would come and look you up."

"It's nice of you," said Bertha, vaguely, taking Constance' hand. "Is Ernst very bad? We had a letter from Frances."

"The doctor is very hopeful."

"Yes," said Bertha, as if it went without saying, "he's sure to get over it."

And she seemed tired from talking so much and said nothing more.

Presently Marianne, when she was alone with Constance, said:

"You'll stay to lunch, of course, Auntie?"

"Yes, dear, if I may."

"Are you staying for the night?"

"At the hotel."

"I'm sorry that we haven't a spare-room. Emilie can sleep here; then I'll sleep on the sofa.... I must just go and see about lunch."

"Don't put yourself out for me, dear."

"No, Auntie, but I must see what there is. You know, with just the three of us, we live very simply."

She flushed; and Constance realized that they had to be careful and that they could not keep the same generous table as in the old days.

They exchanged a sad smile. Suddenly, Marianne flung herself into Constance' arms.

"My darling, how are you yourself?"

"Quite well, Auntie."

"You don't look at all well. My child, how thin you've grown! And how drawn your little face looks! And your poor cheeks: why, they've gone to nothing!... Aren't you happy here, dear?"

"Oh yes, Auntie!"

"No, but tell me, honestly: are you happy at Baarn?"

"Yes, Auntie, I am."

"Do you regret the Hague?"

"Regret?... No...."

"Still, just a little?..."

"No ... no...."

Her eyes were full of tears; she began to sob on Constance' shoulder:

"Forgive me, Auntie. I oughtn't to break down like this."

"My darling ... tell me all about it...."

"No, Auntie, it's nothing, really. I feel so ashamed, but, as you know, I always let myself go with you ... because I feel that you do love me ... a little ... and that you are not angry with me ... and that you forgive me...."

"I have nothing to forgive, Marianne...."

"Yes, you have, yes, you have, Auntie.... Oh, forgive me, forgive me! Tell me you forgive me!..."

"How do you spend your time here, dear?"

"Quietly, Auntie, but I'm quite satisfied. I try to be of some little use ... to Mamma ... and others. I have some poor people whom I look after. But I can't do much, I haven't much.... In the old days, you know, Mamma used to do a lot of good ... in between all her rush and worry; and I try to do a little now. But it is hard work ... and rather thankless work.... However, that's all that's left: to live a little for others ... and do a little for others. But sometimes ... sometimes I find it too much for me...."

"Poor Marianne!"

"Yes, sometimes it's too much for me. I am so young still ... and I feel as if I had done with everything, for good and all!..."

"No, dear, no.... If you only knew! You're a child still, Marianne.... And life, real life, will come later...."

"It will never come for me, Auntie. Oh, forgive me! I feel ashamed of myself. I don't *want* to talk like this ... but with you, just with you, because you're fond of me, I can't restrain myself.... Oh, tell me that you forgive me, say it, say it!"

"My child, if it does you any good to hear me say so, though I have nothing to forgive, very well, I forgive you."

"Oh, thank you, thank you, Auntie!... You are good and kind; you understand."

"Yes, dear, I understand. But the real thing will come later."

"No, nothing will ever come, nothing can come...."

"Can't it?"

"No, how could it?"

"If you had the strength and courage not to give in, Marianne, there would be happiness for you in days to come."

"But I have neither courage, Auntie, nor strength. What am I? Nothing. There is a great, big river, which rushes and flows, carrying everything, everything with it, like a deluge. And then there is ... a tiny twig, a leaf. That's what I am, Auntie.... How can I hope to...?"

"You're talking in parables, my child. Shall I do the same?"

"Do, Auntie."

"Come and sit here beside me. Put your head on my shoulder. There. And now listen to my parable.... There was once a soul, a very small soul, like yours, Marianne. A very small soul it was, quite an insignificant little soul. It knew nothing about anything, it seemed to be walking blindly, walking in a dream, a child's dream, light and airy and fragile. There was water and there were flowers ... and there was a far-away light, towards which it moved. As the soul went on, the flowers and the trees disappeared; and in their stead a palace and every sort of pomp and vanity gleamed in front of the small soul.... But all that glitter was just as much a dream as the water and the flowers; and the small soul ... made its second mistake. It walked blindly in that dream of pomp and vanity and thought that it *saw* all that radiance. It gave itself away, Marianne, gave everything it had to any one who might make it shine still more brilliantly ... gave away everything it possessed, for nothing ... for an illusion. And it already felt unhappy, thinking, 'There is nothing more coming; I've had everything now.' It thought that, even before its fate arrived. It saw its fate arrive and could still have avoided it, but did not, remained blind, blind to everything. Its fate swept it along; and it thought, Marianne, that everything was over, over for good and all; that it would wither like a flower, like a twig, like a leaf; and that the river would carry it along with it. And then, Marianne, then something else came, after it had been swept along by fate: there came a great revelation, a vision of rapture, an ecstasy of glory. And the small soul saw that it was *that*; but its fate forbade it to accept that great happiness, that vision of ecstasy.... And once again it thought, 'Now, *now*, I have really had everything. After *that*, nothing more can possibly come.' And yet something did come. And, after that revelation, it was no longer a dream, but a reality, as tangible as it could hope to be ... for such a poor small soul.... What came, Marianne, was not so very much; but the small soul does not want much: an atom, a grain of absolute truth and reality; a tiny grain, but all-sufficing.... For small souls do not need much.... Just an atom, a grain. And of that grain, Marianne, it even communicated a part ... to others. My child, that is the whole secret: to share your grain, to give, though it be but of your superfluity, to others. But, Marianne, you will have to wait for that grain; it will only come later; and, before you can possess it ... you must first go through everything ... you must pass through all that unreality, that vain dreaming...."

"And, Auntie, have you the grain?"

"Oh, child, the grain is so small, so small! So tiny, so wee, such a very little grain! But what are we ourselves? And, we being what we are, is not that little tiny grain enough?..."

"For happiness ... some day, later, much later, after long, long years?..."

"Happiness? Happiness?... Yes, the happiness of knowing, of understanding; the happiness of resignation; the happiness of accepting one's own smallness ... and of not being angry and bitter because of all the mistakes ... and of being grateful for, what is beautiful and clear and true...."

"Grateful...."

"For the great dream.... And the happiness of satisfying hunger and thirst ... with that one, solitary little grain ... and of no longer yearning for the great, great dream!"

"But yet remaining grateful...."

"Yes, grateful that the dream has been vouchsafed to us, that its radiance ever smiled upon us...."

52

"But, Auntie, suppose it was no dream ... but the very bread of life!"

"My child, who can tell you *now* what is the only bread of life? Now, you are only hungry for your dream ... and, later, much later...."

"Have I hungered then ... after nothing?"

"Perhaps."

"After nothing? Oh no!"

"Who can tell?"

"Auntie, is every one of life's parables so cruel in its worldly wisdom? Do they all teach that the great dream is nothing and the little grain, which comes so late, everything?..."

"I fear so, child."

"Oh, Auntie, it's all words ... soft, gentle words!... I understand you: it is your *own* story, *your* parable. But, until now, mine ... is nothing but the river ... and the leaf...."

"And later perhaps there will come ... the tiny treasure, the grain...."

Then they were silent; and Constance thought: "Every soul must first go through *that*, must have its dream.... Not until very late does it find the grain ... for itself. What another communicates to it never satisfies its hunger as does its own grain ... the grain it has found for itself...."

CHAPTER VI

Addie was nearly sixteen. He did not grow much in stature, he promised to have the same build as his father, for there was something sturdy and yet delicate, something robust and yet gentle about him: strength and refinement combined. He continued to look older than he was, as though he could never quite catch himself up: his face, carved in firm and yet delicate lines, wore an air of calm serenity that did not belong to his years; his cheeks were covered with a golden down: indeed, his mother would have liked him to start shaving, which however he was not willing to do yet; and so the vague strip of golden velvet above his upper lip had become a decided moustache. His hair, with its soft, short, brown curls, was exactly like his father's; and his eyes also were his father's eyes, but they had grown still more serious, if possible, calm and tender, with a smiling sadness in their depths, and, above all, Addie's eyes were of a clear, untroubled blue, with none of the boyishness which shone in Van der Welcke's. Addie's were northern eyes, as his mother said: Dutch eyes, she called them, as distinguished from the creole eyes of all her family, the Van Lowes.

"Addie, how Dutch you are!" his mother would say, meaning thereby that they all, the Van Lowes, were specimens of the languid, less robust East-Indian type and that his father also had become more or less un-Dutch through his long residence abroad. "Addie, how Dutch you are! For a boy born on the Riviera, brought up in Brussels, who had never been in Holland before his thirteenth year, how is it possible that you should be the most Dutch of us all! You have nothing of the cosmopolitan about you!"

His mother used to tease him like this, especially when she looked into his eyes, his clear, calm, Dutch eyes, as into two blue mirrors, with a smile in them like a reflexion ... and beneath that smile, a vague shadow of sadness. And then he would give a sober nod of assent, laughing quietly, as though to say that she was right, that he felt quite Dutch and neither a languid East-Indian nor a mongrel cosmopolitan. He was a Dutch boy above all things, but here, in this little village of Nunspeet, he felt even more Dutch than at the Hague, especially as he looked out of his window at the hotel and saw the glittering white dunes undulating towards those vast skies, saw the piled-up clouds, the immensities of grey-blue rolling clouds, drifting by in their puissant majesty: all the glory of a small land; grandeur and might and majesty towering above the small lowlands, which bowed humbly beneath their awfulness.... Those clouds, those Dutch clouds: Addie loved them, those awful powers throned high above the gently undulating lands ... and Mamma, who teased him so, loved them too, her Dutch clouds, so vast, so vast, as though they were islands and fields, larger than the fields and islands of Holland itself....

It was early, six o'clock; and he looked out of his window into the pearly morning and, with a characteristic gesture of enthusiasm, flung out his arms towards the clouds. Then he laughed at himself, hoped that no one had seen him from the road. No, the peasants going to their work did not look up at his window; and now he dressed himself quickly, ran downstairs, breakfasted hurriedly on bread-and-butter and a glass of milk and went along the high-road and down a shorter road to Dr. van Heuvel's villa. The house stood some way back, in a large garden, quiet and shady; and, as the house stood high, it looked out over the undulating, sparkling dunes, past the dark-green masses of fir-trees on the moor which shimmered purple in the early morning sunshine, towards low horizons of just a streak of green, broken only by the needle-point of a steeple: just a narrow strip beneath the awful majesties of the vast clouds which drifted calmly by, one after the other, on and on, unceasingly, ever vast and majestic.

The doctor came out to meet Addie.

"Here I am, doctor."

"That's right, Van der Welcke, you're in good time. Would you mind going for a walk with your uncle presently?"

"Not at all."

"For I can't manage to come to-day."

"There's no reason why you should, doctor."

"It's the first time you'll have been out alone with him. When will your mother be back?"

"This afternoon."

"Of course, I could send the keeper with you. But it's better that your uncle should not see more of him than's necessary."

"Don't worry, doctor; it'll be all right."

"Don't go too far, you know."

"No, close by, on the dunes."

"I can rely on you?"

"Yes, doctor, absolutely."

"Here he comes."

Ernst came shuffling into the garden from the verandah; he knew Addie and smiled:

"Where's Mamma?" he asked.

"She'll be back this afternoon, Uncle. Are you coming for a walk with me?"

"No, I'm going to wait for Mamma," said Ernst, in a suspicious voice, with a glance at the doctor.

Nevertheless, Addie succeeded in coaxing him outside, down the road. And then Ernst took Addie by the arm and said:

"Do you know what's so rotten? That fellow's hidden Mamma."

"No, Uncle, really he hasn't."

"Yes, he has, my boy. The fellow's buried her somewhere in the dunes. Shall we go and look for her?"

"Uncle, I'm quite ready to go for a walk, but Mamma is not hidden or buried: she's gone to Baarn, to see Aunt Bertha, and she'll be here this afternoon."

Ernst shook his head and grinned contemptuously:

"You people are always so obstinate. Do you mean to say you don't hear Mamma? Can't you hear her moaning? She's been moaning all night. That fellow's buried her, I tell you."

"I don't believe it, Uncle, but at any rate we can go for a walk...."

"Yes, we'll look for her."

They went through a pine-wood: it was cool and dark as a church. Ernst kept poking the ground with his stick, kept listening to the ground:

"She's farther on," he said, "in the dunes. Her voice comes from farther away. Don't you hear it?"

"No, Uncle."

Ernst shrugged his shoulders:

"You people are so dull-witted. You have no senses ... and no souls," he said, roughly. And he immediately added, as though afraid that he had given pain, as though anxious to make atonement without delay, "Mamma is kind. You too, you're a good boy. I may make something of you yet."

They walked along, up and down the dunes, Ernst continually stopping and Addie continually forcing him to go on. At last, Ernst went down on his knees and dug a big hole with his two hands:

"It's here," he said. "I can hear Mamma's voice sighing. O God, O God, how she's moaning! She'll be suffocated, she'll be suffocated. Her mouth, her throat, her eyes are full of sand. What cruel wretches people are! What harm has poor Mamma done them? The wretches, the savages!... It's here, it's here: yes, wait a bit, Constance, wait a bit. I'm digging you out, I'm digging you out!"

He dug away, with his stick and his hands, dug away till the sand flew all round him, making his clothes white with dust. Addie had stretched himself on the ground and was letting him have his way, looking on quietly with his serene blue eyes, which seemed to study each of Ernst's movements. He said nothing more, finding no words with which to dispel the hallucination. At that moment, all words were vain. The hallucination was so vivid that Ernst actually saw Constance through the sand, saw her lying four or five yards beneath the surface, stuck fast in the sand, with its myriad grains pressing so tightly round her that she could not move and that, when, through her sighing and moaning, she was compelled to open her mouth, the sand at once trickled into it. He saw her body, as in a black garment, glued tightly to her limbs, stiff and motionless in that tomb of sand, in that winding-sheet which pressed closer and closer to her until the pressure threatened to choke her, especially now that her mouth was full of sand. Ernst could just see her black eyes faintly gleaming through a screen of sand; sand trickled into, her ears; and the sand, though there was no room for it below, kept trickling faster and faster, till it became an eddy of trickling sand. The trickling grains of sand were now gyrating madly around Constance like a great cyclone ... and Ernst dug and dug, with furious hands. He dared not use his stick ... for fear of hurting Constance. He dug, like an animal, with frantic hands. He dug away, dug out a regular pit; and the sand became wetter and wetter: he was now flinging out great lumps of sand.... Then, as he dug, he saw the dark body sinking, for ever sinking a yard lower: he could not reach his sister. The body sank and sank; and he reflected that, however deep he might dig his pit, he would never reach Constance:

"Addie!" he cried. "Addie! Help me, can't you? Help me!"

Addie, lying at full length, with his chin on his hand, looked quietly at his uncle, with all the serenity of his searching blue eyes. Suddenly Ernst stopped his digging, quickly turned his head halfway towards Addie; and his restless eyes looked into Addie's eyes. Then Addie shook his head gently, as if in denial, as if to explain to Ernst, without words, that it was not as Ernst thought, that there was not a body under the sand....

They looked at each other like that for a few minutes. Ernst lay on his knees by the pit, his fingers still cramped with the effort of digging. Suddenly, his feverish energy seemed to subside; he shivered and cried:

"O my God, O my God, O my God!..."

Then he bent over the pit and looked down. He saw nothing now: the body was not there; there was nothing but the hard, impenetrable subsoil. Then he listened, with his head on one side, for the plaintive voice. There was no voice: there was nothing but the great subterranean silence. There was nothing now: no body, no voice. He looked around: around him lay the sand which he had flung up, those senseless heaps of sand.

"O my God, O my God, O my God!" he cried.

Addie looked at him, very quietly; and Ernst shuddered under the blue serenity of that compassionate, studying glance. Then, with a jerk which shook his whole frame, the tension relaxed and his body seemed to go slack. But he still scraped some sand together and carefully filled up the pit to a certain depth, so that the wet sand was powdered over with dry, white sand. Finally he stretched himself at full length, with his legs straight out and his arms under his head. He was very tired, especially in his head. He could not have spoken a word. Heaving a deep sigh, he lay staring up at the tremendous clouds. They drifted past like something unearthly in their immensity, drifted very, very slowly, before his upturned gaze....

Then he closed his eyes, as if he were becoming frightened, as if it were all too big for him, too tremendous, too unearthly. And at the thought of his smallness he was oppressed with melancholy, a darkness that clouded his soul. He could not help it: under his closed eyes, the slow tears forced themselves; a sob shook him; and he lay weeping, still stretched at full length, still with his eyes closed. A big tear trickled down his cheek....

Addie never took his eyes off him. Now he rose, came nearer and gently stroked Ernst's long, black hair....

And Ernst just raised his eyelids and saw Addie stooping over him: blue eyes looking into black eyes. Then he closed his own again, breathed heavily, let Addie stroke his hair. The big tears trickled slowly....

There was no need, thought Addie, to speak to the tired man. The hallucination had gone; it must have left him utterly fagged out. Round both of them, man and boy, hung the haze of the summer morning; a steady droning filled the sultry air. Overhead, clouds drifted endlessly, everlastingly, cloud after cloud, drifting on and on....

CHAPTER VII

It had gone very, very still. The tired man had dozed off; it seemed as though his nerve-taut limbs had relaxed and lay loose and slack: the thin legs in the wide, creased trousers; the chest sunk under the rumpled coloured shirt; the narrow shoulders, the lean arms in the old coat, with its tired creases. And the features of his face had also fallen in, now that the nerves were at last resting; they had fallen in like an old man's: queer wrinkles furrowed the forehead and etched lines under the eyes and round the nose and mouth; the short, scanty beard formed a stubble around the long chin; and the hair too was thin and stubby, a little thin behind the ears. Addie looked at the hands of the sleeping man: long, thin fingers, in which a nervous tremor still lingered, a very slight tremor, as though quivers were passing under the skin, over the veins.... The boy looked curiously at the hands, for he was always interested in hands, judging people more by their hands than by anything else: he did not exactly know why and certainly could not analyze it. And he could see those long, thin hands not only reaching out vaguely and ineffectually after art, but also laying hold of books with a more confident grasp, turning them page by page. He saw too a tremor of pity in the tapering finger-tips, which seemed not to dare to touch things; and those finger-tips struck him particularly because of the short nails, which nevertheless showed breeding, with their almond shape and the little crescent-moon at the quick; only, the nails were bitten short, as though in fits of nervousness. Then, mechanically, as he always did when studying people's hands, he looked at his own: his father's hands, but still boy's hands, though they were already becoming manlier, short and broad, white and strong, hands that would take a close, steady grip of things. He no longer bit the nails, but would cut them swiftly, with a pen-knife, whenever they bothered him. And from his own hands he glanced once more towards his Uncle Ernst's and seemed to read in them a soul highly susceptible to art and of extreme sensitiveness; a soul ready to assimilate the contents of books; a soul evolved out of loneliness, out of lonely life and lonely knowledge and, above all, out of lonely, very lonely feeling; a soul so lonely and shrinking that it had fallen ill of that loneliness and appeared to see and hear actually the thousand reflexions of all that it had read in books, seen in art and felt in its lonely hypersensitiveness....

The tired man slept on.... And Addie stretched himself at still fuller length, while around him the white dunes rippled away in the summer haze under those wide, unearthly skies. He felt well and not unhappy, though there was just a streak of sadness running through his reverie, sadness because people and things were what they were. It was a pleasant, benevolent sort of secret reverie; and through it all there was the desire to grasp things, to hold them as with the close, steady grip of his own hands, that close, steady grip, firm but tender, with which he meant to grasp everything in this wavering, uncertain life, earnestly and charitably and above all with a great longing for absolutely understanding, for divine knowledge, for the sake both of others and of himself.... And, because he had made up his mind, he ceased dreaming and began to reflect, thinking over how he was going to tell his parents what he knew so well in his own heart. He had loved them with such earnest love from early childhood that he understood them very well, both of them, knew them as thoroughly as it is possible for one being to know another. His father had always remained young, despite what he called the ruin of his life, despite that other thing which had brought great sorrow to him recently. His mother had grown older but more serious and lately, when she talked to him, Addie, had expressed views on all sorts of subjects which he used to think rather ... or was it because he himself was growing older and understood more and fathomed more of the depths of this deep life? Had Mamma always been like this? Were his childish memories at fault and had she always been the serious woman that she now was?... No, that was impossible, he thought; but nevertheless this was more an intuitive feeling than a definite ability to assert it positively and unhesitatingly.... And now he reflected—he had admitted it to himself—that, for as far as his love was greater for one than for the other, it was greater for his father, however much he would have liked it to be equally great for both.... Still, he would not speak to his father this time: he would speak to his mother. She would understand him more quickly than Papa; and what he had to tell her would hurt Papa more than it would Mamma. He would speak to Mamma first.... True, it appeared to him difficult to speak of this matter at all and to destroy in them a thought, an expectation, a hope which they had always cherished. But yet his idea had sprung up with such force from his innermost consciousness that he felt that he could not do otherwise. He would have to speak and tell them what he had resolved to do with his life, whose impenetrable future he saw unfolding before him, clearer every day, as though wide doors were being opened, till he saw what things would be like and where he would go to, a long, long way ahead....

He would tell her that afternoon, would tell his mother first. And, as he made up his mind to this, he felt that in his case it would be a vocation, that the voice was a distinct one, as though it were calling to him and beckoning him, through the wide doors that had opened. The voice that called to him so distinctly he would answer....

But Ernst was stirring and now woke from his sleep.

"Do you feel rested, Uncle?"

Ernst sadly nodded yes.

"Well, then shall we walk a bit? Else the doctor won't be pleased, Uncle."

They rose and walked on, in silence, up and down, down and up the rippling dunes. Ernst was very gloomy and, at last, said:

"You see, it's beyond my powers to help all of you, all of you.... There are so many of you, you see, that I can't possibly take care of every one of you ... however much I should like to. Then again you mustn't forget that there are thousands swarming round me as it is. True, they are no longer alive ... but they feel, all the same. Those are the souls. They never leave me in peace. And then to look after all of you, who are alive, as well ... it's beyond me; sometimes it's beyond me.... There's Mamma, poor woman. The whole world is at her heels; and, if I didn't see to it, they would hide her away and bury her.... Then I have to look after Papa and you and

Uncle Gerrit and Uncle Paul and all the rest of them. I have all of you to look after. You never see anything and you know nothing, you live in a dream, you walk blindly ... to your ruin, all of you.... Who would look after you if I wasn't there? Who would look after you if I died to-morrow?... If I worried about it, instead of quietly doing my duty, it would send me mad to think of it!... And you never stay by me, you keep on running about, with the wretches at your heels, waiting to hide you away and bury you. Why, they had hold of Uncle Gerrit the other day, in chains, under my room! I heard him all through the night and I couldn't release him until ... until...."

He had lost the thread of his thoughts, passed his hand over his hair and said, mournfully:

"Addie, my dear boy, you mustn't come and see me any more. Uncle is in a bad house. It's a bad place, that doctor's house. Terrible things happen there at night. You're too young, Addie, to come to such a bad house. Promise me that you won't come again...."

"Uncle, the doctor's is not a bad house...."

"Of course you would know better than I! You're young; and you don't know and don't see things. There are scandalous goings-on at night, scandalous things in every room in the house. I shall tell Mamma to take you away: I can't look after all of you...."

"Uncle, you should stop thinking of such things and enjoy your walk and the air and the woods and the dunes and the clouds...."

"Yes, that's what you say: stop thinking ... and enjoy ... and enjoy...."

"Yes, enjoy nature around you...."

"Nature?..."

His restless black eyes encountered Addie's clear glance. And suddenly he stopped and said:

"Tell me, do they leave them alone, in my rooms on the Nieuwe Uitleg?"

"Uncle, there's nothing there; and all your books and china are well taken care of...."

"Is there nothing there?"

"No, Uncle, not what you think."

"And in the doctor's house?"

"There's nothing there either, Uncle."

"Here, round about us?"

"There's nothing, Uncle."

"Then what I hear...."

"Is an hallucination, Uncle."

"What I see...."

"That too."

"Why do you say that?"

"Because it's the truth, Uncle."

"How do you know what is the truth?"

"Through my senses, Uncle. Through my reason."

"Are they healthy? Are they infallible?"

"Perhaps not infallible, but healthy. And yours are ailing."

"Are mine ailing?"

"Yes, Uncle."

"My senses?"

"Yes. And your reason too."

"You know that?"

"Yes, I know it for certain."

It was as though the sick man for one moment doubted himself, while he kept his eyes fixed on the boy's steady, blue eyes and read a strange lucidity in them. But something inside him made him unable or unwilling to overstep a certain boundary which was like a line of suffering in his sick mind, a grievous horizon, an horizon which was too near, which he could not look at from a distance, which had neither light nor darkness behind it, but only mist.

"And what about this?" he asked, pointing with his stick to the dune on which they stood.

"What, Uncle?"

"This, this, underneath us! This moaning and sighing and imploring for help!"

He threw himself flat on the sand; he dug furiously:

"Yes!" he shouted. "Wait! Wait a moment! I'm coming, I'm coming!"

And, rooting with his hands, like an animal, he sent the sand flying around him.

"Oh," thought Addie, "if he would only make one more effort suddenly to see, to hear, to feel that he was dreaming ... that he was dreaming! Oh, to have him get well ... to see him get well, all at once, so that one knew it by the brightness in his eyes ... and the untroubled look on his face!..."

Then he put his hand on Ernst's shoulder. The sick man stood up, walked along:

"Come on," he said, beckoning to Addie.

CHAPTER VIII

That evening, in the lane in front of the little hotel, Addie walked arm-in-arm with his mother. The deepening shadows gathered round them, pierced by the bright light of the lamp outside the house.

"Mummy, I want to talk to you...."

They were strolling slowly up and down; and the pressure of his hand urged her gently forward, through the deepening shadows, out of the fierce glow of the lamp and farther along the road, whence, under the starry skies, the meadows receded to remote distances towards the last streak of light on the horizon.

"What about, my boy?"

How old he was for his years and how serious! She felt his hand lying heavy on her arm, like a man's hand; she heard his voice in her ear, full of deep resonance, sounding a little more caressing than usual. He was still a boy, a schoolboy, but that was in years; in his soul she realized him to be a man, her big son; and, though this made her feel very old, it also made her feel calm and contented and safe in the possession of him ... so long as she did not lose him.... And what did he want to talk about now? For he had not spoken yet, but was walking on, silently. And, all at once, she began to be curious, wondering what it could be that he wanted to tell her in that suddenly caressing voice, what he wanted to obtain from her. For she felt that he was going to ask her for something, a favour almost, a gift. Because he was leaning on her like that, she felt that something was weighing on his mind, some oppressive anxiety which he would tell her in order to make it lighter to bear. What could be troubling him? What would it be? It could not be money: he was too sensible; he knew exactly how much she could spare. Was he in love? A boy's love-affair? Yes, she was convinced that that was it. She had always said that, when Addie fell in love, it would be once and for all; and she had grown a little afraid for her big son, with that serious heart of his....

"Well, what is it?" she asked; and she added, playfully, "Are you in love?"

He only laughed:

"No, I'm not in love. But still I have something very important to say to you, something that will distress you perhaps, because you always pictured it differently...."

"What is it, Addie?" she asked, feeling a little frightened and bewildered.

"It's this, Mamma," he said, quietly and very calmly. "I can't go into the diplomatic service ... because I want to be a doctor."

She was silent, walked on, with his arm in hers; and it seemed to her that new vistas suddenly opened out before her. No, she never thought that he was going to speak to her of his future. It had always been so positively settled, from the very beginning, that her son should take up the life and the career which she had ruined for his father. She had always looked upon it as a vague form of compensation which Addie, her son, would pay to her husband, to his father. She had never imagined that it would be otherwise. It could be done: he bore a distinguished name, he would have money later on and, once he had entered the profession which in their set had always been considered so eminent and honourable and illustrious—the most eminent, honourable and illustrious of all—he would console his father for the ruin of his career and restore to his mother something of her old position in society.... She had always, almost unconsciously, looked at it like that. And then there was still a grain of vanity in her, dormant, it was true, of late, but still an eternal, ineradicable germ: the vanity inherent in her, the vanity of thinking that *her* son would pursue that most eminent, honourable and illustrious career. Now her whole world seemed to be turned upside down: the shock, the surprise, the disappointment made her dizzy; and through it all there came a sudden impulse to say no, no, no, that it was impossible, quite impossible, that it would give too much pain to Papa, to herself, to poor old Grandmamma and certainly to his grandparents as well; and, if he insisted, to say to him imperiously, almost in a tone of command, that it was out of the question, out of the question. But for the moment she said nothing; and he said nothing either; and they walked on, along the grey ribbon of the road, which ran on through the meadows fleeing on either side to the last streak of light on the horizon, under the great starry skies. He said nothing, as if he had said all that he had to say, quietly and simply. And she was too much under the influence of that tumult of shock, surprise and disappointment....

"Does it upset you, Mamma?" he asked, at last.

"It comes as a blow, Addie.... I never expected it...."

"Can't you understand that I...?"

"Understand? I don't know, Addie. We always thought...."

"Yes, I know: you and Papa always thought differently. I understand that it must upset you and that it is a disappointment."

"You had better speak to Papa first...."

"No," he said, calmly and quietly. "I want to speak to you, first, Mamma. You know how fond I am of my father, what chums we are. But I can't speak to him first, because he would not understand. And I want to speak to you first, Mamma, because you will understand."

There was something soothing to her vanity in his words, but also something deeper underlying them, which was not at once clear to her; for she knew that he loved his father more than her and yet he wanted to speak to her first....

"You will understand, Mamma, when I tell you. I don't feel in any way cut out for a career in which, no doubt, one can rise very high if one happened to be one of the four or five great men who stand out in it.... And even so ... even if I were one of those four or five—always supposing I had the brains or the genius for it, which I haven't and never shall have—then there would still be something in me which would make me feel that I had missed my vocation, that it was all purposeless, that I had got into the wrong path, into the wrong sort of work. I should always be too simple, Mamma, and too natural, your Dutch boy...."

He turned towards her with a little laugh; and she suddenly pictured him, faultlessly attired, in a white tie and a dress-coat, among the young diplomatists whom she remembered in the old days, in Rome. No, he did not resemble his father as much as all that....

"Whereas the other thing, doctoring, I feel quite different about. It's the only thing which attracts me and in which I feel that I shall do well. Let me just tell you what I do feel about it. First of all, there's nothing that interests me more than people ... and studying them, both their outsides and their insides. That's my *head*, Mummy. And, as well as that, there's something else, a question of *feeling*. I feel for nothing so much as for any one who suffers, physically or mentally. And then I get a sort of impulse, which comes to me as naturally as sitting or walking or talking, to help as much as I can. That's how I feel; and I can't tell it you in any other way. It's no use my trying to explain it in a lot of words; I couldn't say more than I have already said. But, just telling it you like this, I do hope that you understand it, Mamma, and that you get the same feeling as I do.... And then, Mummy, there's something else, something I hardly dare say to you, because you will perhaps think that I am imagining...."

"Say it, dear...."

"It's this, Mamma: I feel inside me the power of curing people. And I feel that that power is growing...."

His great seriousness startled her.

"But I'm only saying this to *you*, Mamma; I won't say it to any one else ... not even to Papa, because I feel that he would not understand. I am only saying it to you; and I shall never say it to any one but you; and I'm only saying it to you as a sort of justification for what I mean to do. And, if I'm wrong and it doesn't turn out as I think, then you'll forgive me, won't you? For I'm quite in earnest now."

"My darling...."

"Who can tell me for certain that I am mistaken, Mamma, and that I have *not* that absolute conviction deep down in my soul? It is a wonderful thing to have an absolute conviction like that about yourself. I would almost say that to be certain about other people ... is not so wonderful as to be certain about yourself.... But still ... but still.... I *feel* that this is my vocation. Who can deny the existence of what I feel so very plainly within me, even though I am sometimes amazed at my own consciousness of it?... I know, Mamma, that all this sounds very strange and that I am not talking like a boy of my age. But that is because I am being very, very confidential and letting you know my most private thoughts.... It is so calm and peaceful out here this evening, Mamma, and the stars are shining so bright, as if *they* knew everything for quite certain. I ... I do not know for certain: I only feel ... and I wish. And I am telling you my most private thoughts, just freely and in the strictest confidence, so that you may not be unhappy...."

A thrill of tenderness went through her.

"Darling, I am not unhappy."

"What I have told you ... is a disappointment."

"A disappointment?... Is it a disappointment? I don't think so now, dear.... Not after the first shock of hearing it. It's not a disappointment any longer. If there is clearly something inside you which tells you what your vocation is ... oh, why shouldn't you follow it? So few of us feel clearly about anything.... Let's sit here, on the sand, under the trees.... So few people feel things clearly. Everything was vague with me ... until quite late in life, dear. We all cling to small things, to small interests ... both in our own case and in the case of the small people around us.... Do you still remember ... that friend of ours ... whom Mamma liked so much? Things weren't clear to him.... Darling, if they're clear to you, already, and if you are almost certain that you are not mistaken ... then obey your vocation. No one has the right to hold you back; and why should I hold you back ... for small reasons, while much greater things perhaps are urging you on? For small reasons ... for a touch of vanity, perhaps ... Ah, you see, darling, I *am* small. I should have loved to see you, you my own boy, in the diplomatic service. Papa would have been satisfied; and you would perhaps have given me back something of the past.... Do you understand? It would not be honest of me if I did not confess that I should have been glad to see it. But that is because I still cling to small things ... while you are urged on by greater things. And, if it is really so, then I am proud of you, proud of you. You see, my darling, there's always that about your mother: her little bit of vanity. She is so glad that you did not inherit it ... that perhaps she gave you other things—something very small, but the best she had—which may become very great in you, an atom which in you will grow into a world.... No, I am not disappointed any longer...."

"You see, Mamma, I feel it so clearly when I am alone with Uncle Ernst: not that I can do anything yet, but I am certain that I shall be able to, later.... I feel that, if he were to come a fraction of an inch towards me ... and if I had the power to go another fraction of an inch towards him, we should get near to each other, he and I.... It doesn't happen now; but I feel ever so clearly that I am looking for something in him, the secret spot from which I could cure him if ... if I was older, more advanced and stronger...."

But he pulled himself up:

"Perhaps it's better not to say that."

"Why not, dear?"

"One shouldn't say those very private things.... But I wanted to talk quite frankly to you...."

"You have, darling. Don't force your words, if they won't come. Just tell me quietly, when talking comes to you more easily. Mamma will try to understand you. Mamma does understand you."

"And you forgive me ... for the disappointment?"

"It has gone."

"Then what is left?"

"A great sense of peace, dear. It will all be for the very best, I think. Do as you think, go to what calls you."

She leant against him, laid her head on his shoulder. He kissed her. A kindly, health-giving stream seemed to be flowing through her.

"He knows already, he is certain about himself," she thought, looking up at the understanding stars. "He knows his own mind ... definitely, definitely. O God, let him always know his own mind!"

CHAPTER IX

Old Mrs. van Lowe had taken a furnished villa at Nunspeet for a few weeks and gone to stay there with Adeline and her flaxen-haired little tribe. She wanted to be near Ernst; and the doctors had not objected to her going to Nunspeet and even seeing him once or twice: there was no question of an isolation-cure; on the contrary, the patient had always been too lonely; and something in the way of kindly sympathy, which would counteract his shyness, might even have a salutary effect.

Gerrit ran down once or twice from the Hague. But there was hardly room for him in the villa, which was full up with the children's little beds; and also he was secretly hurt that Ernst had taken a dislike to him. And, when he was back at the Hague, alone in his house, he pondered over it all, over the difference and the resemblance between them: Ernst belonging to the dark Van Lowes, Papa's blood; he, like Constance and Paul, to the fair ones, Mamma's blood, though they all had black or at least very dark-brown eyes, with that rather hard, beady glance. But what struck him as very singular was that he more or less understood why Ernst had become as he was: a little odd, he called it, nothing more; whereas Ernst saw nothing in Gerrit, saw nothing but a nature entirely antipathetic to his own: no doubt his deceptive muscular strength, which was antipathetic to the morbid sensitiveness of the shy, lonely, studious brother.... But did any one see him, Gerrit, really as he was? And had it not always been so, from the time when he was a child, a boy, a young man? It gave him a melancholy sense of security, in these days; that he was living by himself, living a life taken up exclusively with his military duties, captain for the week, out very early, in the stables from six to seven seeing to the grooming of the horses, the cleaning of their boxes, thinking even more of the horses than of the men and caring more, hussar that he was, for a fresh, clean-smelling stable, with a litter of fresh, clean-smelling straw for the animals, than for the details of the troopers' mess. When the horses had been fed and watered came the ride with his squadron: drilling, target-practice or field-duty; then back again, handing in his report, finishing any business in the squadron-office. This took up the whole morning; and in the exercise of those minor duties which he loved he had hardly time for thinking; and the officers for the week saw him as they had always seen him: the big, strong, yellow-haired Goth, brisk in his movements, flicking his whip against his riding-boots, broad-chested in his red-frogged uniform, his voice loud and domineering, with a note of kindliness under the bluster, his step quick and firm, giving an impression of energy.... That was all that officers and men saw of him; and he, for the time, was what he appeared, even to himself.... But then he would go home and bolt his sandwich, alone, and would ride his second charger, before going back to barracks in the evening, to supervise the foddering of the horses again. And it was during this afternoon interval that he was accustomed to pick out lonely roads, where he would meet none of his brother-officers; it was then, in that afternoon interval, when loneliness was all around him, that he saw himself and knew himself to be different from what he seemed to his acquaintances, different even to himself.... He saw himself again as a child in Java, a small boy playing with his sister

Constance, on the great boulders in the river behind the palace at Buitenzorg. He could see her still in her white *baadje*,[4] with the red flowers at her temples. The thought of it gave him a curious sentimental pang, which made him melancholy, he did not know why. Then he saw himself grown a few years older and in love, perpetually in love, with the earnest amorousness of East-Indian schoolboys for girls of their own age, little *nonnas*[5] who learn so rapidly that they are women and that they attract the boys who ripen so rapidly into men under the burning sun. He, Gerrit, had always been in love, sometimes in romantic fashion, like the fairy princes in the stories which his little sister Constance used to tell him, but more often in rougher style, longing to satisfy his greedy mouth and greedy hands, the gluttonous senses of his lusty, growing body, the body of a schoolboy and of a young man in one.... Oh, he still laughed at those recollections. He could see the school distinctly and, at play-time, the boys slyly looking through the reeds by the ditch-side at the schoolgirls' little carts; the young *nonnas*, in their white *baadjes*, peeping through the curtains of the rickshaw; the boys throwing them a kiss with quivering fingers, the girls throwing back the kiss to their boyish lovers in the reeds. And the assignations in the great, dark gardens; the burning and glowing in the childish breast: oh, he remembered it all!... And he saw, as he went on his lonely ride—although he now laughed the laugh of his mature years—he saw before his eyes all the girls with whom he had been in love, as a schoolboy, at Buitenzorg....

There was one delicate, fair-skinned girl, very pale and very pretty. She soon acquired the purple, laughing lips of the child who, by the time that she is thirteen, becomes a full-grown woman, with a ripe bust and riotous black curls.... And he also remembered a coffee-plantation in the hills, with a young married woman of barely twenty, who had taken him, a lad of fifteen, in her arms and had not released him until the boy had become a man. She had taught him the secret that was seething in his blood, throbbing in his veins, the secret that flushed his cheeks and took away his breath the moment he approached anything in the shape of a woman: the secret which the boy knew by hearsay but not by experience. And, ever since she taught it him, there had been in him, like a healthy hysteria or vigorous sensuality, a great lustiness of his adolescent body; a surplus of strength which he must needs dissipate: he never came near a woman now but he at once swiftly appraised her arms, her swinging gait, her bust, the look in her eyes, the laugh on her lips; if he passed her in the street, a quick glance printed her whole figure like a photograph on his sensual imagination until the next woman whom he met effaced it with her own, later print.

And, when he came to Holland as a young man and entered as a cadet at Breda, the need for lust had developed into an overpowering obsession, as it were an unquenchable thirsting of those new-found senses which were fermenting in the young male body. Afterwards, as a young officer, he had known one quick sensual

---

[4] Shirt.

[5] Half-castes.

passion after the other, taking each laughing enjoyment with all the carelessness of a youthful conqueror. His strong constitution and open-air life had enabled him to triumph like that with impunity, for years on end; but even at that time he had often suffered from sudden fits of depression, a secret, silent hopelessness, when everything seemed to be going black before him with needless, useless, menacing gloom. None of his fellow-officers saw it; none of his brothers or sisters. If he put in an appearance on one of those days, he was the same blunt, jovial soldier, the fair-haired, burly giant, rough and noisy, with the mock fierceness in his voice and the love of women in his brown, questing eyes, that went up and down, doing their appraising in a moment. But, secretly, there was within him so great a discontent with himself, that, as soon as he was alone, he would think:

"O God, what a rotten, filthy life!..."

Then he would fling himself on a couch, under his sword-rack, and wonder whether it was because he had drunk champagne yesterday, or because of something else ... something else ... a strong feeling of discontent. He did not know, but he made up his mind on one point, that he must knock off champagne: the damned fizzy stuff didn't suit him and he wouldn't drink it again. Indeed, he wouldn't drink much at all: no beer, no cocktails, for it all flew straight to his temples, like a wave of blood, and throbbed there, madly. And so it came to a secret abstemiousness, of which he never spoke and which he calculated so cunningly that his friends, though they knew that he was no great drinker, did not know that he could not support a drink at all. Sometimes he was fierce about it, allowed the drink to be poured out and emptied the glass under the table or broke it deliberately, knocked it over. That beastly drinking drove him mad; the other thing, on the contrary, kept him calm and cool, cleared his blood and his brain. It was after drinking, especially, that he felt depressed; after the other thing, he felt as if he were starting a new life. He was like that as a young officer, like that for years at Deventer, Venlo and the Hague; and his sudden rough outbursts—of insolent gaiety rather than anger—had given him his name as a big, blustering, brainless sort of ass: a pane of glass smashed, without the slightest occasion; a quarrel with a friend, without occasion; a duel provoked for no reason and then a reconciliation effected, with the greatest difficulty, by the other officers; a need sometimes to go for houses and people like a madman and destroy and break things, more from a sheer animal instinct of wanton gaiety than from anger. When he was angry, he knew what he was doing; a kind of soft-heartedness prevented him from becoming really angry; it was only that madness of his which allowed him to go really far, letting himself be carried away by a strange intoxication, the same intoxication which he felt on horseback, when riding in a steeplechase: a longing to rave and rage and go too far and trample on everything under him, not out of malice but out of madness. That again cooled him, made him feel clear and calm: it was only the confounded drink that drove him mad....

But, as he grew older, he quieted down and mastered his hot blood, so that he was satisfied with a quiet *liaison* with a little woman whom he went to see at regular intervals; and suddenly, in his secret fits of gloom and blackness, it was borne in upon him that he must get married, that it was that confounded living alone in rooms which gave him the deep-lying discontent which he never spoke about, for it would never have done to let the others notice things which they would think queer and of which he himself was at heart ashamed. And then, as he lay quietly, under his sword-rack, he would think, ah, to get married, to have a dear little wife ... and children, heaps of children ... and not to dissipate your substance for nothing!... But children ... Lord, Lord, how jolly, to have a whole tribe of children round you!... All that was kindly in him and friendly, not to say very romantic and extremely sentimental, now made him wax enthusiastic, under the sword-rack, the great, strong fellow who made the couch crack under him with his weight: Lord, Lord, how jolly! A whole tribe of children: not two or three, but a tribe, a tribe!... He smiled at the thought; after his riotous youth, it was a pleasant prospect: a nice little house, a home of his own, a dear little wife, children.... He talked to his mother about it; and she was delighted; because she had long been thinking that he ought to get married.... He was thirty-five now; yes, really, it would be a good thing to get married.... And she looked about and found Adeline for him: a good family, of French descent; connections in India, which was always nice; no money, but the Van Lowes never looked at money, though they hadn't so very much themselves, comparatively, professing a laughing contempt for the dross which, all the same, they could very well do with. A dear little girl, Adeline, young— she was thirteen years younger than her husband—fair-haired and placid: a regular little mother even as a girl. And Gerrit, though he had had a brief vision of other women, other girls, had thought:

"Oh, well, yes, a bit bread-and-buttery; but you want a different sort for your wife than you do for your mistress!"

And, after all, she was round and plump, a little round ball, even as a girl, and nice to hug, even though she was a bit short and though her figure was badly deficient in the lines that set his blood tingling. He never for a moment fell in love with Adeline; but he saw her for what she was: his wife and the mother of his children, the little tribe for which he longed, because it was such a pity and almost mean to go dissipating your substance for nothing, especially when you were getting a bit older and sobering down. He would have a healthy little wife in Adeline; she would give him a healthy little tribe.... She, in her placid way, had come to love him, very simply, because he was big and good-looking and because he was offering her, a penniless girl, a modest position. They had got married and were still living in the same little house, quite a small house, but big enough to harbour what Gerrit had looked for from the start, one citizen of the world after the other.

He thought it rotten now to be alone; and, when Mamma had asked Adeline and the children to the little villa at Nunspeet, he had grumbled that they were leaving him all alone, but gave in: a few weeks in the country would do the wife and the children good; and he ran down once or twice to Nunspeet on Sundays. But the loneliness was bad for him; and the house that had suddenly become lifeless and silent oppressed him with a gloom which weighed upon him so heavily that he could not throw it off: a cursed heavy weight which bore down on his chest. Add to this that, in order not to be alone in the evenings, he allowed the other fellows, at whose mess he dined these days, to persuade him to go with them and have a drink at the Witte ... and it was those confounded drinks which finished him, simply finished him.... He was home by one, at the latest; but he felt, after those drinks, as if he had been up all night: he could not sleep; if he fell asleep at last, he kept on waking up; his heart bounced as if it were trying to reach his temples; he turned about and turned about, dabbed his face and wrists, lay down again, ended by splashing cold water all over his body; then he crept into bed again, huddling himself up, with his knees drawn up to his chin, like a child; he stuffed the sheets into his ears, hid his watch, so as not to hear it ticking louder and louder, and at last went to sleep. When he woke in the early morning, whole landscapes of misty mountains pressed upon his brain, as though his poor head were the head of an Atlas supporting the world on his neck; persistent, slow-rolling, rocky avalanches crumbled all the way down his spine; and, with his legs stretched out wide in bed, he was so horribly depressed by that waking nightmare that he felt as if he could never make a move to get up, as if he could not stir his little finger. Then, at last, with a groan, he got up, cursing himself for drinking the damned stuff, took his bath, did his dumb-bell exercises, full of wondering admiration for his powerful arms and ingenuously thinking, if he was so strong in his muscles, why couldn't he carry off a drink or two?... Then he would look at his arms with the smiling vanity of a woman contemplating her beautiful curves; and, though his eyelids still hung heavy and round, too weary to roll up, the waking nightmare vanished under the influence of the water and the exercises and the misty mountains rose higher and higher till they vanished out of sight and the avalanche of rocks just tickled his back with a last gritty hail of pebbles. Then he became himself again: his orderly was waiting outside with his horse; in barracks he was the zealous captain, who carefully performed his military duties; none of the officers saw anything the matter with him....

But, though, of course, there were always the other fellows, loneliness seemed to envelop him, an almost tangible loneliness that pressed upon him, something that alarmed him. What was it this time, he would ask himself: was he ill, or had he the blues? Blast those moods, which you couldn't understand yourself! Was he ill, or had he the blues? Was it that beastly worm, rooting away in his carcase with its legs and eating up his marrow, or was he just thinking it rotten that his wife and children were away?... His brain was whirling with it all: first that rotten feeling and then the beastly worm. Sometimes it became such an obsession with him that, during his afternoon rides when he let his horse gallop wildly, he would see the thing wriggling along in front of him.... Then he would think of Ernst; and he felt sorry for the poor chap. What a queer thing it was, a diseased soul; and could he ... could he himself be diseased ... in his soul ... or at any rate in his body?... If he told people what he suspected, nobody would believe him. Outwardly he was such a sturdy fellow, such a healthy animal. But if only they could take a peep inside him!... That wretched worm thing had been at it again, rooting away in his carcase with its beastly legs, its hundreds of legs, never leaving him in peace. Was it just a queer feeling, was it an illusion, like Ernst's hallucination ... or could it really be a live thing?... No, that was too ridiculous: it wasn't really alive.... And yet he remembered stories of people who always had headaches, headaches which nothing could cure; and, after their death, a nest of earwigs had been found swarming in their brains.... Imagine, if it should be some beastly insect! But no, it wasn't alive, it wasn't alive: he only called it a worm or centipede because that described the beastly sensation.... Should he go and see a doctor, some clever specialist at Amsterdam?... But what was he to say?

"Doctor, there's something crawling about inside my carcase like a beastly centipede!"

And the doctor would tell him to undress and would look at his carcase, still young and fresh, notwithstanding his earlier rackety life, with the muscles in good condition, the joints flexible, the chest broad, the lungs expanded, and would stare at him and think ... he would think ... the specialist would think that he was mad! He would ask questions about his brothers and sisters ... and he would want to see Ernst ... and he would draw all sorts of learned conclusions, would the clever specialist.... No, hanged if he would go to a doctor; he would be ashamed to say:

"Doctor, there's something crawling about inside my carcase, like a beastly centipede."

He would be ashamed, absolute ashamed....

Or to say:

"Doctor, a gin-and-bitters upsets me."

"Well, captain," the doctor would say, "then you'd better not take a gin-and-bitters."

What was the use of going to a doctor, or even a specialist? He would not do it, he would *not*.... The best thing was to be abstemious, certainly not take any drinks ... and then grapple with that damned sensation—come, he wasn't a girl!—and not think about it, just stop thinking about it.... He must have a little distraction: he was leading such a lonely life these days. And, in that loneliness, without his wife and children, he began to think, with that incurable sentimentality which lay hidden deep down in him, of the comfort it was to belong to a large family, of the way it cheered you up.... Theirs had been a big family: but how it was scattering now! Bertha's little tribe had all broken up.... The others Mamma still kept together; and that Sunday evening was a capital institution of Mamma's.... And so he would look in on Karel and Cateau towards dinner-time, hoping that they would ask him to stay and that for once he would not have to dine with the other fellows at the mess; but they did not ask him and, when it was nearly six, Gerrit, feeling almost uncomfortable, heaved his big body out of his chair and went and joined the others, reflecting that Karel and Cateau had little by little become utter strangers.... And, though he was not awfully keen on Adolphine, he sank his pride, invited himself to her house and stayed on for the whole evening; and he had to confess to himself that, upon his word, Adolphine was at her best in her own house and that the evening had not been so bad. Constance was at

Baarn one day, at Nunspeet another; Van der Welcke was abroad; but Aunt Ruyvenaer was at the Hague—Uncle had gone to India—and Aunt Lot was always jolly:

"Yes, Herrit.... You showed a ghood nose to come here.... We're having *nassi*[6].... You'll stay and lhunch, take pot lhuck, eh, Herrit, what?"

He accepted gratefully, felt a sudden radiant glow inside him, just where loneliness gave him a feeling of icy cold. Yes, he would stay to lunch: he loved the East-Indian "rice-table," the way Aunt and Toetie made it; and he was secretly glad that Uncle was away, for he didn't like Uncle. In Aunt Lot's big, roomy house there was a sort of genial warmth that gave him a delicious sensation and almost left him weak, as though a smell of Java pervaded everything around, reminding him of his childhood. The house was full of Japanese porcelain; there were stuffed birds of paradise; under a big square glass cover was a whole *passer*,[7] with tiny dolls as toys: little *warongs*,[8] little herds of cattle; there were Malay weapons on the walls; in Aunt's conservatory there were mats on the floor, as in Java; and Gerrit thought it fun to tease Alima, though she was dressed as a European, and he was only sorry that she was not *latta*,[9] because that reminded him of the *latta* servants whom he used to tease, in Java, as a child:

"*Boeang, baboe; baboe, boeang!*"[10]

And from the Japanese porcelain and the birds of paradise and the *passer* there came that same smell, the smell that pervaded the whole house, a smell of *akar-wangi*[11] and sandalwood; and, while Aunt was making "rice-table" and Alima running from the store-room to the kitchen with a basket full of bottles of Indian spices, Gerrit felt his mouth water:

"Aunt, we're going to have a great tuck-in!"

"*Allah,*[12] that boy Herrit!" chortled Aunt Lot, looking terribly fat, with her vast, pendulous bosom, wearing no stays, indoors, but with brilliants the size of turnips in her ears. "*Allah,* that Herrit: he'd murder his own father for *nassi!*"

And Aunt went into ecstasies: Aunt, turned into a mobile Hindu idol, ran from kitchen to cellar and store-room; Toetie ran too; Alima ran too. The aromatic fragrance filled the whole house. There would be *petis,* black and scented and hot.

"Oh, for rice, with a dried fish, and *petis!*" Gerrit rhapsodized.

And Aunt laughed till the tears came, happy and glad because Gerrit was fond of *nassi.*

---

[6] Malay: rice, currie.

[7] Market-place, bazaar.

[8] Booths.

[9] Attractive, pretty.

[10] "Put the baby down, nurse; nurse, put baby down."

[11] Cedarwood, or any other scented wood.

[12] Lord!

But there would also be *kroepoek*,[13] golden and crisp: the dried fish which, when heated, swelled up into brittle flakes, flakes that cracked in your fingers as you broke them and between your teeth as you crunched them; and then there would be *lodeh*,[14] with a creamy sauce full of floating vegetables and *tjabé*; and, to follow on the rice, Aunt had made *djedjonkong*, the Java sugar-cake, with the icing of white *maizena*[15] on the top; only Aunt was sorry that she could get no *santen*,[16] in "Gholland," and had to do the best she could with milk and cream....

And, when at last they sat down to table—Aunt, the three girls and Gerrit, the enthusiastic Gerrit—Aunt and the little cousins would laugh aloud:

"*Allah*, that boy Herrit!"

And they vied with one another who should help him, very carefully, so that the rice should not make a messy heap on his plate:

"No, *don't* mix up your food!" Aunt Lot entreated. "That Dhutch *totok*[17] way of mixing up everything together: I can't stand it. Keep your rice clean, as clean as you can."

"Yes, Aunt, as maidenly as a young girl!" cried Gerrit, with sparkling eyes.

And Aunt again laughed till the tears came: too bhad, you know!

"And now your *lodeh* in the little saucer ... that's it ... so-o! ... And the *sambal*,[18] neatly on the edge of your plate: don't mix it up, Herrit ... Oh, that boy Herrit! ... Take a taste now: each *sambal* with a spoonful of rice ... that's it ... so-o! ... The *kroepoek* on the table-cloth ... that's it ... so-o! ... And now ghobble away ... *Allah*, that boy Herrit: he'd murder his own father for *nassi*! ... *Kassian*, Van Lowe!"

This last exclamation was meant to convey that Van Lowe, Gerrit's father, was dead long since and that Gerrit therefore could not murder his father for *nassi* if he wanted to; and this time Aunt's eyes filled with tears of real emotion, not of laughter: *kassian*, Van Lowe!

Gerrit no longer felt lonely and ceased thinking of those queer feelings of his. He ate his rice with due respect, ate it slowly, so as to spin out the enjoyment as long as he could; but it was an effort, you know, with Aunt and Toetie and Dotje and Poppie vying with one another in turns:

"Herrit, have some more sambal-tomaat[19]... Herrit, fill up your *lodel*-saucer.... Herrit, take some *ketimoen*:[20] that's nice and cool, if your mouth's burning...."

---

[13] The dried fish known in British India as Bombay duck.

[14] A sort of cocoa-nut.

[15] Indian cornflour.

[16] Cocoa-nut milk.

[17] The nickname given by the half-castes to the pure bred Dutch.

[18] Red pepper, capsicum.

[19] Tomato-capsicum.

[20] Cucumber, gherkin.

And, though Gerrit's palate was on fire, though the *sambal* rose to his temples till it congested his brain like a cocktail, Gerrit went on eating, took another spoonful of clean rice, took another taste of black *petis*....

"Herrit, there's *djedjonkong* coming!" Aunt warned him. "You won't leave me in the lurch with my *djedjonkong*, will you, Herrit?"

And Gerrit declared that Aunt was making heavy demands on his stomach, but that he would manage to leave room for the *djedjonkong*; and he banged one fist upon the other, to express that he would bang the *nassi* together in his stomach, to make room for the sugar-cake. Aunt was radiant with pleasure, because Gerrit thought everything so delicious; and, after the *djedjonkong*, as Gerrit sat puffing and blowing, she suggested:

"Come, Herrit, *nappas*[21] a bit now!"

And Gerrit took the liberty of loosing a few buttons of his uniform and dropped, with legs wide outstretched, into a wicker deck-chair, while Aunt invited him to be sure and not leave her in the lurch, next day, with the remnants.

The curry lunch at Aunt Lot's put Gerrit in good spirits for the whole day. He puffed and blew more in fun than in reality; he extolled the "rice-table," which is never heavy, the *tjabé*, which clears your blood and your brain; and it was as though Aunt's aromatic and very strong *sambals* filled him with the joy of life, for that day, and also with a certain tenderness, because it all reminded him of his childhood at Buitenzorg. He took his afternoon ride quietly and pleasantly: excellent exercise, after the generous meal; arrived at the mess in good spirits and did not eat much, gassing about Aunt Lot's *nassi*; and, when he went home, at a reasonable hour in the evening, he asked himself:

"If I can have such good days, why should I have such rotten ones? I shall tell Line to give us *nassi* every day; but Line can't do it as Aunt Lot does...."

Another day, Gerrit, with that sentimental longing for his own people, went and looked up Paul. He found him in his sitting-room, the place beautifully tidy, Paul lying on the sofa in a silk shirt and a white-flannel jacket, reading a modern novel. And Paul was very amiable, even allowed Gerrit to smoke a cigar: one of his own, for Paul did not smoke; only, he asked Gerrit not to make a mess with the ash and to throw the match into the wastepaper-basket at once, because he couldn't stand used matches about the place.

"Aren't you going away this summer?" asked Gerrit.

"Not I, my dear fellow!" said Paul, decidedly. "It's such dirty work, travelling: your skin gets black, your nails get black in the train; your clothes get creased in your trunk; and you never know what sort of bed awaits you. No, I'm getting too old to go away...."

"But aren't you even going to Nunspeet?"

---

[21] Take breath.

"Oh, my dear Gerrit," Paul implored, "what *is* the use of my going to Nunspeet? Mamma has Adeline and the children with her; Constance is devoting herself to Ernst: what earthly use would it be for me to go to Nunspeet?... All that travelling is such a nuisance; and going to Nunspeet would make me almost as dirty as going to Switzerland.... No, I shall stay where I am. The landlady's very clean and so is the maid; and, though I have to see to a lot myself, of course, things are fairly well cared for ... and not *too* dirty...."

"But, Paul," said Gerrit, with a sort of "Look here, drop it!" gesture, "that cleanliness of yours is becoming a mania!"

"And why shouldn't I have a mania as well as any one else?" asked Paul, in an offended voice. "Every one has a mania. You have a mania for bringing children into the world. Mine is comparatively sterile, but has just as much right to exist as yours."

"But, Paul, you're becoming an old fogey at this rate, never moving, for fear of a speck of dirt. If you go on like this, you'll get rooted in a little selfish circle of your own, you'll cease to take an interest in anything ... and you're young still, only just thirty-eight...."

"I've taken an interest in the world for years," said Paul, "but I consider the world such a vile, dirty rubbish-heap, such a conglomeration of human wretchedness, such a rotten, scurvy, stinking, filthy dustbin...."

"But, Paul, you're absurd!"

"Because I choose at last to retire into my room, where at least things are clean!" said Paul, with a gesture of irritation.

"My dear chap, you don't mean what you say: I can't tell if you're serious or humbugging."

"Serious? You say I'm not serious?" cried Paul, grinning scornfully and working himself into a real temper. "Do you think I'm not serious?"

"Well, if you're serious, then I say that you're simply diseased."

"Diseased?"

"Yes, diseased: just as much as Ernst is diseased. That tidiness of yours is a mania; that way of looking upon the world as a dustbin is a disease. You were always a humbug, but at least you used to be good company, you used to be a brilliant talker; and nowadays, for some time past, you show yourself nowhere, you shut yourself up, you're becoming impossible and a bore...."

"I'm becoming older," said Paul, soberly. "A brilliant talker? I may have been, perhaps. But it's not worth while. The moment you fashion a thought into words and try to express it, no one listens to you. People are just as sloppy and messy in their conversation as in everything else. It's not worth while.... And yet," he said, with a touch of melancholy, "you're right: I used to be different. But it's really not worth while, old fellow, in my case. You have your wife and your children: not that I'm yearning for a wife and children, especially such an ant-hill as you've brought into the world. But what have I? The club bores me. Doing anything bores me. I am too modern for the old ideas and not modern enough for the new ones."

His eyes lit up as he heard himself beginning to talk:

"Yes, the old ideas," he repeated; and his voice became fuller and recovered the rather sing-song rhythm of earlier days, when he used to unbosom himself at great length of all sorts of ironical theories and mock philosophy, very often superficial, but always brilliant. "The old ideas. There's rank, for instance. I've been thinking about it lately. I like rank. But do you know how I like it? Just as Ernst loves an antique vase, even so I am sometimes attracted by an old title. I should like to be a count or a marquis, not from snobbery: don't imagine that I want to be a count or a marquis out of snobbery, for that's not the idea at all. But just as Ernst admires an antique vase, or an old book, or a piece of brocade, I admire a count's or marquis' title; and my title, besides, would be much cleaner than the piece of brocade, which is full of microbes. But, for goodness' sake, don't run away with the idea that I want to be a count or a marquis out of snobbery. You understand, don't you? I should only care for it from the decorative and traditional point of view.... But a modern title of *jonkheer*,[22] Gerrit, dating back to William I.,[23] I wouldn't have if you paid me! To begin with, I think *jonkheer* an ugly word; and then I think that a title of that sort looks like a modern-art signboard, like one of those *art-nouveau* posters with their everlasting stiff, upright, squirmy lines; and those conventional poppies are positively revolting to my mind because they symbolize to me the cant and hypocrisy of our modern world.... Yes, there's a great deal of poetry, Gerrit, in old ideas. We people are crammed full of old ideas: we inherited them; they're in our blood. And we live in a society in which the new ideas are already putting forth shoots, the real, new ideas, the true, the beautiful ideas, the three or four beautiful ideas that already exist. But I, for my part, have my blood so full of old ideas that I can't advance with the rest.... New ideas: look here, one new idea, a really beautiful new idea, in our time, is pity. Gerrit, what could be more beautiful and more delightful and newer than pity: genuine pity for all human wretchedness? I feel it myself, even though I never leave my sofa. I feel it myself. But, even as I feel it and never leave my sofa, so the whole world feels the new idea of pity ... and never leaves its sofa.... Lord, my dear chap, there's blood sticking to everything; the world is nothing but mean selfishness and hypocrisy; there's war, injustice and all sorts of rottenness; and we know it's there and we condemn it and we feel pity for everything that is trampled underfoot and sucked dry.... And what do we do? Nothing. I do just as little as the great powers do. The Tsar does nothing; there's not a government, not an individual that does a thing. You don't do anything either.... Meanwhile, there is war, there is injustice, not only in South Africa, but everywhere, Gerrit, everywhere: you've only to go outside and you'll come upon injustice in the

---

[22] The lowest title of nobility in Holland, ranking after the barons and hereditary knights or *ridders*. The highest title is that of count. There are no marquises or dukes in the Northern Netherlands.

[23] 1814.

Hoogstraat; you've only to go travelling and get black with grime and dirt ... and you'll find injustice everywhere.... And, meanwhile, that idea is stirring in this filthy world of ours: the idea of pity.... And, just as I am powerless, everything and everybody is powerless.... Then am I not right to withdraw from the whole business into my room ... and to stay on my sofa?..."

He went on talking; and at last Gerrit got up, glad that he had been to see Paul and that Paul had talked as usual, long-winded though he might have been. But he was hardly gone, before Paul rose from his sofa. He flung open the shutters, to air the room of Gerrit's smoke; he rang the bell, to have the ash cleared away; he put the chairs straight and removed every trace of Gerrit's visit:

"There, I let myself be persuaded into talking!" thought Paul, irritably. "But d'you think the chap grasped it and valued it for a moment? Of course he didn't: not what I said of the old and not what I said of the new ideas!... It's not worth while taking the trouble to be a brilliant talker.... The world is dirty and stupid ... and Gerrit is stupid also, with his nine children, and dirty, with those cigars of his ... and besides he's a melancholy beggar, who has his manias ... just as Ernst has ... and I ... and everybody...."

And he flung himself angrily on his cushions and read his modern novel, all day long, without so much as stirring....

CHAPTER X

Dorine also, Gerrit remembered, had remained in the Hague; and he looked her up at her boarding-house, where she occupied two small, comfortless rooms. He had not seen her for days ... or was it weeks? He called twice without finding her in: the servant did not know where she had gone, for Miss van Lowe was nearly always out. At last, Gerrit caught her at home, at twelve o'clock, when she was hurriedly having a makeshift lunch, on the edge of the table, with her chair askew, taking nervous bites and timid sips.

"My dear Dorine, where have you been hiding all this time?" asked Gerrit, with boisterous geniality.

She was out of sorts at being taken by surprise:

"Where have I been hiding? Where have I been hiding? I never have a moment to hide anywhere. I'm far too busy for that!"

"But what have you got to do?"

"What have I got to do? The day flies ... and I never have time to do what I've got to do."

"But what *have* you got to do, Dorine?"

"My dear Gerrit, I won't bore you with a list of my doings. Take it from me that my life is sometimes *too* busy and that I *never* know a second's rest...."

He sat down and looked at her lunch.

"I came to take a snack with you and just to have a chat. But I see that you're in a great hurry and that you haven't a great deal to eat, so I don't expect you want me...."

"Do you think I sit down to an elaborate meal all by myself? No, Gerrit, I've no time for that."

"Have you a mouthful for me?"

"A mouthful, yes. I'll ring and order a couple of eggs for you."

She rang, ordered the eggs; and Gerrit was given a plate on the edge of the unlaid table:

"I'm glad to see you again, Sissy," said Gerrit. "I never see you at all, now that we don't meet at Mamma's."

"Well, you don't miss much."

"I can't say you're very amiable to-day. Have you such a thing as a glass of beer for me?"

"No, I haven't any beer."

"What are you drinking then?"

"Water, as you see."

"Oh, do you drink nothing but water? Well, then I'll have a glass of water too. I'm not very hungry either," said Gerrit, fibbing, for he was always hungry. "And, tell me, Dorine: don't you intend to run down to Nunspeet?"

"Ye-es," said Dorine, dubiously. "I ought really to go to Nunspeet.... Mamma's written to me, so has Adeline ... but I don't know how to fit it in."

"How do you mean, to fit it in?"

"Well, with the things I've got to do here."

"But what is it you've got to do?"

"Oh, Gerrit, nothing really that would interest you!... The point is that I'm good enough for Nunspeet ... but then of course they only want me to be nurse to your children."

"Why, Dorine!"

"That's it, of course!" she said, tartly. "To be nurse to your children!"

"I don't think you need be afraid of that. Line has the governess with her...."

"Well, then why does everybody want to get me down to Nunspeet: Mamma, Adeline, you?... I can't do anything for Ernst, because Ernst upsets me too much...."

"But, Dorine, to give you a change ... as you're so lonely here...."

"Lonely?... Lonely?" echoed Dorine.

She drank her last sip of water and said:

"I don't mind being lonely...."

"Yes, I know that, but still it's rather comfortless."

"I like being lonely. I think it very cosy and comfortable."

"You think it cosy?"

"Yes."

"Here, in this bare room of yours?"

"Yes, here, in this bare room of mine."

"But, Dorine, that's not possible!"

"But, good gracious, Gerrit, don't I tell you that it is!"

She stamped her foot angrily and gave him a resentful glance. Behind her dark eyes he saw a whole world of secret bitterness, a fierce grudge which smouldered in the depths of her soul. And it suddenly struck him that she looked very old, though he knew that she was only just thirty-nine. Her hair, drawn into a knot at the back, was beginning to go grey, there were deep wrinkles in her forehead, now that she was out of temper; and the lines of her cheeks and chin and her sharp, bitter mouth gave her almost the look of an old woman. Her figure too appeared withered and shrunken. And he suddenly thought her so much to be pitied in her lonely life as an unmarried woman without interests, over whose head the years had passed bringing none of the sweetness of the changing seasons—for it seemed as if she had never known a spring, as if she would never know a summer, as if there would only be the dreary autumn which was now beginning to loom dimly before her, as if there had never been anything for her in life, as if there never would be anything for her, never anything but that weary passing of the monotonous, lonely days, so lonely and so monotonous that she created for herself a bustle and flurry that did not exist, interests that were not there, an activity which she imagined, running in and out of shop after shop, for a box of stationery or a skein of thread, with, in between, a casual charitable call, done in a fussy, unpractical fashion—he suddenly thought her so much to be pitied in her loveless, cheerless life that he said:

"Shall I tell you what would be nice of you? And sensible?... To pack up all your traps, say good-bye to your landlady below ... and come and live with *us!*"

She stared at him with angry eyes and pressed her thin lips together:

"Come and live with *you*?" she asked, in astonishment. "What do you mean?"

"What I say. The house is small, but we can manage with the children; you would have a tiny bedroom: that's the best I could do for you. Line is very fond of you and so are the children. And then you'd be living with us and have a jolly time."

"*Live* with you?" she repeated.

And he saw a shadow of hesitation in her eyes, for, indeed, it seemed to her that a heavenly warmth suddenly lapped her round; and she felt her dark, angry eyes grow moist, she did not know why.

"Yes. Wouldn't you think that jolly?"

"But what put it into your head, Gerrit?"

"Because I don't think it's jolly for you here."

"I'm all right here, I'm quite contented."

"Yes, I know; but surely you'd be more comfortable with us?"

She made an effort to force back the tears in her eyes. It was always so, with those tiresome, nervous tears: they came for nothing, for no reason at all. It was not sensitiveness in her, it was sheer miserable nervousness, so she herself thought; and she hated herself for it, hated herself for those tears which sparkled so readily. But Gerrit's words had surprised her and touched her, surprised and touched her to such an extent that she was ashamed to let him see it and so blazed out, purposely, in order to hide herself behind that assumption of bitter resentment and ill-temper:

"More comfortable? More comfortable in your house? I'd be a *nursemaid* in your house, that's what I should be! No, I've had enough in the end of living for everybody who wants me and who can make use of me! I'm going to live for *myself* at last, for myself and nobody else...."

"But, Dorine...."

He did not complete his sentence. He did not wish to be cruel and tell her that she had never lived for anybody but herself: not because she was selfish, for she was not that at heart, but because she had never found the right path, along which she could have trudged valiantly, urging her lonely steps towards a point which would have formed a centre for her small life, for the small circle of herself and that which she would have loved. Year after year had passed over her head, bringing none of the sweetness of the changing seasons: the illusion of spring she had never known; the fierce heat of summer she had never known; kindly shelter she had never known; nor had she ever known aught of blowing winds and raging storms: all that was sensitive in her had shrivelled like flowers which no sun has ever shone upon; what was feminine in her had withered like flowers which no dew has watered; and everything in her had become soured and embittered into an almost unconscious exasperation at her aimless existence, at her loveless life, which had gone on for years and years. Was it now nothing but autumn in front of her and around her, like twilight in her soul, like twilight around her soul?...

He stood up, she made him feel sad. He went away; and his parting words were merely:

"No, Dorine, you would not be a nursemaid in our house. If you care to think it over, do; and be sure that Line and I will think it very jolly if you do come to us...."

And he took his afternoon ride, picked out his lonely road. With a horse, like that, it was like being with a friend. He patted the animal's neck; and it shivered, like a woman under a caressing hand. He talked to it; and it shook its pointed ears, as though it understood, as though it answered with a graceful movement of its neck and head. And, while he let the horse go at a foot's pace, with the reins held loose in his hand, he thought how lonely it had all become, now that the twilight was deepening around them. In bright flashes he thought just once more of his childhood, out there: Buitenzorg; the white palace; the delicious garden, unique of its kind and world-famous, with its precious trees, its clustering palms, its giant ferns, its strange, huge giant creepers with stems as thick as pythons slung from tree to tree.... And, behind it, the river ... where he used to play with Karel and Constance.... Oh, how vivid it all was! To think of it almost brought the tears to his eyes, now that the twilight was gathering round him and these memories were but the last reflection of those sunny days when they were all children together!... It had begun very slowly, slowly but irrevocably: the gradual separation and drifting apart, the ties loosened until they were all detached ... now, just now, in the sombre twilight that was drawing nigh.... Slowly, slowly, with every year in which the brothers and sisters grew bigger and older, in which they developed from children into persons who themselves drew a circle around them, their own circle of marriage, their own circle of children, of which they themselves were now the centre, even as his father and his mother had been in their family-circle, in their circle of children and even grandchildren.... Slowly, slowly it had happened, year by year, really almost unnoticeably, that all the brothers and sisters who had been one family in the white palace over there—which in that garden yonder, so very far away in miles and years, seemed to him part of the fairy-tale of his boyhood, with Constance' fairy figure flitting through it, red flowers at her temples—that all the brothers and sisters had drawn a circle round about themselves, a circle of their families or of themselves alone; and, though those circles for the first few years had sometimes intersected one another, slowly, slowly they had shifted farther and farther apart; and, just as that gloomy twilight drew nigh, they retreated still farther.... Had Mamma always secretly foreseen it; and was that why she had clung so obstinately to that one evening a week, the evening at which formerly he had laughed and joked with the others: always that Sunday evening of Mamma's, the "family group," that gathering at regular intervals, with cards and cakes, which they all sometimes thought extremely boring, but never neglected, for the sake of the old mother, who wished to keep the children together? Had Mamma always foreseen it? Oh, it still existed, the family-group, with the cards and cakes, every Sunday; but was it not really losing its significance more and more ... because the circles had shifted so very far apart?... The twilight was gathering around them all, sombre and menacing; and he felt its chilling influence even now as he rode along on that warm summer's day: the twilight was deepening around Dorine and around Paul, growing darker and darker with their growing loneliness, the loneliness of a lonely man and a lonely woman who had not sought or had not found the warm light for their later years, the still young but yet later years of the small soul that just exists and, consciously or unconsciously, is for ever asking itself the reason of its small existence.... The twilight was perhaps not yet so dark around Adolphine, for she still had her own circle; but even that circle had already shifted far from the original family-circle, was moving farther and farther away.... And the twilight had fallen, black as night, so suddenly, around poor Bertha, now that she was dozing away in a small house in a village where she knew nobody and did nothing but look out of her window at the garden, while the roar of the trains deadened her already dull memories. It seemed too as if Bertha's circle had broken up, like a ring of light that breaks up into sparks which die out in the distance, now that she had no one with her but Marianne, poor girl, pining away in her unhappy lot, the victim of a destiny too big for her small soul.... Karel, his brother: was Karel his brother still? Or had not Karel, with his wife, who had never been admitted to the family as an intimate, also shifted his circle far, far away from the circle of them all?... And, as for poor Ernst, had the twilight not deepened around poor Ernst, his gloomy solitude growing ever darker, until he had fallen ill, ill in his soul and in his senses?... And, now that all those circles were shifting so far away from one another and becoming ever wider, what consolation would there be for Mamma, around whom loneliness and darkness were closing, closing just around her, poor Mamma, to whom the family circle meant so much, who had always wanted to remain the centre of the love and warmth of all her children?... And it was strange that, when he thought of Constance, her circle, on the contrary, seemed to be moving closer, as though there were a new light dawning for her and Addie; and strangest of all was when he thought of himself and of his little tribe, which, it was true, had left him for the moment, but still belonged to him and was always, always round him ... as if there were no twilight there at all ... as if it were always dawn, a radiant dawn, flinging wide its golden beams.... Oh, children were everything! Had he not done wisely to create his golden dawn?... He did not think of his wife: he thought of his children; he was a father more than a husband.... Had he not done well? Was it not there that hope smiled upon him, upon all of them, upon poor Mamma: upon poor Mamma who, at that very moment, was sunning her lonely old age in the light of that golden dawn?... Had he not done wisely? But why, if he had done wisely, must he doubt sometimes and be astonished and even anxious about all that young, radiant life which he had begotten and which shed forth a warmth and light in which he now felt his strange soul happily basking, warmer and lighter than the sunlight in which he was riding?

84

Why should he doubt and be astonished and even anxious?... Oh, he saw it, suddenly: because, later on, the rays of that golden dawn also would shine far away from their centre and that golden radiance would gradually become dim and dark in its turn!... But, suppose it were a law of nature, suppose it were bound to be, that all that was united at first in sunny affection and sunny fellowship should scatter in all directions; suppose it were bound to circle away and fade into sombre twilight; suppose it were a law of nature that brothers and sisters should become estranged, as though they had not been born of one mother and begotten of one father! Suppose that had to be! Then why have so many doubts, why feel astonishment and anxiety and why not enjoy the warmth, as long as the morning sun still shone, after the first gleams of the cheerful dawn?... Oh, how he longed for his dawn, his little tribe of laughing children! He would go to them to-morrow, to-morrow! To see them all around him, to hold them all in one vast embrace, to toss them in his arms, to let them ride on his back and on his shoulders, to dandle them on his knee, to romp with them till they all rolled in a heap, to press his lips to their soft childish skins, giving himself sheer ecstasy in those simple caresses! He would go down to-morrow, to-morrow!...

Yes, the gloom might deepen around all the rest, but light was still dawning before him, as it had shone, long years ago, before his father and mother, when they had all—he and his brothers and sisters—been children together and their sunny radiance had been their parents' dawn yonder in India, in the grand white palace, in the fairy gardens.... Yes, light was still dawning in front of him ... and, though later that light would surely circle away from him also, though the twilight would gather around his head, around his soul, as it was now beginning to gather, with such gloomy darkness, around his poor mother, there was still the present and he had no right to feel doubt or anxiety.

He rode back; and the evening dusked along the wooded roads. But straight before his eyes was a whirl of golden dust, because he had forced his thoughts to be glad and sunny: his fair-haired little tribe, at Nunspeet, whirled before his eyes. It whirled all radiant light, straight before his eyes.

When he was back in town, seated at the officers' mess, where he dined these days, not one of them noticed that he had seen that deepening twilight, nor that he had seen the first gleam of dawn; and he was just a big, yellow-haired fellow, a great, burly officer, with a jovial, blustering voice and rough movements that made his chair creak and his glass in constant danger of breaking; and all the time a stream of noisy oaths came from his mouth and his jokes set the whole table ringing with laughter....

CHAPTER XI

Months had dragged by, when Gerrit, riding out with his squadron, had a meeting that gave him a shock. It was on the Koninginnegracht, one dank autumn morning, dull and dark at that early hour, as if it would not get light all day; the whole roadway was taken up by the horses, whose hoofs clattered in rhythmical trot over the even cobbles; the maids, in their lilac-print dresses, hung out of the windows to look at the fine hussars. A closed cab came towards the squadron and had to pull up beside the pavement to let the horses pass. And, with a swift glance, Gerrit saw through the dimmed panes of the carriage the face of a woman with a pair of laughing eyes: two brown-gold sparks of laughter, lasting scarce two or three seconds, those two gleams of gay gold. The laughing eyes were all that he saw in the vague expanse of face, pale in the shadow of the cab, under the dark frame of a large hat; but that laughing glance gave him such a shock that he flushed purple, while his blood flew to his temples and set them throbbing as if he had taken a cocktail. He felt a stinging sensation in his neck; and the thought flashed through him:

"I'll be hanged if that wasn't Pauline! I'll be hanged if that wasn't Pauline! Can she be back at the Hague?"

But he pulled himself together, settled himself stiffly and firmly in the saddle and tried to forget his shock and the two brown-gold sparks of those laughing eyes. Well, suppose it were she: what about it? It was all so long ago; and did he not often come across the live memories of his past, looming up suddenly on his path, just like that, in the street, and did he not pass them with hardly a smile of reminiscence lurking under his moustache and just lingering in his glance? Suppose it were she: what then? Was he, who had brought all his old madness within respectable, middle-aged bounds, going to let himself be shocked by a pair of laughing eyes out of the past?... No, he felt himself quiet and strong, in the soberness of his later years. If his blood went coursing through his veins like that at the glance of a woman, at a memory looming up on his path, he couldn't help it.... Nevertheless, all that autumn day—a day which had opened dull and dark and which had remained dull and dark, with its heavy, clouded sky—was lighted for him by the two or three seconds' gay, golden gleam from those eyes. Yes, what eyes that girl Pauline had ... Lord, what a pair of eyes! Eyes that laughed even when her mouth did not, eyes full of golden mockery, eyes which knew that they sent him raving mad with their glance, as if he were a brand which a spark from them set on fire!... And she knew it, she knew well enough that she sent him mad with her eyes!... Was she back at the Hague? At the time, she had suddenly gone to Paris and he had not seen her for years ... for at least twelve years. He was twelve years older now; she was twelve years older. How rotten, that getting old, that wearing out of your miserable carcase, of the one body which you got in this world and which you took to the grave with you and which you couldn't change, as you change into a new uniform!... Well, his was still fit and strong; and Pauline's eyes laughed as they used to do....

Twelve years? Come, he wouldn't think about it any longer! If he once started remembering everything that had happened years and years ago, the day would be too short for his recollections!

And, in the staidness of his riper years, he forgot the meeting on the Koninginnegracht and even thought that he might easily have been mistaken and that it wasn't Pauline at all.... He was no longer lonely in his house, now that his wife and the children filled the home once more; and he felt that he must always have it like this in future: the warmth of the snug home around him; that otherwise he would feel unhappy and queer and lonely, as in those months last summer. And the first Sunday evening at Mamma's sent a cheerful glow all through him; and yet it seemed empty here and there in the once crowded drawing-rooms. For the two old aunts no longer came: Mamma, it was true, had not held them accountable for the upset which they had caused with their shrill, childish voices on that most unfortunate evening, when poor Constance had been so excited as it was; Mamma had forced herself always to remain nice to them; but gradually they had fallen into their dotage altogether and never went out now, living in their little villa with a nurse; they had become very badly-behaved and fought and quarrelled with each other; they slept in one bed and refused each other a fair share of the sheets; and once Aunt Rine pushed Aunt Tine on the stairs, so that she fell down and hurt her old ribs severely. So they no longer came. And it was strange, but Gerrit missed the queer, old figures of those two antiquated spinsters, who used to sit, each with a great piece of crochet-work in her bony hands, on either side of the conservatory-doors all through the Sunday evening, now and again hissing into each other's ears spiteful observations which the children heard and understood and laughed at; looking with their greedy old eyes, sweet-toothed old ladies that they were, at the cakes and lemonade; consuming them at last, with gloating satisfaction; then getting up suddenly, both at the same time, and going downstairs, under the careful conduct of the little nieces, to the four-wheeler with the reliable driver, who always brought them safe home. The Sunday evenings were no longer the same, thought Gerrit, without those two characteristic, traditional figures, about whom they all cracked a lot of jokes, but who nevertheless had so long retained something of life's immutability and pathetic monotony ... until suddenly the change came and the two figures disappeared.... They would go on living for years, perhaps, wrangling and quarrelling, clinging desperately to the world with their bony hands: for years, as though death couldn't get at them; but they would never sit there again, one by each of the conservatory-doors....

But a great void had been caused by the dispersal of Bertha's little band. For Bertha never came to the Hague now; and all who had been to see her at Baarn were agreed that she was becoming very strange and sat in a very strange way at her window, almost without moving, as if, after her busy, stirring life, she, the society-woman, had suddenly, upon her husband's death, felt that there was no need to do anything more and had let that atmosphere of listlessness and apathy submerge her and become the element in which she vegetated. She hardly ever spoke, took no interest in anything, just sat and looked out of the window, never going outside the house; and, though she had the full use of her senses, she had lapsed into a sort of staring torpor, submitting to the passing of the years, the unnecessary, sombre years that would glide noiselessly over her soul, bringing with them the dreary twilight, unillumined by a ray of hope, in which her soul would sit, waiting for the coming darkness.... In that house of mourning, in her silent, passionless grief, she had kept no one with her but Marianne, though Marietje was to come home later. The family knew about Emilie and Henri now, for Emilie, proud of her new life, had been unable to hold her tongue, had bragged of what they were doing and how they were making money in Paris; and the whole family had been astounded and shocked at it. Adolphine and Cateau had made them all swear never, whatever they did, to let out that Emilie painted fans or that Henri had become a circus-clown! True, they had not been able to hide Emilie's fans from Mamma van Lowe, because Emilie herself had presented her grandmother with one; but that scandal about Henri the old woman fortunately had not heard: it might have given her a shock that would have been fatal.... Gerrit knew that people at the Hague were incessantly telling stories about Emilie and Henri and he would rather have told the thing out, so that people should know the truth; but the others, even Constance, implored him to hold his tongue and so he would hold his tongue with the rest, as if it concerned a disgraceful family-secret....

Ernst, it is true, had never come regularly to the Sunday evenings; but none the less his absence—down at Nunspeet—cast a sad shadow. What was even sadder was that Aunt Lot still came with the girls, but was full of bitter lamentation, saying that things were going altogether wrong with the sugar and that these were r-r-rotten times. And, as a matter of fact, suddenly, one Sunday, Aunt came with much emotion and tears, the girls more resigned, good, simple souls that they were; and Aunt told in a torrent of words how they were as good as ruined—Uncle had sent cable after cable from Java—as good as ruined: they were leaving their big house at once; they already had in view a tiny little house at Duinoord; and they would manage there till better times came. It created great consternation in the family, where money never counted but had always been very useful; yet Gerrit, in spite of Aunt Lot's tragic attitude and the tearful voice in which she lamented her fate all through the evening, admired a certain keen practical sense in her; in the girls there was also an unruffled calm, a quiet determination to accept the situation sensibly, without keeping up the appearance of former luxury, and to retire into poverty with a modest resignation that left no room for false shame.... A tiny little house, one servant: yes, Herrit, but Aunt would ask him to *nassi* all the same, for there was no living without *sambal*, eh, Herrit?... And Gerrit admired it all, admired that practical notion of at once cutting your coat according to your cloth in spite of the tragedy of tears and gestures and exclamations of "Ye-es, *kassian!*"[24] And he said, speaking to Constance:

---

[24] Oh, dear!

"Do you think that real Dutch people could ever behave like that? No, to begin with, they wouldn't trumpet it forth; then they would go quietly abroad; but good old Aunt Lot trumpets it forth and started being practical yesterday and isn't ashamed to move into a smaller house; and, as I live, she's already asking me to *nassi!*"

Yes, that was the good, old-fashioned East-Indian way; the simple soul, the simple views of life; the real thing, without show; the cordial hospitality surviving, even though there was no money left; and all this attracted Gerrit, for all Auntie's East-Indian accent, for all her look of a Hindu idol, with the capacious, rolling bosom and the brilliants as big as turnips.... And the three girls, no longer young—why had those good children never married, in "Gholland"?—so quiet and practical, laughing already at the thought of the one servant: they'd make their own beds; but Alima, of course, was remaining—dressed just like a lady, stays and all, splendid!—sharing prosperity and misfortune with her *njonja,*[25] just simply, without stopping for a moment to think whether she hadn't better look out for a better place.

"Yes, Constance, say what you like, it does me good, in this cold Dutch air of ours, a glimpse like that of the simple, warmhearted, old-Indian way!"

And, in spite of all, there were still cards and cakes on Sunday evenings; but, though Mamma stuck to it, though she was still the centre of her circle, though the children left her outside most minor quarrels and difficulties, she still seemed to feel that something was cracking and tearing and breaking. No, she could no longer deny it to herself; and her once bright old face had changed, had lost its cheerfulness and had come to wear, with those new wrinkles round the mouth, a melancholy, moping look: the family was a *grandeur déchue!*

And things were no better when Constance, making her voice as gentle and sympathetic as she could, spoke to her about Addie; and, on one of those Sunday evenings, the old woman said to Van der Welcke, in a harsh voice, which was beginning to tremble with the sound of broken harp-strings: "So Addie ... has changed his mind. Constance has told me."

It had been a great disappointment to Van der Welcke too, so great that he could not forgive Addie and would hardly speak to him. And he also shrugged his shoulders, angrily, as if he couldn't help it:

"What am I to say, Mamma? Addie is such a very determined boy. He spoke to his mother at Nunspeet and his mother agrees with him. I don't."

The old woman's head dropped to her breast and went nodding softly up and down.

"The older we become," she said, "the more disappointment we find in life...."

She looked up; there was resentment in her eyes. She beckoned Addie to her, with that imperative gesture which she sometimes employed even to the oldest of her children.

---

[25] Mistress.

The boy came:

"What is it, Grandmamma?"

She looked at him; and something within her at once grew softer, when she saw him standing before her, with a grave, gentle smile on his fair boyish face, the face which was at the same time so virile in its strength. Still, she shook her grey head, as though to say that she knew all about it; and there was reproach in her flickering eyes.

"Well, well," she said. "Mamma has been speaking to me, Addie. And Mamma tells me that you have changed your mind ... that you want to be a doctor."

"Yes, Granny."

"Well, well ... and Papa and Mamma and Grandmamma, who would so much have liked to see you make your way in the diplomatic service."

"Granny, really, I don't feel that I have the vocation."

"And as a doctor?"

"As a doctor, yes, Granny."

"Then I suppose it can't be helped, Addie," said the old woman; and she suddenly broke down and began to sob quietly.

Van der Welcke looked gloomy. The boy looked down upon them where he stood, in front of his father and his grandmother. He liked the old woman and he adored his father and had been hurt by his father's fit of sulkiness. But he couldn't help seeing that it was their vanity that was wounded; and, without wishing to be cruel, he couldn't help saying, very gently:

"Granny, Mamma understood. I should be so glad, Granny, if you and Papa could also understand...."

But Van der Welcke's jealousy of Constance stabbed ruthlessly at his heart: he rose and moved to the card-table.

"Mamma understood, Addie?" the old lady repeated, resentfully. "Oh, Mamma knows that she can't refuse you anything, you see. Papa too; and now he's upset, poor Papa.... Our illusions become fewer and fewer, Addie, as we grow older; and therefore it's so terribly sad, dear, when we have to lose the very last of them. We had all placed our hopes in you, my boy."

"But, even if I don't go in for the diplomatic service, Granny, that's no reason why I...."

The old woman raised her hand almost angrily, imposing silence upon him:

"Diplomacy is the finest profession in the world," she said, sharply. "There's nothing above it.... It's just those new ideas, dear, which Granny can't keep up with and which make her so sad, because she doesn't understand them...."

"Granny, I can't bear to see you crying like this."

He sat down beside her, took her hand, looked into her eyes. She mistook his gentleness:

"Won't you think it over, Addie?" she asked, softly and coaxingly:

"No, Granny," he said, in a calm, decided tone. "I can't do that."

"You mean, you won't."

"I can't, I mustn't, Granny."

"You mustn't?"

"No, Granny. Do try to realize, Granny dear, that I *mustn't.*"

The old woman's head went up and down, nodding bitter reproaches....

"Granny, may I promise you to try my hardest ... to do you credit, one of these days ... as a doctor?"

She gave an angry, contemptuous smile through her tears. He kissed her very tenderly....

"Ah," he thought to himself, "how we all drag with us—every one of us—that burden of vanity in our souls ... which prevents us from living, from really *living!*..."

CHAPTER XII

Yes, Gerrit had quite forgotten the golden glint of those two laughing eyes which he had seemed to recognize; he had only just reflected, lightly and vaguely, that he must have been mistaken. And great was his surprise, a few days later, when, on his way to the Witte after dinner, a woman came up to him near the club, in the dusk of the evening, and, as she passed, flashed a laughing glance into his eyes and whispered very tenderly, almost in his ear:

"Good-evening, Gerrit!"

He knew the voice, even as he had known the eyes: a drowsy, deep-throated note, with a slight roll of the "r's." Yes, he recognized her: it was really Pauline; she was back at the Hague. After twelve years' time!... Well, he took no notice of her, walked on, turned the corner and reached the Witte at once. He ran up the steps, almost as though fleeing from something outside; and his face was red, his temples throbbed. He stayed talking to his friends for an hour or so, curious to learn whether they too had happened to see Pauline. But the others—younger officers than himself, he reflected— did not know her; and he did not hear her name mentioned....

He went home early. The impudent wench, to *dare* to speak to him! He went to bed early, man of regular habits that he had become in the course of years; and, while Adeline was already asleep in the other bed, he saw the golden eyes laughing, heard his name murmured by that drowsy, provocative voice, heard it whispered almost close to his ear.... He fell asleep and, in his dreams, saw the golden eyes....

Well, he thought next morning, if he was to start dreaming of all the eyes into which he had looked, his sleep would be one great firmament of eyes! And, as he got up and took his bath, he threw the thing off him, washed those eyes out of his mind.... Then he breakfasted, quickly, with his pretty children, vigorous and fair-haired, around him; and then he rode to the barracks....

But, two days later, walking back from barracks with a couple of officers, at six or half-past, he came upon Pauline under the fading trees beside the Alexandersveld. He repressed a movement of impatience and thought:

"Is she mad? Is she pursuing me deliberately?" But he did not let the others notice anything. One of them said:

"A fine girl. Who is she?"

But none of them knew; and they went on. Gerrit did not look round.

The thing began to get on his nerves. What did the damned wench want to come back to Holland for and why must she look at him and speak to him, why must she go walking past the barracks? Was she mad, was she mad?... He felt angry and uneasy.... And, a day or two after, as though he had a presentiment, he hung about the barracks, so as to go away alone, quite late.

He met her; and, in the dim light under the fading trees, her eyes laughed towards him through the distance like gold, with that gay, wicked glint of mockery.

"Damn it all!" he cursed.

And, resolved to take up a firm attitude, he squared his chest, put his shoulders back, apparently wishing to fill the whole lane with his manly determination to force his way through every ambush and snare. But she stopped right in front of him and said, in that drowsy, seductive voice:

"Good-evening, Gerrit!"

"Look here, clear off, will you? And be damned quick about it!" said Gerrit, angrily.

"It's so nice, meeting you again!"

"Yes, but I don't think it a bit nice, see? So be off!"

And he tried to walk on, broad-chested and imposing, the strong man who would trample on every smiling and mocking temptation that blocked his way under the fading trees.

"Gerrit, I *must* speak to you," she implored.

"Yes, but I don't want to speak to you."

"Oh, but I *must* speak to you, Gerrit!" murmured the languorous, maddening voice. "I must, I must speak to you. Not here, but just ... just inside the Woods."

"What do you want to speak to me about?"

"Only for a second.... I can't tell you here."

"Well, no, d'you see?" said Gerrit, roughly. "I don't want to have anything to do with you."

"Yes, yes, Gerrit.... Please, Gerrit ... only for a second...."

And he walked on.

She followed him:

"Gerrit...."

"I say, if you don't hurry up and clear out...!"

"Gerrit, just let me tell you something ... let me speak to you for three minutes ... in the Woods...."

The voice coaxed him and he saw that deep glint of mockery in the laughing eyes.

"Only for three minutes ... and then I sha'n't worry you any more...."

"Well ... go ahead then!" said Gerrit. "You go on.... I'll follow you.... But be quick ... I've no time...."

"Where are you going?"

"Home."

"Are you married, Gerrit?"

"Yes. Go ahead now."

"And have you any kiddies?"

"Yes, I have.... *Ajo!*..."[26]

"I expect they're charming kiddies, Gerrit?"

Once again the deep glint in those golden, mocking eyes leapt out at Gerrit ... and then she had turned, walked away quickly, gone down the Timorstraat, disappeared in the Woods. It was quite dark there.

"Well, what is it?"

"I haven't seen you for twelve years, Gerrit."

"Is that all you have to say to me?..."

"No, listen," she said, swiftly, understanding that she must make the most of this precious moment. "Listen. I've been twelve years in Paris, Gerrit; I've had a lot of trouble there, I can tell you.... But a lot of fun too. I was all the rage: my photo used to be in the shop-windows between the Tsar and the King of the Belgians and under Otero's. That shows, doesn't it?... But a lot of trouble too, Gerrit. Men are beasts, Gerrit: they're not all like you, so kind, so nice. I often used to think of you...."

"Yes, but I don't care a hang about all this...."

"I often thought of you, how nice you were and how kind, though you often pretended to be rough and put on such an angry voice.... Well, Gerrit, I had to go back to the Hague—you see, it's too long a story to tell you—and now, Gerrit, now I want to tell you, I'm very hard up ... I haven't got a penny just now.... Please, Gerrit, can you give me fifty guilders?"

"Look here, if you think I'm well off, you're very much mistaken. I can't give you anything."

"Well, Gerrit, couldn't you give me twenty-five guilders? You'd be doing me a good turn."

"I haven't got it."

"Oh, but, please, Gerrit, can't you give me *something*?"

Gerrit fumbled in his pocket:

"Here's two rixdollars ... and a ten-guilder piece. That's all I've got. I'm not rich and I don't go about with sheaves of notes in my pocket."

He gave her the fifteen guilders.

"Oh, Gerrit, thank you ever so much! Oh, Gerrit, how sweet of you!"

And, before he could stop her, she had thrown her arms round his neck and was kissing him wildly on the mouth.

He almost flung her from him:

"Look here, are you mad?"

"No, Gerrit, but I love you and you're such a dear. Thank you, Gerrit, thank you ever so much."

---

[26] Malay: forward!

He saw the golden eyes jeering.

"And now clear out!" said Gerrit, shaking with fury, while sparks seemed to dazzle his eyes. "And never speak to me again and don't go thinking that you'll get any more money out of me, for I haven't got it. So it's finished: understand that. You look out for a young, rich fellow ... and leave me alone...."

"Oh, Gerrit, they're all beasts ... all but you ... all but you...."

"Well, beast or no beast," roared Gerrit, "you go this way now and I that, see?"

And he released himself, panting, snorting, quivering. He walked as fast as he could; and, when he looked round, she was out of sight, must have gone up the Riouwstraat. He breathed again, managed to catch a tram, stood on the front platform to get the wind in his face and cool his throbbing temples.... And all the time he was thinking:

"The girl's mad, to speak to me ... to go kissing me!... I'd have done better not to give her any money.... Twelve years!... She looks older, but she's still a fine girl.... She's put on flesh and she was painted, which she never used to be. But she's still a fine girl...."

Her kiss lingered on his mouth, like a burning pressure, as if she had sealed his lips with wax, the hot, melting wax of her kiss. And suddenly he had to admit to himself that, for years and years, for twelve years, *no one* had kissed him like that; and the admission sent his blood racing through his veins and set all sorts of memories, like swift spirals, swarming before his eyes, in curving, waving lines, between him and the wet autumn street, down which the horse-tram jogged along, toiling slowly on its rails. Memories flashed before his eyes, in glowing visions before him and inside him and around him, until it was as though he were standing there, on the platform of the tram-car, in a blaze of recollections which the wind fanned rather than extinguished.... But the tram was passing his house; and he jumped down, wildly, almost stumbling over his sword, hampered by his military great-coat, which blew between his legs. He rattled with his latchkey against the door, like a drunken man, could not find the keyhole at once.... The door of the dining-room was open, sending forth a soft light of domesticity; the table was laid for dinner. Gerdy and Guy ran out to meet him. Adeline, inside the room, called out:

"Is that you, Gerrit? How late you are!"

"I missed the tram," he fibbed; and he thrust the two children away from him, a little roughly. "Wait, children: Papa must go upstairs first and wash his hands."

He stormed up the stairs, again nearly stumbling. The noise shook the whole house; the door of his bedroom slammed. He feverishly felt in his pocket for matches, couldn't find them; his trembling hands groped all round the room, knocking things over, almost breaking things; at last he found the box, lit the gas, looked at himself in the glass. He saw his face red with fierce, raging blood, which glowed under his cheeks and beat up towards his temples. His eyes started from their sockets and contracted to pin-points. He looked at his mouth, to see if the kiss was visible that still burnt on his lips like a hot seal of purple wax. His uniform felt too tight for him and he undressed himself, savagely. He washed his head in a basin full of water; he rubbed his mouth with a handkerchief till his lips glowed, went on rubbing them, as if they were dirty. He crunched the handkerchief into a ball and flung it on the ground. Then he quickly put on his indoor-jacket and then ... then he went downstairs....

"How late you are!" Adeline said again, very gently.

He did not answer, made no jokes with the children. He now, deliberately, let Gerdy kiss him, with cool lips; and it was as a cool flower, pressed flat on his glowing cheek. It calmed him; and he suddenly felt safe, in that small room, under the circle of light from the hanging lamp, with in front of him the great piece of beef, which he began to carve, with great art, and advised Alex to watch how Papa carved, so that he could do it too when he was older. He now gave all his mind to the beef, carved it in clean, regular slices, while Adeline and the children looked on.

He ate heartily and, after dinner, fell into a heavy sleep.

CHAPTER XIII

No, nobody saw it in him. He could admit that now without hesitation. Around him there appeared to be—he became more and more conscious of it—an opaque sphere, like a materialized phantasm, through which no one could see him, through which no one could penetrate and know him as he knew himself. This evening, as he sat with Constance, Constance did not see that he had met Pauline yesterday and gone back with her to her room. His wife did not notice it; Van der Welcke did not notice it. There was nothing around him but the everyday circumstances of an after-dinner chat in Constance' drawing-room, in the soft, cosy light of the lace-shaded lamps, while the wind outside blew from a great distance and howled moaning round the little house.... In his easy-chair, with the glass of grog mixed by Constance at his side, he was just a big, burly, light-haired fellow in his mufti; and his movements were brisk, his parade-voice sounded loud.... His wife was sitting there, gentle and placid, the quiet, resigned little mother; the children were asleep at home. Oh, his children, how he loved them!... Certainly, all of that existed, it was no phantasm, it was most certainly the truth; but behind that truth lay hidden another truth; and that was why it seemed a phantasm, his outward life as an officer, a husband, a father, while the real truth was what he always kept to himself: his strange gloom; the great worm that gnawed at him; his hot, racing blood; his sentimental and melancholy soul; that wriggling horror in his marrow; that recrudescence of sensuality in his blood.... The quiet, kindly words fell softly round the room, like small, sweet things between a brother and a sister who still have sympathy and affection for each other amid the inevitable slow moving apart of the family-spheres; but he—though he talked, though he was lively, though he cracked joke—he saw Pauline before him, as he had held her in his arms the day before.... Heavens, he couldn't help it: why was he built like that? A handsome woman, standing before his eyes, drove him crazy! Well, for years, all the years of his marriage, he had remained sober and sedate, but he had gradually begun to feel that this sedateness did not really suit him. It was no good his thinking it rotten; it was no good his telling himself that he was a husband and a father—the father of such jolly children too—and that he oughtn't to think of those things, that all that sort of thing belonged to his youth, to which he had said good-bye. It had been all very well to say it. But a thousand memories had gone curling into the air before his eyes, like swarming spirals; and, when he met Pauline again—by accident?—he had made an appointment with her for the next evening, in her room, cursing himself as he did so and swearing at her, with a torrent of rough words.... No, nobody had kissed him like that for years! Besides, he was sentimental. Didn't he himself know, damn it, what a sentimental ass he was? Didn't he know that sometimes, when he read a book or saw a play, when Mamma told him her troubles, as she had now got into the habit of doing, when he saw Dorine and felt sorry for her: didn't he himself know, damn it, that he was a sentimental ass and that he must pull himself together and not let the tears come to his eyes.... And Pauline, whether she did or did not know how sentimental he was: he couldn't see as far as that—not only kissed him as no one else did and knew how to drive him crazy, but she also worked upon his sentimentality. Was she making a fool of him, or did she mean all she said? He had never been able to trust those eyes of hers: they always retained a glint of mockery; but, when she said to him, "Men ... men are all beasts, every one of them, Gerrit ... except you.... You're not ... you're so nice and gentle ... however rough you may be," then she had him by his sentimental side and he did not know how to shake her off....

"I tell you, Gerrit, that's why I was so glad to see you again ... oh, I *was* so glad, Gerrit!"

He had cursed her, asked why she didn't go after a young, rich fellow rather than him, who was neither young nor rich; but her golden eyes had gleamed and she had merely repeated:

"Oh, men are all beasts, Gerrit ... beasts, beasts ... every one of them!"

And—perhaps that was the stupidest thing of all—he had believed her, believed that he was the only one whom she did not think a beast; and, when a woman got hold of him by his crazy side and his sentimental side as well, then he did not find it easy to wrench himself away: oh, he knew himself well enough for that!

Not one of them knew it, you see, while he sat talking so quietly with them, while he sipped his grog with enjoyment, his legs stretched out wide in front of him, and while he heard the raging wind outside come howling up from the distance.... And now Paul came in, rubbing his hands: he had driven up in a cab, declaring that he was too old to walk from the Houtstraat to the Kerkhoflaan in that weather and through such dirty streets. Why didn't he take the tram? Thank you for nothing: was there ever such a filthy conveyance as a tram, in wind and rain too? And a volley of sparkling witticisms flashed out for a moment: tirades against his dirty country, where it was always, always raining; against people, against the whole world, all dirty alike.... When he sat down, he looked round, with a glance that had become a second habit, to see that there were no bits of fluff on his chair. And he at once ceased talking, the battery of his words exhausted, sat still, not thinking it worth while to talk, because nobody appreciated what he said. Gerrit heard Constance chide him, in her gentle voice, in a sisterly but serious fashion, because he was growing so elderly, shutting himself up, giving way to his mania for cleanliness and for thinking everything dirty. He answered with a couple of whimsical sallies....

Then Constance said that she had asked Dorine also, but that Dorine did not seem to be coming; and that Aunt Ruyvenaer was too tired, because she was fixing up the new small house with the girls. And Gerrit felt—now that Mamma was getting old, very old—how Constance was trying to keep the elements of the family together in her place. Not in such a wide and comprehensive manner as Mamma used to do— and still did—but with some measure of sympathy. Ah, she wouldn't succeed, thought Gerrit! The circles were not moving closer together: each was just himself; he was no different from the rest. Was he not thinking of Pauline? Had he not his silent secret?

Had not each of them perhaps his silent secret, while they sat talking together with such apparent sympathy?...

Addie came in, after finishing his school-work upstairs; and Gerrit noticed the conciliatory smile with which he at once went up to his father, who had been sulking of late because his boy had made a choice of which he altogether disapproved. But for weeks and weeks he had seemed unable to resist the conciliatory smile; and Gerrit had noticed that it was Van der Welcke himself who suffered most from his sulking, which went on because he did not know how to manage a gradual change of attitude, while the boy's calm smile meant:

"Daddie will have to give in, for what I want is only reasonable...."

And Gerrit enjoyed looking at Addie, hoping that his own boys would grow up like that; but Paul, as soon as he saw his nephew, flashed forth into chaff, a chaff which had a speculative interest underlying it and which the boy took quietly, looking at Paul with his serious, blue eyes, which gazed so steadily out of his fresh, boyish face.

"Well, learned professor *in ovo*, my dear doctor *in spe*, how are the patients? Are they keeping you busy just now? Has mankind increased in vitality and primordial vigour since you entered the therapeutic arena? O great healer, on whom are you going to try your powers first, Æsculapius? On members of your family, I suppose? Are you going to make us live for ever, Addie? Well, you needn't trouble about me.... Can't you manage to make the human body work a little more cleanly in future? That's the thing before which we're expected to kneel in admiration: the Creator's masterpiece, the human body; and what is dirtier than the human body? A nasty house of flesh, with our poor small soul pining away inside it.... Addie, when you grow very clever later on, just remove all that: entrails, intestines, the whole bag of tricks; and put in its place a little silver machine which a fellow can polish at least ... if there must be a machine of some sort!"

The boy never got annoyed, but stood in front of his uncle and put his hand on Paul's shoulder and looked at him and said:

"Why aren't you always so lively, Uncle?"

"Lively? Do you think me lively? He thinks I'm lively, while I sit here cursing human filthiness! Is that your diagnosis, professor? Well, you're quite out of it, my boy! You'll never get your ten guilders for that! Lively? Heavens, boy, I'm far from that!... As long as life remains as dirty as it is, I shall be as melancholy as melancholy can be.... Cure me, if you like, but first clean the Augean stable.... There's just one little clean spot left in our soul; but all the rest is dirty!... Tell me now: whom will you start on? Couldn't you cure Uncle Gerrit? Give him a better appetite? Sounder sleep? A healthier complexion? Teach him to buck up that big carcase of his a bit?... Just see how wasted he looks!..."

There was something in Paul's chaff that grated on Gerrit very unpleasantly; but he laughed, as though he thought it the best joke he had ever heard, that Paul should be wishing him a better appetite and sounder sleep. Was Paul getting at him? Did

Paul see through his sham strength? And would Addie do so, later?... No, nobody saw through it: the centipede rooted in him unseen by them all....

And he got up, to mix himself another grog; but he mixed it so that it was hardly more than hot water and lemon.

CHAPTER XIV

He had never quite understood her, not even in the old days. In the old days, as a young officer, he had seen in her a fine girl, a delicious girl, of whom he had been madly enamoured. He had never understood her eyes, never understood her soul; but formerly he had not thought so very much about those eyes and that soul, because in those days he didn't know much about himself either, did not know what he knew now. In those days, he only now and then had a vague glimpse of his own latent sentimentality: to-day, he knew that sentimentality to be there most positively, as a blue background to his soul. And he was so much afraid of that sentimentality, so much afraid lest he should miss the truth, the naked, mocking reality of that courtesan's soul, so much afraid lest he should make it out to be finer than it really was, kinder above all and gentler and more tender, that he could never speak to her without abusing her or swearing at her, his voice as rough as if he were roaring at one of his hussars.

"I mustn't let myself be put upon by her ... or by myself either," he constantly reflected.

And he kept on his guard. Add to that a vague resentment, at not having been able to keep away from her, at having gone to see her in her room; a vague resentment at the thought of his home, of his children, of all that he went back to when he left her room. The way you got used to anything, he would reflect! Now, when he had been to her, he would put his latchkey calmly into his front-door, without feeling his heart beating with nervousness, would undress calmly, would walk into the room where Adeline lay in bed! The way you got used to everything and by degrees came to do things which at first you thought rotten! You did it because you couldn't very well help it ... and also because your ideas about things, day by day, as you did it, slumbered away into a feeling that you weren't responsible, that it was no use resisting what had got such a hold of you.... Nevertheless, when he was with her, he always felt that resentment keenly: it did not slumber away.... At Pauline's, he had a keen apprehension of being still more imposed upon, of seeing kindness and charming tenderness in that girl, whereas of course she was nothing but a courtesan who meant to get money out of him. And then, in her small, shabby room, he would roar at her and ask:

"Look here, why can't you leave me alone?"

Her golden eyes gleamed; and he read a secret mockery in them. No, mark you, he'd take jolly good care that his sentimentality didn't make him see her as a chocolate-box picture! You only had to look at her eyes!

"But, Gerrit," she said, nestling at his feet, "I never ran after you! I met you by accident, really by accident, I assure you. Don't you remember? Yes, once when I was driving: that was the first time; then near the Alexander Barracks...."

"But what were you doing near the barracks, damn it?"

She looked at him coaxingly, stroked him caressingly:

"Oh, well ... I thought...!"

"There, you see!... You thought...!"

"Yes, you won't believe me.... Even towards the end ... in Paris, Gerrit...."

"Well?"

"I used to think of you sometimes."

"Oh, rot, you're lying!... Do you think I believe you?"

"No, you don't believe me, but, Gerrit.... I assure you ... men are beasts ... and you...."

"Oh, yes, you tell everybody that: do you imagine I don't see through it?"

Then she laughed merrily; and he laughed too.

"I'm laughing," she said, "because you're pretending to be so cynical. ... Tell me, Gerrit, why do you pretend to be so cynical?"

"I?"

"Yes, you: why do you do it? You're putting it on, aren't you, on purpose?"

"Purpose be blowed!... If you think I'm going to be taken in by all your pretty speeches!... If you come to me with pretty speeches, it's because you want money and I've ... I've told you, I haven't any...."

"But, Gerrit, I don't ask you for money ... and I'm not getting any from you either...."

He flushed, a deep glow overspreading his red, sunburnt face and the white neck on which the tight collar of his uniform had left a plainly-visible line. What she said was quite true: she asked for no money and he gave her no money. He had none to give her.

"Now let me tell you," she said, nestling still closer against his knees. "You see, in Paris, towards the end, I got the blues badly.... You understand, Gerrit, don't you, one has enough of the life sometimes ... and a fit like that isn't very cheerful?"

"Oh, rot!" he said, gruffly. "And you, who are always laughing!"

"I'm always laughing?"

"Yes, you, with those eyes of yours, those eyes which are always laughing."

"That's my eyes, Gerrit: I can't help it if they laugh."

"And you want to make me believe that you get fits of the blues?"

"Well, why shouldn't I?"

"Very likely. But you're not the sort...."

"To what?"

"To sit moping for long."

"Well, I didn't. I came to Holland."

"Weren't you doing well in Paris?"

"Not quite so well, perhaps," she said, hesitating between her vanity and certain strange feelings which she did not clearly realize.

"So *that's* why you came to Holland!"

"I might have gone to London."

"To London?"

"And from there to Berlin."

"Berlin?"

"And then to St. Petersburg."

"Look here, what are you talking about?"

"And next to Constantinople."

"Oh, shut up!"

"And do you know where we finish?"

"What do you mean, finish?"

"At Singapore. You know that's the regular tour."

"Oh, well.... I've heard it; but that's nonsense."

"So many of us go on that tour. It's not a circular tour, Gerrit. It doesn't bring you back ... to Paris."

"What a queer way you have of saying those things!" said Gerrit, laughing uncomfortably. "You were always a strange girl. Tell me, your father ... was a waiter, wasn't he?"

"No, a gentleman. My mother was a laundress ... in Brussels."

"And those twelve years of yours in Paris...."

"Made me into a Parisian, you think?... Gerrit, I longed for Holland!"

"I'll never believe that."

"Yes, Gerrit, I longed for Holland."

"You're a great liar ... with those eyes of yours! I never believe a word you say."

"Gerrit ... and for you!"

"What's that?"

"I longed for you."

"Yes, of course. Tell that to the marines."

"I remembered the old days...."

"Oh, drop it!"

"Don't you know, when...."

"Yes, yes, I know everything. Stow all that, you and your recollections! You've taken me in enough, as it is. Why don't you look out for a young, rich chap?"

"You're not old, Gerrit."

"Oh, I'm not old!"

"No. I am. I've grown older, haven't I, Gerrit?"

"Your eyes haven't."

"But the rest of me?"

"Yes, of course.... You have grown older..."

"Gerrit, I don't want to get old.... I think it terrible to get old.... Am I still pretty and...?"

"Yes, yes, yes...."

"But, very soon, I shall...."

"You'll what?"

"I shall be plain ... and old."

"Oh, don't sit there bothering!"

"I'm very fond of you, Gerrit. You're so...."

"Yes, I know what you're going to say. I'm off now...."

"Must you go?... I say, Gerrit, you have children, haven't you? I expect they're charming children."

He seemed to see mockery in the gleaming eyes.

"You drop it about my children, will you?"

"Mayn't I ask after them?"

"No."

"I saw them out walking the other day."

"Shut up!"

"I thought them so charming."

He swore at her, roughly and hoarsely:

"Shut up, blast it, can't you?"

"Very well. ... Are you going?"

"Yes."

He was outside the door.

"Are you cross with me?"

"No, but this talkee-talkee bores me. That's not what I come to you for...."

"No, I know you don't. ... But, still, you can't mind my talking to you sometimes, Gerrit?..."

"Very likely, but not such twaddle. And I won't have you mention my children."

"I won't do it again. Good-bye, Gerrit."

"Good-night."

He looked round, in the passage, and nodded to her. In the dim light of the room, he saw her standing, framed in the half-open doorway; she stood there, a handsome, slender, willowy figure, in a shimmer of dull gold: the light, the yellow tea-gown, the touches of gold lace round the very white neck, the strange gold hair round the powdered white face and, under the sharp line of the eyebrows, the golden eyes, with a golden gleam. Her voice, all the evening, had sounded very soft and coaxing in his ears, as though crooning a plaintive song, of youth, of memories, of the past, of longing for her native country ... and for him: all unnatural and impossible things in her, things which he only heard in her voice because of his confounded sentimentality, a sentimentality which, however deeply it might be hidden from everybody else, was clearly perceptible to himself....

And, outside, he thought:

"I must be careful with that girl. ... She is as dangerous as can be ... to *me*...."

CHAPTER XV

Well, if he treated it like that, he thought, he could reduce the danger to a minimum. He had allowed himself to be taken in; and the only thing now was to disentangle himself, slowly, gradually; and he would certainly succeed in this, for none of them, not even Pauline, had ever held him for long. Though she had got him to come and see her, though he had gone back once or twice, he had shown her that she had no sort of power over him and that he remained his own master. His voice roared hers down, so that he did not even hear the coaxing, brooding tones; his robust cynicism was more than a match for his sentimental tendencies; and so her only hold was on his recrudescent sensuality, glowing with the memories that had been smouldering in his blood. But that would run its course in time; and meanwhile, as he would never really recapture those old sensations after twelve years, the charm, the enchantment of it would wear off ... and pretty quickly too.... Yes, she had grown old. She had not gone through her twelve years in Paris with impunity. All that former freshness, as of a fruit into which he used to bite, had vanished; he could not endure the musty smell of the paint which she smeared on her face: he once roughly rubbed a towel over her cheeks till she had grown angry and locked herself in; and he had to go away and apologize next time. And he was struck above all by her timidity in revealing her body, her artfulness in retaining, even when in his arms, those laces and fripperies which were supposed to create a filmy haze all around her: a haze through which he was well able to see that she was no longer the girl of twelve years ago.... And, when he compared his recollections of that time with what she gave him now, he could not understand that he had allowed himself to be caught like that by her eyes, which had remained the same, though she now smeared black stuff round them; he did not understand how he had gone into the Woods with her; he did not understand how he had yielded to her entreaties that he should come to see her.... No, he would disentangle himself from this woman, from this faded courtesan, who was complicating his life, his life as a respectable husband and father, especially father. He would disentangle himself. It would not be difficult, now that the present gave him back so little of what had glowed in his memory.... But, just because of that, because it would be so easy, because the present was such dead ashes, a heavy melancholy fell around him like a curtain of twilight.... Great Lord, how rotten it was: that slow decay, that getting old, that dragging on of the days and years! How rotten that you had to pay for everything that life gave you, first with your youth and then with your prime, as if your life were a bank on which you drew bills of exchange, as if your existence were a capital on which you lived, without ever saving a farthing, so that, when you died, you would have squandered every little bit of it. Lord, how rotten! Not dying, which was nothing, after all; but just that slow decay, that confounded spending of your later years, for which you got nothing in return; for you had had everything already: your youth, your strength, your good spirits; and, as the years dragged and dragged along, you just jogged on towards the cheerless end; and there was nothing to do but look on while every day you spent one more day of your capital of later days and got nothing in return, while nothing remained but your memory of the youth which you had also squandered.... Lord, Lord, how dark it all grew around you, when you thought of such rotten things!... Oh, of course, there was one streak of light: he knew it, he saw it, saw the golden dawn, the dawn in his own house, the dawn of his children: light still shone from them; their circle was still moving within his circle, just for a time, for so long as their shining sphere touched his own sphere ... until later it would circle away, ever farther and farther, describing wider and wider revolutions, even as every sphere rolls away, rolls away from the centre!... That was how it would be ... when he had grown old, very old. It was not so yet: for the present, the bright-haired little tribe was still in its golden dawn.... Yes, for its sake too he would like to disentangle himself, to disentangle himself. The thing that had never been able to hold him, would it hold him in his old age?... Well, there was no question of old age yet, even though he was getting on for fifty. But still it wasn't as it used to be: nothing was as it used to be, no, not even Pauline....

No, not even Pauline. When he went to her now, he took a malicious pleasure in telling her so, with rough words, in making her feel it ... both in order to make himself appear rougher than he was and because of the resentment which always kept pricking him sharply.

"I say, you're not a bit like those old photographs of yours now!"

It gave her a shock when he said this. Nothing gave her such a blinding shock, as if the shock had plunged her into darkness and made everything go black and menacing as death.

She felt that it was cruel of him to throw it in her face like this; and she couldn't understand it in him. But, because her eyes were always laughing, even now they laughed their golden laugh....

"Ah, you don't believe it!... You just think you're exactly as you were, the same young and pretty girl.... Well, my beauty, you never made a greater mistake in your life!... But I see you don't believe me, you grin when I tell you, you think your charms are going to live for ever.... Everything wears, child.... However, you won't believe it: I can see your eyes mocking me now...."

Indeed, her eyes were laughing and the smouldering spark of mockery seemed to leap into flame. And, because he spoke like that, she laughed, a loud laugh with a shrill note which annoyed him, in which he heard mockery ... because, after all, though she no longer resembled her old photographs, she had caught him badly.

"Just come here," he said, roughly.

"Why?"

"Just come here."

She went up to him, trembling.

He took hold of her, a little more roughly than he intended, took her between his knees, looked her in the face:

"What do you make up for?" he asked.

"I don't make up."

"Oh, you don't, don't you? Do you think I can't see it?"

"No, I don't make up."

"Then what's that?"

He pointed to her cheek.

"That's only powder, which stays on because I use a face-cream first."

"Oh, really! And isn't that making up?"

"No."

"And what's that?"

He pointed to her eyes. She shrugged her shoulders:

"That's done with a pencil, just a touch. It's nothing. That's not a make-up. Make-up ... is something quite different."

"Oh, really! Well, I don't like all that messing. What do you do it for?"

She looked at him in dismay; and again the blinding shock bored an endless, dead-black perspective before her ... of death. But he saw only the laugh of her golden eyes.

"What do you do it for?" he repeated. "You usedn't to."

"No."

"Then why do it now?"

She made an effort, so as not to cry. She laughed, shrilly; and it sounded like a jeer, as though she were saying, jeeringly:

"I make up my face, but I've got you all the same."

"Give me a towel," he said, roughly.

"No," she said, struggling and releasing herself from his grip.

"Give me a towel."

"No, Gerrit, I won't, do you hear?"

Her eyes just flashed an angry look of dark reproach. But they laughed and mocked immediately afterwards.

He snatched a towel from the wash-hand-stand:

"Come here," he said.

Her first impulse was a storm of seething rage, a rage as on the last occasion, when she locked herself in and he had to go away.... But there was something so cruel and vindictive in his voice, in his glance, in the abrupt movements of his great body that she grew frightened and came:

"Gerrit," she implored, softly, timidly.

"Come here. I don't like all that muck...."

He had wetted the towel. He now washed her face; and he became a little gentler in his movements, glance and voice ... because she was frightened and meek. He washed her face all over:

"There," he said. "Now at least you're natural."

Something like hatred gripped at her heart, but she could not yield to it: her nerves had become too slack for hatred. Besides, she had always, always been very fond of him, just because he was such a strange mixture of roughness and gentleness. She remained standing anxiously in front of him, with her hands in his.

Like that, like that, at any rate, she no longer looked like the picture on a chocolate-box. He was safe now against his sentimentality. But, Lord, how old she looked! Her skin was wrinkled, covered with freckles and blotches. Was it possible that a drop of wet stuff out of a bottle and a touch of powder could cover all that? And the golden eyes of mockery, how ghastly they looked, without the shadows about the brows and lashes!... And yet she kept on mocking him.... But then, suddenly, he felt pity, was sick at having been rough, at pretending to be rougher than he was. He was always like that, always made that pretence, putting on a blustering voice, squaring his broad shoulders, banging his fist on the table ... for no reason, save to be rough ... and not sentimental. And, seeking for something to say to her, he said, in a voice which she at once recognized, a voice of pity, the gentleness now tempering the roughness, that mixture which she had always loved in him:

"Really, Pauline, you look much prettier like this...."

But she saw the dark vista opening out before her, black as night.

"You're much prettier now. You look a fresh and pretty woman."

Her eyes were laughing.

"You haven't the least need to smear all that stuff on your face."

Her lips were laughing now.

"Come and give me a kiss.... Come...."

He caught her in his arms. He felt her flesh, soft and flabby, as though he were grasping wadding or lace, not as though he were grasping the woman whom he remembered in his glowing memories, a woman of warm marble.

She roused herself, in her desire. She strained her muscles, embraced him with force, with all the science of passion which she had acquired during the years. They embraced each other wholly; and their embrace was full of despair for both of them, as though they were both plunging with their intense happiness into a black abyss, instead of soaring to the stars....

She now lay against him like a corpse. Never had he felt so full of heavy melancholy in his heavy, heavy soul. Never had his whole, whole life passed before him like that, suddenly, in a flash: his boyhood, Buitenzorg, the river, Constance; his young years as a subaltern, his reckless period, the period of inexhaustible, gay, brutal, young life; and, after that very youthful period, still many long years of youth, with Pauline herself still young, warm marble; and then the sobering down, his marriage and oh, the golden dawn of his children!... He was not old, he was not old, but everything had arrived.... Nothing, nothing more would come but the dragging past of the monotonous years; and, with each year, the bright circles would shift farther and farther apart and the gloom would deepen around him.... Never had he felt so full of heavy melancholy in his heavy, heavy soul.

She, against him, lay like a corpse. He felt her like a bundle of down, of lace, soft and flabby as a pillow, still in his arms. He would have liked to fling her away from him, weary, sick of that tepid flabbiness. But he kept her in his arms, made her lie against him, suffered the tepid heap of lace and down on his chest. Her eyelids hung closed, as though she would never raise them again. Her mouth hung down, as though she would never laugh again. And yet he continued to hold her like that. It was not because of his sentimentality, for she was anything but a chocolate-box picture now, and it was not out of a sudden recrudescence of rough sensuality that he now held that flabby bundle in his arms: no, it was from a real, genuine, but heavy and melancholy feeling, a feeling of pity. He had been able to wash the make-up from her face with a towel, but he couldn't fling her from him now, before she herself should raise herself from his arms. And she remained lying, like a corpse. God, what a time it lasted!... Still, he couldn't do it: he continued to suffer her there, on his heart. He looked down at her askance, without moving; and his eyes grew moist.... Those confounded eyes of his, which grew moist! He couldn't help it: they just grew moist. He screwed them up, wiped them with his free hand, before Pauline could see them moist. And he remained like that, so long, so long!... At last he gave a deep sigh and she drew breath; he could not go on: not because of her weight, but because of her softness, that soft flabbiness, that stuffiness, that crumpled lace against him. His chest rose high; and she awoke from her lethargy. She lifted her heavy eyelids, she pinched her lips into a smile. It was a smile of utter despair....

She released herself from his arms, stood up; and he made ready to go.

"Gerrit," she said, faintly.

"What is it, child?"

"Gerrit," she repeated, "you don't know how glad I am that I ... that I met you again ... here ... that we have seen each other again.... I used to think of you so often ... in Paris ... because I was always ... a little fond of you ... because you are so gentle and rough in one.... That's how you are ... and that was why I was fond of you.... Oh, it was so nice to see you again ... after so many, many years ... those dirty, dirty years!... It has made me so happy, so happy!... Thank you, Gerrit ... for everything. But I wanted to say...."

"What, child?"

"You had better not come back again.... You know, you had better not come back.... We have seen each other again now: not often, perhaps ten or twelve times, I can't remember.... It was such heavenly, such heavenly happiness ... that I forgot to count the number of times.... But you had better not come back any more...."

"And why not, child? Are you angry ... because I washed your face with that towel?"

"No, Gerrit, it's not that, I'm not angry about that.... I'm not angry at all...."

Indeed, her eyes were laughing. Then she repeated:

"But still ... you had better not come back."

"I see. So you've had enough of me?"

She gave a shrill laugh:

"Yes," she said.

"Oh! And have you found a young, rich chap, as I advised you?"

Her laugh sounded still shriller and her golden eyes were full of mockery.

"Yes," she said.

Under his heavy melancholy, he was angry and jealous:

"So you don't want me any more?"

"Want you?... I shall certainly want you, but...."

"But what?"

"It's better for every reason, better not. You mustn't come back, Gerrit."

"Very well."

"And don't be angry, Gerrit."

"I'm not angry. So this evening was the last time?"

"Yes," she said.

They both looked at each other and both read in each other's eyes the memory of their last embrace: the stimulus of despair.

"Very well," he repeated, more gently.

"Good-bye, Gerrit."

"Good-bye, child."

She kissed him and he her. He was ready to go. Suddenly he remembered that he had never given her anything except on that first evening in the Woods, a ten-guilder piece and two rixdollars:

"Pauline," he said, "I should like to give you something. I should like to send you something. What may I give you?"

"I don't mind having something ... but then you mustn't refuse it me...."

"Unless it's impossible...."

"If it's not possible ... then I won't have anything."

"What is it you'd like?"

"You're sure to have a photograph ... a group ... of your children...."

"Do you want that?" he asked, in surprise.

"Yes."

"Why?"

"I don't know; I'd like it."

"A photograph of my children?"

"Yes. If you haven't one ... or if you can't give it me ... then I don't want anything, Gerrit. And thank you, Gerrit."

"I'll see," he said, dully.

He kissed her once more:

"So good-bye, Pauline."

"Good-bye, Gerrit."

She kissed him hurriedly, almost drove him out of the room. It was ten o'clock in the evening. Gerrit, in the street outside, heaved a great sigh of relief. Yes, this was all right: he was rid of her now. It had not lasted very long; and the best part of it was that none of his brother-officers, of his friends or of his family had for a moment suspected that connection, for a moment noticed that the past, his memories, his youth had loomed up before him, haunting him and mocking him in Pauline, in her body, in her golden eyes. It had remained a secret; and what might have been a great annoyance in his life as husband and father had been no more than a momentary and unsuspected effort to force back what was long over and done with. It was now over and done with for ever. Oh, it was the first time and the last: never again would he allow himself to be entrapped by the haunting recollections of former years!... But how sad it was to reflect that all that past was really over and done with ... and that everything had been!

During the days and weeks that followed, he went about with heavy, heavy melancholy in his heavy soul. Nobody noticed anything in him: at the barracks he blustered as usual; at home he romped with the children; he went with Adeline to take tea at Constance' and laughed at the tirades of Paul, who was daily becoming more and more of an elderly gentleman. Nobody noticed anything in him; and he himself thought it very strange that the eyes of the world never penetrated to the shuddering soul deep down within him, as though sickening in his great body, with its sham strength. Sick: was his soul sick? No, perhaps not: it was only shrinking into itself under the heavy, heavy melancholy. Sham strength: was his body weak? No, not his muscles ... but the worm was crawling about in his spine, the centipede was eating up his marrow.... And nobody in the wide world saw anything—of the centipede, of the worm, of all the horror of his life—even as nobody had seen anything of what had come about during the last few weeks between himself and his past: the last flare up of youth, Pauline.... Nobody saw anything. Life itself seemed blind. It jogged on in the old, plodding way. There were the barracks, always the same: the horses, the men, his brother-officers. There were his mother, his brothers and sisters. There were his wife and his children.... He saw himself reflected in the blind eyes of plodding life as a rough, kindly fellow, a good officer, a big, fair-haired man, just a little grey, a good sort to his wife, a good father to his children.... Lord, how good he was, reflected in the blind eyes of plodding life!... But there was nothing good about him and he was quite different from what he seemed. He had always been different from what he seemed. Oh, idiot people! Oh, blind, idiot life!

CHAPTER XVI

It was a steadily grey and rainy winter. A winter without frost, but with endless, endless rains, with a firmament of everlasting clouds hanging over the small, murky town, over the flooded streets, through which the gloomy people hurried under the little roofs of their umbrellas, clouds so preternaturally big and heavy that everything seemed to cower beneath their menace, as though the end of the world were slowly approaching. Black-grey were those everlasting clouds; and it seemed as if they cast the shadow of their menace from the first hour of the day; and so short were the days that it was as though it were eternal night and as though the sun had lost itself very far away, circled from the small human world, circled very far behind the immeasurable world of the clouds and the endless firmaments. And, lashing, ever lashing, the whips of the rain beat down, wielded by the angry winds. Gloom and menace hung over the shuddering town and over the shuddering souls of the people. There were but few days of light around them.

The old grandmother sat gloomily at her window, nodding her head understandingly but reproachfully, because old age had not come in the nice and peaceful way which she had always, peacefully, hoped. The shadows of old age had gathered around her like a dark, dreary twilight, were already gathering closer and closer because she saw that, however hard she had tried, she had not been able to keep around her all that she loved. Was the supreme sorrow not coming nearer?... Just as the shadows were gathering around her, so they had already gathered around Bertha, over at Baarn, far away, too far for her, an old woman, to reach her; and, in a sudden flash of clairvoyance, she saw—though no one had ever told her—Bertha sitting at a window, listlessly, with her hands in her lap, saw her sitting and staring, even as she herself stared and sat. In a flash of clairvoyance she saw Karel and Cateau and Adolphine's little tribe far, far away from her, even though they lived in the same town and came regularly on Sunday evenings. Far away from her she saw Paul and Dorine. Very far away from her she saw her poor Ernst, whom she knew to be mad; and her old head nodded in understanding but yet in protest against the cruelty of life, which brought old age to her in such a sad guise and made it gather so darkly and menacingly around her loneliness.... Yes, there was Constance, there was Gerrit: she felt these two to be closest to her; but, though they were closer, it grew black around her, black under the black skies, with the glimpses of light, the flashes of clairvoyance, in the midst of them.... She saw—though no one had told her—a pale, thin girl, Marianne, pining away by Bertha's side.... She saw—though no one knew it—Emilie and Henri toiling in Paris, struggling with life, which came towards them hideous and horrible, bringing with it poverty, which they had never known. She saw it so clearly that she almost felt like speaking of it.... But, because they would not have believed her, she remained silent, enduring all that gloomy life even as the town endured the black skies and the lashing of the rain....

And yonder, far away, too far for her, she saw a woman, old like herself, dying. She saw her dying and by her bedside she saw Constance and she saw Addie. She saw it so clearly, between her eyes and the rain-streaks, as though flung upon the screen of the rain, that she felt like speaking of it, like crying it out.... But, because they would not have believed her, she remained silent, enduring all that gloomy life even as the town endured the black skies.

Then things grew dull around her and she saw nothing more; and the nodding head fell asleep upon her breast; and she sat sleeping, a black, silent figure, while the rain tapped as though with fingers—which would not tap her awake—at the panes of the conservatory-window at which she used to sit....

For hours she would sit thus alone in the shadow of her day and the shadow of her soul; and, when any of her children or friends called, they would find her in low spirits.

"Mamma, don't you feel lonely like this?" Adolphine asked, one afternoon. "We should all like to see you take a companion."

The old woman shook her head irritably:

"A companion? What for? Certainly not."

"Or have Dorine to live with you."

"Dorine? Living with me? No, no, I won't have her in the house with me. Why should I?"

"You're so lonely; and, though you've had the servants a long time, somebody ... to sit with you, you know...."

"Somebody sitting with me all day long? No, no...."

"We should like to see it, Mamma."

"Well, you won't see it."

And the old woman remained obstinate.

Another afternoon, Adeline said:

"Mamma dear, Constance asked me to tell you that she won't be able to see you for a day or two."

"And why not? What's the matter with Constance?"

"Nothing, Mamma dear, but she's been sent for to Driebergen...."

"To Driebergen?..."

"Yes, dear. Old Mrs. van der Welcke hasn't been quite so well lately...."

"Is she dead?"

"No, no, Mamma. ... She's only a little unwell...."

The old woman nodded her head comprehendingly. She had already seen Constance standing yonder by the dying woman's sickbed, but she did not say so ... because Adeline would have refused to believe it....

Another afternoon, Cateau said:

"Mamma ... it's ve-ry sad, but *old* Mrs. Friese-steijn...."

"Oh, I haven't seen her ... for ever so long; and...."

"Yes. And it's ve-ry sad, Mam-ma, because she *was* a friend of yours. And, Mam-ma, peo-ple are saying that she's *ill* and that she won't last very *long.*"

The old woman nodded knowingly:

"Yes, I knew about it," she said.

"Oh?" said Cateau, round-eyed. "Has somebody *told* you?...."

"No, but...."

The old lady had seen her, had seen her old friend dying; and she nearly committed herself, nearly betrayed herself to Cateau.

"What?" asked Cateau.

"I suspected it," said the old lady. "When you are old, old people die round you...."

"Mam-ma, we should ve-ry much like...."

"What?"

"Adolph-ine would like it ... and so would Ka-rel."

"What?"

"If you would take a compan-ion to live with you."

"No, no, I don't want a companion."

"Or Do-rine. She's ve-ry nice *too....*"

"No, no. Not Dorine either."

And the old woman remained obstinate.... The old people were dying around her; she was constantly hearing of contemporaries who had gone before her. Her old family-doctor was dead, the man who had brought all her children into the world, in Java; now an old friend was gone; the next to go would be Henri's old mother, who had been unkind to Constance and none the less had sent for Constance to come to her.... Who else was gone? She couldn't remember them all: her brain was sometimes very hazy; and then she forgot names and people, just as the old sisters always forgot and muddled things. She did not want to muddle things; but she could not help forgetting.

"So I sha'n't see Constance for quite a long time?" she said to Cateau.

"Con-stance?"

"Yes, you said she was going to Driebergen."

"No, Mam-ma, I never men-tioned Con-stance."

The old woman nodded her understanding nod. Nevertheless she no longer remembered who it was that had told her about Constance; but she preferred not to ask....

And she thought it over, for hours....

CHAPTER XVII

An icy shudder swept over Constance when she arrived at Driebergen and saw the carriage waiting outside the station, with the coachman and the footman:

"How is mevrouw?" she asked, as she stepped in.

But she hardly heard the answer, although she grasped it. She shuddered, icy cold. She shivered in her fur cloak. It had rained steadily for days upon the dreary, wintry trees, out of a sky that hung low but tremendously wide and heavy, as oppressive as a pitiless darkness. Drearily the wintry roads shot forward as the carriage rattled along them. Drearily, in their bare gardens, the houses rose, very sadly, because they were deserted summer dwellings, in the ice-cold winter rain.

The day was almost black. It was three o'clock, but it was night; and the rain, grey over the road and grey over the houses and gardens, was black over the misty landscapes which could be dimly descried through the bare gardens. The dreary trees looked dead and lived only in the despairing gestures of their branches when a wind, howling up from the distance, blew through them and moved them.

The carriage turned into the bare front-garden, round the beds with the straw-shrouded rose-bushes. Constance had driven in like this only a few times before, with the careful coachman always describing the same accurate curve round the flower-beds: the first time, when she came back from Brussels, and two or three times since, after the old woman had been to the Hague, on one of Henri's birthdays. And suddenly a strange presentiment flashed through the black day right into her, a presentiment that she was destined very often, so many times that she could not count them, to drive with that curve round those beds....

She stepped out of the carriage; and the strange presentiment flashed into her that she would often, very often, stand like that, waiting for that solemn front-door of the great gloomy, solemn villa to open to her.... Then she walked in; and the long oak entrance-hall stretched before her like a strange indoor vista, with at the end a dark door that led to ... she did not quite know what.... And she felt that she would often, very often, go through that hall and stare at that dark door, knowing full well what it led to.... And it was very strange indeed now, but she imagined that she had, unconsciously, had this presentiment before—really unconsciously, so vaguely that she had not felt it yet—from the first time that she had come and waited in this hall, sitting on the oak settle, with her hand on the shoulder of her boy, the grandchild whom she had come to introduce to his grandparents.... Oh, what a gloomy house it was, with that long hall and that dark door at the end of it, with those portraits and those old engravings, only brightened by the gleam of the Delft on the old oak cabinet! Oh, what a gloomy house it was and how strange was the presentiment that she would so often be coming here now, that she would have to mingle some part of herself with this gloomy Dutch domestic atmosphere!... Shuddering, shivering, still in her fur cloak, she was thrilled with a very swift and fleeting home-sickness for her dear, cosy house in the Woods, at the Hague, and she did not know when she would go back to it now.... The old woman was ill; Henri had gone first; Addie had followed him.... Then she had asked for Constance; and Constance had taken the first train....

She had asked Piet in the hall how mevrouw was, but she had not taken in his answer either. She now went up the stairs, which wound in their ascent and were quite dark; and, because the strange presentiment also forced itself upon her on the stairs, she resisted it, put it from her. How strange everything seemed around her and within her! Was that the approach of death, skulking along with the wind, as it were tapping at the windows on the staircase and knocking in the heavy oak presses in the hall? Was that the approach of death, of the death which she already felt around her? Or was it only because the day was black and the house gloomy?...

And now everything seemed to make her shudder. A dark door had opened, slowly; and she started; and yet it was simply her child, her boy, coming out to meet her.

"How is Grandmamma?"

But again she did not take in the answer; and, as though in a shuddering dream in which she already felt the approach of death, she entered a room. There sat the old man; and Henri sat beside him, like a child, with his hand in his father's large, bony hand. She herself did not hear what she said ... to the old man. She was only conscious that her voice sounded soft and sweet, as with a new music, in the gloomy house. She was only conscious that she kissed the old man. But she felt herself growing strange, frightened and shuddering, in the dark room, in the gloomy house, with the vast, low, heavy skies outside. The black rain rattled against the panes. The old man had taken her hand, awkwardly; he held only two of her fingers; and they trembled, pinched in his bony grip. He led her in this way to another room, dark with the curtains of the window and the bed, lighted only by the reflected gleam of an old-fashioned looking-glass wardrobe. The black rain rattled against the panes. Oh, how she felt the approach of dread death, that great, black death before which small people shudder, even though they do not value their small lives! How she felt it rustling in the rain against the window, how she felt the ghostly flapping of its cloak in the shadows among the heavy furniture, how she felt death reflected in the reflex light of that looking-glass! She shivered, in her fur cloak. But in the shadow of the bed-curtains two eyes smiled at her gently from out of the suffering old face.... The old man had gone.

"Here I am, Mamma...."

"Is that you?"

"Yes."

"I had to send for you...."

"I thought it would be too much for you.... That's why I let Henri and Addie come without me...."

"Are we alone?"

"Yes, Mamma."

"Tell me, you didn't stay away ... because you were angry ... because you still bore a grudge?..."

"Oh, no! I was not angry. I thought it would be too much for you."

"Is that true?"

"Quite true."

"The simple truth?"

"The simple truth."

"Yes, I can tell: you're not angry. But you were angry...."

"Hush, Mamma, hush!"

"No, no, let me speak. I sent for you to speak to you.... There was a time when you were angry. And we could not talk together. Let us talk now, for the first and last time."

"Mamma...."

"There were those long, long years, dear. The years which are now all dead.... There was your suffering ... but there was also our suffering, Father's ... and mine."

"Yes...."

"It was a day like to-day, gloomy and black; and it was raining. I was restless, I had such a strange presentiment: I had a presentiment ... that Henri was dead, my child, my boy, in Rome. It was a gloomy day ... seventeen or eighteen years ago. And in the afternoon, about this time—it was quite dark, the lights were not yet lit—a letter came: a letter from Rome ... from Henri.... I trembled ... I could not find the matches, to light the gas ... and, when I looked for them, the letter dropped from my hands.... I thought, 'He's writing to me that he is very ill. I shall hear presently that he's dead.' I lit the gas ... and read the letter. I read not that he was ill ... but that he had to resign his post. He wrote to me about a woman whom I did not know, he wrote to me about you, dear. I breathed again, I thought to myself, 'He is not dead, I have not lost my son.' But Father thought differently: he said, 'Henri is dead, we have lost our son.' Then I knew that my presentiment was right, that he *was* dead.... He was dead ... and he stayed dead for years and years.... Oh, how I longed for him to come to life again! Oh, how I kept on thinking of my child!... But year followed upon year; and he remained dead.... Then by degrees I began to feel that it would not always be like that, that things would be a little brighter one day, that he would come back out of that distant death.... He came back; I had my boy back.... I saw you ... for the first time. Long dead years lay between us; and, when I wished to embrace you, I felt that I could not, that I did not reach you. My words did not reach you. They remained lying between us, they fell between us like hard, round things.... I knew then that you had suffered much and also that for long, long years you had been full of grief and resentment ... grief and resentment.... You brought us your child: you brought him grudgingly.... Hush, don't cry, don't cry: it couldn't be helped. There was bound to be that feeling, that grudge, inside you ... oh, I knew how it rankled! People are always like that: they never understand each other as long as there is no love; and, when there is no love and no understanding, there is bitterness ... oh, and often hatred!... No, it was not hatred yet, it was bitterness: I knew it. Don't cry: the bitterness couldn't be helped. We did not reach each other across that bitterness.... Also you were young still, dear, and it was *I* who had to go to *you* on Henri's birthday ... and yet I do not believe that there was any wrong on my side. Tell me, was there any wrong on my side? Was it not your bitter, implacable youth that refused the reconciliation?... Hush, don't cry: reconciliation always comes, sooner or later; sooner or later, all bitterness melts away ... if not here ... then *there*.... But with you and me, dear, it is *here*. With you and me it is here. I am certain that you gradually felt the bitter grudge melting away in you, because you learnt to understand ... learnt to understand that old people have different ideas from young people; you learnt to understand their ideas, the ideas of the older people, folk before your time, old-fashioned folk, my dear. You learnt to understand them; and your soul became more gently disposed towards them ... and you said to yourself, 'I understand them: they could not be any different.' You can even understand, can't you, dear, that the old man has not yet, has not even now forgiven and forgotten as completely as I forgave and forgot, long, long ago? I am right about that, am I not? You must even learn to understand ... that he will *never* forgive and forget—hush, child, don't cry!—you must learn to understand that; you do understand it.... We must understand that together, however much we may regret it, but we will not tell anybody and we will both of us forgive him, dear, for now and for the time to come; for, if he can't do otherwise, then he is not to blame.... And, once we are *there* ... when we meet again ... oh, what will all the old bitterness and all the old suffering amount to? Nothing! *There*, all the old bitterness and the old suffering are lost in love. Then Father too will no longer be bitter.... That's why I sent for you, you see: to tell you all this; because of the words which I could not keep in, because I longed to say to you, 'My dear child, you have suffered ... but we have suffered too! My dear child, I ... I want to forgive you, now, with my last kiss. But let my forgiveness count as two; and do you, my dear child—it is my last request— forgive the old man also ... now and always ... always...."

The room was quite dark. The rain clattered in the darkness against the window. Constance had dropped to her knees beside the bed; she was sobbing quietly, her tears falling upon the old woman's hand. And there was a long silence, interrupted by nothing but the clatter of the rain and the soft, heaving sobs. The dark room was full of the past, full of all the things which the old woman's words had brought to life out of the dead years. But through that past the dying woman saw the morrow breaking, as in a radiant dawn. She saw it breaking in radiance and she said:

"Tell me that you forgive him ... now ... and always ... always."

"Yes, yes, Mamma ... now ... . now and always."

"For he will *never* forgive, he will *never* forgive."

"No, no ... but I forgive him, I forgive him."

"Even if *he* never forgives?"

"Yes, yes ... even if he never forgives!"

"For he will *never* forgive, he will *never* forgive."

"No ... but I forgive him..."

"And I, dear..."

"You forgive me ... you forgive me!"

"Yes, I forgive you ... everything. From first to last. Your bitterness...."

"Oh, I have long ceased to be bitter!"

"Yes, I know that you had learnt to understand.... We could have become very fond of each other, if...."

"Yes, if...."

"But it was not to be. Let us become fond of each other *now*. Love me, Constance, in your memory...."

"Yes...."

"Just as I shall continue to love you. There! Just because we suffered through each other in this life, we shall *now* love each other."

"Yes, oh, yes!"

"Kiss me, my dear. And ... and forgive the old man."

"Yes...."

"Even if he...."

"Yes, oh yes!..."

"Never forgives. For he will *never*, he will *never* forgive!"

"I forgive him, I forgive him!"

"Then all is well. Let him come in now: him ... and my child, my son, Henri ... and *him* ... the child ... our child...."

Constance rose from her knees; she stumbled, sobbing, across the dark room. She groped for the door, opened it: the light of the lamps streamed in.

"Mamma is asking for you," she stammered through her tears. "For you ... and Henri ... and Addie...."

Death entered the room with them....

CHAPTER XVIII

Constance and Henri returned to the Hague a week after Mrs. van der Welcke's funeral. Constance went straight to her mother.

"Oh, you mustn't leave me alone again so long!" Mrs. van Lowe complained. "I can't do without you for so long. It's so dark, so gloomy when you're not here, my Connie!... Yes, yes, they all came to see me regularly. But they are not like you, dear. It seems they no longer understand me. And, when they're gone, I sit here feeling so lonely, so lonely!... They're now all bothering me, wanting me to take a companion, or to have Dorine to live with me ... but I *won't* have any one here. It's such a trouble. An extra person in the house means such a lot of trouble. I can't see to everything as I used to. I just sit here at my window.... So the old lady, down there, is dead? People are dying every day. I can't understand why I need remain. I am no use to anybody now. I just sit here, giving all of you trouble: you all worry about me ... you all have to come regularly to see how I am. I can't understand why I need go on living. It would be much better if I just died.... There is nothing more to come for me. I've no illusions left. Not one. Even your boy, Connie: what an idea, to want to be a doctor How do we know if he's suited for it?... It's a good thing that you're back. I couldn't do without you.... Is the old man over there going to remain all alone, in that big house ... just as I remained all alone here?"

"No, Mamma, he won't be alone. There's a cousin coming to live with him: you know, old Freule[27] van der Welcke...."

"No, I don't remember. I often muddle people and names."

"Cousin Betsy van der Welcke...."

"No, I don't remember...."

"She's coming to live with the old man. We would have liked him to have had a companion to keep house for him ... because Cousin Betsy herself is so old."

"A companion, a companion: you want everybody to have a companion. So the old man will be all alone...."

"No, Mamma, the old cousin's coming."

"Which old cousin?"

"Cousin Betsy van der Welcke."

"Who?"

"Cousin Betsy, Mamma."

"Oh, yes, Cousin Betsy ... *and* a companion?..."

"No, not a companion...."

"Well, then he'll be well looked after ... with Cousin Betsy and a companion. Better than I. I'm here all by myself."

---

[27] The title borne by the unmarried daughters of the Dutch noblemen.

"But that's not right. You must have some one with you."

"No companions for me, thank you!"

"Or Dorine...."

"So you're beginning with Dorine too! No, I won't have Dorine. She's too fidgety and restless for me."

"But she's out so much."

"No, she's fidgety and restless.... It's not nice of me to say so, dear, but really Dorine is too fidgety and restless, child.... Oh, child, if you yourself could come and live with me!"

"But, Mamma, that would never do."

"Yes, with your husband ... and your boy...."

"No, Mamma, it really wouldn't do."

"Yes, it would, yes, it would ... with your husband and your boy.... Then I would put up with the extra trouble."

"No, Mamma, really, it wouldn't do. Whereas Dorine...."

"No, no, I don't want Dorine. I want you."

"Why?"

"I want you. I want Addie. I want youth around me. It's all so gloomy here. Dorine.... Dorine's gloomy too.... So will you come?"

"Mamma ... really...."

"You don't want to. I see you don't want to.... You are all of you selfish.... Children always are.... Oh, why need I go on living?"

"Dear Mamma, do be reasonable. You say you would find Dorine too much trouble ... and, after all, there are three of us...."

"Yes, three of you. Well?"

"And the rest of the family?"

"What about them?"

"They wouldn't approve."

"It's none of their business to approve or disapprove."

"And my husband...."

"Well?"

"My husband ... no, really, it wouldn't do."

"Yes, I see you don't want to come.... You're all selfish alike...."

No, it was not feasible. Constance foresaw all the difficulties: the old woman still always moving aimlessly about the house in the mornings ... and coming upon a cigarette of Van der Welcke's ... a book of Addie's lying about ... a hundred trifles.... Adolphine, Cateau, Dorine disapproving, beyond a doubt, that Constance, of all people, should come to live with her mother: Constance, of all people ... with Van der Welcke.... No, it was not feasible ... because of all those trifles ... and also because of a strange feeling of delicacy: she did not want to come and live at Mamma's with her husband, with Van der Welcke, long as it was since it had all happened....

"Very well, dear, don't," said the old woman, bitterly; and she nodded her head repeatedly, in sad comprehension of all the disappointments of lonely, melancholy old age. "Yes, yes ... that's how it is ... always.... And so the old man; down there, is left all alone?..."

Constance's heart shrank within her. She saw the old woman's dim eyes look vaguely into her own eyes and she read in the vague glance the uncertain memory of things that had just been said. And, while the eyes gazed dimly, the plaintive voice went on lamenting, with that inward sighing, a broken sound of broken strings, and with a keener note of bitterness through it, so that, with that voice, with that glance, the old woman suddenly aged into the semblance of her old sisters, Auntie Tine, Auntie Rine....

Constance went home through a dismal, heavy rain, hurrying along under the shelter of her umbrella, from which the drops fell in a steady cataract. She could not shake off the gloomy anxiety that haunted her in these days, through which flashed strange premonitions and presentiments; and, since she had been to Driebergen, in response to the old woman's dying summons, she could no longer free herself from this haunting dread, as though it were all a magic web in which she was caught. Oh, what could be threatening, now that the old woman yonder was dead? What sort of change would come looming up, day after day, gloomy day after gloomy day, in her small life, in the small lives around her?... For herself, in the late aftermath of life, she had found a tiny grain of true philosophy—small, oh, so small, but very precious!—and she did not think of herself, because she believed that what might still come, in her own life, she would be able to bear philosophically. Sometimes even, at such times, she would think of the worst that could happen to her: if Addie were suddenly to die. In that case, perhaps, in that case alone, the grain would not be sufficient to enable her to bear it with philosophy.... But, for the rest ... for the rest, she was no longer afraid of life. And yet what were these vague terrors which chilled her soul, which enveloped her nowadays in that magic web of anxious speculation concerning the future? Would she be involved or would others? Was it illness ... money trouble ... an accident ... a catastrophe ... or was it death?... Was it to do with Addie ... or was it to do with her mother? Oh, she wanted to be prepared for anything ... but what ... what would it be? And these haunting terrors which gathered around her so menacingly, like a gloomy twilight, with all those ghostly premonitions and presentiments of what was coming, was it because the days themselves were so gloomy, because it was always raining out of fateful skies? Why should there be deeper gloom around her soul in these days than around others, perhaps hundreds and thousands of people? Was it not the reflection of that gloomy winter in and around her and was not that reflection casting its gloom around all the people who were now, like herself, walking under dripping umbrellas or else, like spectres, looking with pallid faces out of their windows at another dark and dreary day?... Oh, how vast, how immense it all was and how small were they all! To think that, if the sun happened to shine, she would perhaps think and feel quite differently! To think that possibly she was divining, with a shudder, something of days and things to come and went flying off to distant cloud-lands, to all ... and that possibly she was divining nothing!... How ready people were to play with their emotions, their sensitiveness! How ready they were to delude themselves that they had seen invisible things, that they had foretold the most profound secrets!... No, she could foretell nothing, she saw nothing invisible ... but still, argue as sensibly as she might, a haunting fear oppressed her, a chill shudder ran through her, as though she had brought something of death back with her from Driebergen, as though its shadow continued to follow her, indoors and out of doors. Was it only because it was raining?...

Well, she was glad to be at home, to change her wet things, to slip into a tea-gown and warm herself by the fire. Hark to the wind howling round the house and down the lane, the wind that came tearing on from afar that was far, wide and mysterious, wide and mysterious as the heavens, above houses small as boxes, above people as insects small!... How mighty was the wind!... How often had she not thus listened to the wind, her mighty Dutch wind, as though it would carry all sorts of things to her ... or, not heeding her smallness, swoop right down upon her!... What calamity was there that could happen? Addie brought home unexpectedly: an accident on his bicycle; run over by a motor-car; murdered? Henri telling her that they were ruined; that he would have to work for his bread: he who had never been able to work after his shattered career? The house on fire, at home ... or at Mamma's? Mamma dying?...

Oh, what thoughts of shuddering horror they all were and of sombre misfortune and of death, always death!... Something happening to one of the brothers or sisters or to their children. For, in spite of everything, she was fond of all of them, they were still her brothers and sisters. Despite all the misunderstanding, the lack of harmony, the ill-feeling, she was fond of all of them, felt herself to be of one blood with them.... Oh, how lonely she was!... And perhaps, very soon, she would have to be all alone like that, all her life long: without Mamma, dead; without Henri, dead; without Addie, dead!...

She stared into the fire and shivered in its ruddy glow, while the shuddering horror gripped her in its sharp clutches. But a bell jangled loudly ... and she felt a shock of apprehension passing through her; her breath was almost a scream: were they bringing Addie home dead?...

Truitje opened the hall-door: thank goodness, she heard his voice. She sank back in her chair; the door of the room opened; and he stood on the threshold, laughing:

"I daren't come in, Mummy, I'm dripping wet. I'll go and change first. Did you ever see such weather?"

She smiled; he shut the door; and—she couldn't help it—she began to sob. When he came down a quarter of an hour later, healthy, vigorous, smiling, he found her in tears:

"What is it, Mummy?"

"I don't know, dear...."

"But why are you crying? Surely there must be something!..."

"No, it's nothing.... It's nothing ... I think...."

She leant against him. She told him how the dread horror was clutching at her. She was very much unstrung and she felt as if something was going to happen: a great sorrow, a disaster, an accident, she didn't know what.... She poured out her anxious soul to him, nestling in his arms:

"It's too silly, Addie. I must try to be calmer."

She became calmer under his steady gaze. Oh, what delightful eyes he had! As she looked into them, she became calmer:

"Addie ... your eyes...."

"What about them, Mummy?"

"They are growing lighter in colour: they are serious, as always, but they're becoming lighter...."

"What's the matter with my eyes now?"

"They've become grey."

"Oh, nonsense!"

"Yes, they're turning grey, blue-grey...."

He laughed at her a little. She remained with her head on his shoulder, looked into his eyes. She became quite calm, now, gave a last, deep sigh:

"Dear, listen ... listen to it blowing...."

"Yes, Mamma."

"I'm afraid of the wind sometimes...."

"And sometimes you love it."

"Yes."

"You're a very sensitive little Mummy."

"I wonder, Addie, if I'm so strange ... because of a presentiment...."

"A presentiment?"

"Don't you believe in them?"

"I don't know ... I never have 'em...."

"Are you awfully matter-of-fact, Addie?... Or...."

"I don't know, Mamma...."

"No, you're not matter-of-fact.... It's very strange, but you have a magnetism about you which matter-of-fact people never have. You calm one. When I lean against you, I grow calmer.... Listen, listen to it blowing!"

"Yes, it's very stormy. Let's listen to it together, Mamma. Perhaps we shall hear something ... in the storm."

She looked into his eyes. His eyes were smiling. She did not know if he was serious or joking.

"Yes," she said, nestling closer in his arms, feeling that she still had him, that she had not yet lost him. "Let us listen to the storm ... and see if we can hear anything ... in the wind...."

And they remained still, without speaking. The lamps were not lit; only the fire in the open hearth cast its dancing gleams and shadows on the walls. The wind tore on from very far away, out of mysterious cloud-laden skies. It shrieked round the house, rushed past the windows, howled in the chimney, spread its wide wings and flapped on through the clattering rain, leaving its howl like a trail in the air....

By the flickering firelight, playing upon their small souls, they listened attentively.... He smiled.... Her eyes were wide and staring....

CHAPTER XIX

The next day, a Sunday, Constance felt a strange longing for youth and laughter, for merry voices and sunny faces. Addie and his father had gone out early, trying the bicycles on the sodden roads; and she was so lonely, still obsessed by that unaccountable sense of depression, that she felt that she must have laughter around her, that she must watch the romping of children, or she would be perpetually bursting into tears. And she took advantage of a lull in the rain to go to Adeline's in the Bankastraat.

As she entered the house, it seemed to her that the sun was shining. Adeline was sitting downstairs in the living-room, with the children round her. Marie, the eldest girl, was just twelve. All the others followed her at regular intervals of age, like the steps of a staircase. Marie was a sort of little mother to the rest: she was a great help to Adeline with the three youngest, those with the ugly names, Jan, Piet and Klaasje. These were now six years, four and two; and they formed a little group within the big group, because Jan insisted on ruling over Klaasje and Piet, looking upon them as his vassals, imitating Papa's voice, playing at horses with Piet and Klaasje, both very docile, while Jan was the tyrant, trying to impart a roar to his shrill little cock-crow of a voice ... until Marietje had to come in between as a supreme referee, giving her decision in all sorts of difficult questions that arose out of the merest trifle.... Adèletje, ten and a half, was a delicate, ailing child, mostly sitting very quietly close to Mamma, hiding in her skirts: a puny little thing, a great anxiety to her mother; and Adeline was uneasy too about Klaasje, as the child remained very backward and dull: the uncles and aunts called it an idiot.... But a merry little couple were Gerdy and Constant, nine and eight years old, always together, adoring each other, good little flaxen-haired kiddies that they were: very babyish for their age, blending their resemblance to Papa and Mamma into one soft mixture of pink and white and gold, almost like a coloured picture, and seeming a couple of idyllic little figures by the side of the rough, sturdy elder brothers. For, while Jan already was turbulent and tyrannical, Alex and Guy were regular "nuts;" had become indifferent to Marietje's judicial decisions, no longer even submitted to Adeline's restraint and had lost all sense of awe except when the stairs creaked under Gerrit's heavy footstep or when he bellowed at them. Though even then they knew, secretly, with a knowing glance of mutual understanding, that Papa might raise his voice, but never raised his hand; that, when Mamma decreed a punishment, he would say something to her in French, so that the punishment became very slight. And this precocious worldly wisdom had turned them, in their little nursery world, into two intractable, cheeky, swanking young reprobates, putting on big boys' airs, striking terror into little Gerdy and Constant, who would run away together and hide and play at mothers and fathers behind the sofa standing aslant in the drawing-room, chuckling quietly when Mamma or Marietje looked for them and could not find them. But, however intractable, Alex and Guy were two handsome little fellows, with cheeky mouths, but gentle eyes, dark eyes, the Van Lowe eyes: not their hard, but their soft eyes; and, when they were impudent and troublesome, with lips stuck out cheekily, but with those eyes full of dark, soft gentleness, then Constance felt in love with them, spoilt them even more than Gerrit did, put up with everything from the rascals, even allowing the two great boys to hang all over her and ruffle her clothes and hair. This time too, they rushed at her the moment she came in; and Constance, glad to see them so radiant, glad that everything became bright around her, as though the sun were shining, flung open her arms; but Adeline cried:

"Alex! Guy! Take care: Auntie's good cloak!... Boys, do take care: Auntie's beautiful hat!"

But neither Alex nor Guy had any regard for Auntie's good cloak or Auntie's beautiful hat; and Constance was so weak in their rather rough and disrespectful embrace that she only laughed and laughed and laughed. Oh, sunshine, sunshine at last! Passionately fond as she was of her own big son, this was what she needed in these days of rain and gloomy skies and gloomy feelings: this almost overwhelming sunshine, this almost pitiless blaze of radiant youth; this rough gambolling around her of what was young and healthy and bright, as if the shock brought her out of her gloomy depression....

When the boys, after behaving like young dogs jumping up to kiss her face, were at last satisfied, she and sober Marietje looked all through the house for Gerdy and Constant, who had purposely hidden themselves and who, she knew, had crept behind the slanting sofa in the drawing-room. She would not find them too quickly, wished to prolong their enjoyment, called out in the drawing-room:

"But where can they be? Wherever can they be? Constant! Gerdy!..."

Then at last the giggles of the little brother and sister behind the sofa made her look over the back:

"Here they are! Here they are!"

Oh, how young those children were! Excepting wise and sedate Marietje— Mamma's help—and perhaps quiet Adèletje, how young they were! Those two rascals, what children they were for their eleven and ten years! That little father-and-mother pair, Gerdy and Constant, what babies for their nine and eight! And then the nursery proper, Jan tyrannizing over Piet and Klaasje!... How pink and young and fresh and sunny it all was!... Now those were real children, even though Klaasje's laugh was very dull and silly. She had never known Addie like that. Addie had never had that sort of youth. No, his childhood had been spent amid the outbursts of temper of his father and mother, amid their jealousies, amid scenes and tears, so that the child had never been a child. And yet ... and yet, though he had grown up early, how well he had taken care of himself and what kindly powers had watched over him, making him into their one great joy and happiness and consolation!...

But, though this melancholy just passed through her, still the morning, that Sunday morning, had begun sunnily for her, with all that golden hair, all those soft, pink cheeks, all that mad, radiant gaiety; and Constance forgot her gloomy depression, caused by she knew not what, in the glow of childish happiness in that living-room.

The stairs now groaned under a heavy tread.

"There's Gerrit," said Adeline.

"How late he is!" said Constance, laughing. "Gerrit, how late you are!" she cried, even before he opened the door.

And she was surprised that his step should sound so sluggish and heavy, accustomed as she was to hear him fill the whole house with the brisk noise of his movements. Sluggishly and heavily his footsteps came down the passage. Then he slowly opened the door of the dining-room, which was also the living-room.

He remained standing in the doorway:

"Ah, Constance! Good-morning."

"Good-morning, Gerrit. How late you are!" she repeated, gaily. "You're in no hurry to get up on a Sunday, I see!"

But she was startled when she looked at him:

"Gerrit, dear ... what's the matter?"

"I'm feeling rotten," he said, gloomily. "No, children, don't worry Father."

And he pushed aside the playful-rough hands of the two cheeky rascals, Alex and Guy.

"Gerrit hasn't been at all well for a day or two," said Adeline, anxiously.

"What is it, Gerrit?" asked Constance, smiling her smile of a moment ago, when the sunny warmth of the children had made her smile through her own gloomy depression.

"I feel beastly rotten," he repeated, gloomily. "No, thanks, I don't want any breakfast."

"Haven't you been well for the last two days?" asked Constance.

He looked at her with dull, glassy eyes. He thought of telling her, with bitter irony, that all his life he had not been well; but she would not have understood, she would have believed that he was joking, that he was vexed about something; she would not have known. And, besides, he did not want to hurt her either: she was so nice, he always looked upon her as the nicest of his sisters, though they had gone years without seeing each other. What a good thing it was that she had come back! She had been back in Holland three years now, his little sister; he was fond of her, his little sister; he had an almost mystic feeling for her, the sympathy which has its origin in kinship, that sharing of the same blood, the same soul, apportioned so mysteriously in the birth of brother and sister out of one and the same mother by one and the same father; and he felt so clearly that she was his sister, that he loved her as something of himself, a part of himself, something of his own flesh and blood and soul, that he went up to her, laid his hand on her head—she had taken off her hat; and her hair was all ruffled with the boys' romping—and said to her, in a voice which he could not possibly raise to a roar and which broke faintly with emotion:

"It's good to see you, Sissy, with your dear, kind face.... I don't know about being unwell, child: I've had a couple of bad nights, that's all."

"But you sleep well as a rule."

"Yes, as a rule."

"And your appetite is good."

"Yes, Connie, I have a good appetite as a rule. But ... I don't feel like breakfast this morning."

"Your face is so drawn...."

"I shall be all right presently," he said, brightening up. And he struck his chest with his two hands. "My old carcase can stand some knocking about."

"Gerrit came home dripping wet two days ago," said Adeline. "He had been standing on the front of the tram, in a pelting rain, and he was wet to the skin."

"But, Gerrit, why did you do it?"

"To get the wind in my face, Sissy...."

"And to catch cold."

He laughed:

"There, don't worry about me. My old carcase," striking his chest, "can stand some knocking about."

"But you're looking ill."

"Oh, rot!"

"Yes, you're looking ill."

"I want some air. The weather's not so bad. It's not raining, it's only blowing fit to blow your head off. Are you afraid of the wind, or will you come for a walk with your brother?"

"Very well, Gerrit ... but first eat a nice little egg."

He gave a roar of laughter which made the whole room ring again. The children also laughed: they always laughed when Papa laughed like that; and the laughter gave courage to Gerdy, who had looked frightened at first. She crept up on Gerrit's knees, mad on being caressed, clung on to Gerrit, kissed him with tiny little kisses; and Alex and Guy hung, one on his arm, the other on his leg, while his Homeric laughter still rang long and loud.

And his laughter never ceased. He laughed till the servant peeped round the door and disappeared again, perplexed. He laughed till all the children, the nine of them, were laughing, for his laughter had tempted the three little ones—Jan, the tyrant, and his two small vassals—from the stairs, where they were playing. He laughed till Adeline, the dear quiet little mother, also got a painful fit of giggling, which made her choke silently in herself. And he could not stop; his laughter roared out and filled the house: even a street-boy, out of doors, flattened his nose against the window in an attempt to peer in and discover who was laughing like that inside.

And at last Gerrit got up, released himself from the three children, kissed Constance; and, with a red face, tears in his eyes and a mouth still distorted with merriment, he caught her two shoulders in his great hands and said, looking deep into her eyes:

"Don't be angry, Sissy, but I c-couldn't help it, I c-couldn't help it!... You'll be the death of me with laughing, if you go on like that!... And when you put on that kind little voice and or-order me ... to eat a n-nice little egg ... before you consent to go for a walk with me...! ... Oh, dear, oh, dear! I shall never get over it!... Very well ... all right ... just to please you ... but then ... but then *you* must ... b-boil the n-nice little egg for me ... and put it before me ... put my n-nice little egg before me!..."

Constance was laughing too; the children all kept on laughing, like mad, not really knowing what they were laughing at, now that they were all laughing together; and Adeline, Adeline....

"L-look!" said Gerrit, pointing to his wife. "L-look!"

And, while Constance took the egg out of the boiler, she looked round at Adeline. The little mother was still overcome with her fit of silent giggling; the tears rolled down her cheeks; the children around her were screaming with the fun of it.

"I n-never in all my l-life, Connie," said Gerrit, "saw Line laugh ... as she's laughing at that n-nice little egg of yours...."

And he started afresh. He roared. But she had put his plate in front of him. He now played the clown, took up his spoon, said in a pretty little voice that sounded humorously in his great roaring throat:

"Thank you kindly, Constance ... for your n-nice little egg.... It's too sweet of you!..."

And he nipped at his nice little egg with small, careful spoonfuls, pretending to be very weak and very fragile; and the children, seeing their big, burly father nipping at the nice little egg with dainty little movements, were wild with delight, thought it great fun of Papa....

He had finished and was ready for his walk with Constance.

"Papa, may we come too? Do let us come too, Papa!"

"No," he said, bluntly. "No, don't be such limpets. You're just like a pack of octopuses, winding one in their suckers. No, Father wants to go out with his sister alone, for once...."

And he went out alone with Constance, after she had managed to conceal the disorder of her hair under her hat and veil.

Outside, she said to him:

"Gerrit, how bright it all is in your house, how sunny, how happy!"

"Yes," he said.

"You have every reason to be thankful, Gerrit."

"Yes."

"Do you feel better now, in the air?"

"Yes ... especially after your nice little egg."

"No, don't be silly, Gerrit. You don't look half as well as usual."

"And I feel simply rotten ... if you really want to know."

"Still?"

"Yes ... but it'll pass off.... I ... I always sleep very well; and just because of that a bad night upsets me...."

"But that's an exception, isn't it?"

"Yes, of course, it's an exception. Don't be anxious about me, Sissy. I've a hide like a rhinoceros. I'm the pachyderm of the family. I haven't got your dainty little constitution...."

"I am so glad when I come to you, Gerrit. I always brighten up in your house."

"You haven't been gloomy, surely?"

"That's just what I have been, quite lately."

"And why, Connie?"

"I don't know. Because of the weather...."

"Are you afraid of it? It's beginning to rain again."

"As long as it doesn't pour, we can go on walking...."

"It does me good, especially the wind blowing about one. Do you like wind?"

"Yes, I do ... but...."

"But what?"

"Sometimes I hear too much in it."

"My little fanciful sister of old! What do you hear in it?"

"Gloomy things, melancholy things ... but always very big things ... whereas we ourselves are so small, so very small...."

"People never change.... You're just the little sister that you used to be ... in the river ... with your fairy-tales...."

"But what I hear in the wind is not a fairy-tale."

"What do you hear?"

"Life: the whole of life itself.... Things of the past; things of the future; and all big and tremendous.... When I listen to the wind, the past becomes immense and the future tremendous ... and I remain so small, so small...."

"What you remain, child, is a dreamer...."

"No, I haven't remained so.... I may have become one again...."

"Yes, you have become one again.... I recognize you like this absolutely, just as you were as a slim, fair-haired little girl, the same little fairy-like vision.... How long ago it all is, Connie!... How everything melts away in our lives!... How old we grow!..."

"But all your children: they keep you young. They all ... they all belong to the future...."

"Yes, if only I myself...."

"What?"

"Nothing."

"What were you going to say?"

"I was going to own up to something. I was going to confess to you. But why should I? It's better not. It would be very weak of me. It's better not. It's better that I shouldn't speak."

"Gerrit ... Gerrit, dear ... tell me ... is there ... is there...?"

"What?..."

"Is there anything?..."

"No."

"Is there anything threatening you?"

"Why, no, child!"

"Aren't you well?... Do you feel ... unhappy?... Have you some big trouble?... Tell me, Gerrit, tell me!... I'm your sister after all!"

"Yes, you're my sister, the same flesh and blood, soul of my soul.... No, there's nothing, Constance, there's nothing threatening."

"And there's no secret trouble?"

"No, no secret trouble."

"Yes, I'm sure there is."

"No, old girl. It's only that I've slept badly the last night or two. And I feel rotten. That's all."

"But your health is good, isn't it?"

"Oh dear, yes!"

"There's nothing serious the matter? You're not seriously ill?"

"No, no, certainly not."

"Then what is it?"

"Nothing."

"No, no, I feel that you have a trouble of some kind. Gerrit, aren't you happy? Is there some private worry? Aren't you happy with Adeline?"

"Why, of course I am, Connie! She's awfully sweet. I'm very happy with her."

"Then what's wrong?"

"Nothing."

"Yes, Gerrit, there's something wrong. Oh, do tell me about it! Don't keep it to yourself. Sorrow ... chokes us ... when we keep it in."

"No, it's not sorrow.... It's ... I don't know what it is...."

"You don't know?"

"No."

"But there's something, you see. What is it?"

"Constance, it's ... it's...."

"What?"

"Constance, it's ... an overpowering *melancholy*."

"An overpowering melancholy?"

"Yes."

"What about?"

"About ... myself."

"Yourself?"

"Yes.... Because I'm rotten."

"Because you haven't felt well the last few days?"

"Because I'm never well."

She now thought that he was exaggerating, that he was joking, that he was pessimistical, hypochondriacal; and she said:

"Why, Gerrit!..."

He understood that she did not believe him, that she never would believe him. He laughed:

"Yes," he said, "I've a gay old imagination, haven't I?"

"Yes, I think you're imagining things a bit."

"It's this confounded weather, you know."

"Yes, that makes people out of sorts. It doesn't affect children, fortunately."

"No, not children."

"When you see them presently, you'll.... But you mustn't let our walk make you gloomy. Gerrit, will you try to keep your mind off things and not to be melancholy? I had no idea that you were like this!"

"No, old girl, but what does any one of us know about the other?"

"Not much, I admit."

"Each of us is a sealed book to the other. And yet you're fond of me and I of you. And you know nothing about me ... nor I about you."

"That's true."

"You know nothing of my secret self. And I know nothing of your secret self."

"No," she confessed softly; and she blushed and thought of the life that had blossomed late in her, blossomed into spring and summer, the life of which nobody knew.

"It has to be so. It can't be otherwise. We perceive so little of one another, in the words we exchange. I have often longed for a friend ... with whom I could feel his secret self and I mine. I never had a friend like that."

"Gerrit, I did not know ... that you were so ... sensitive."

"No. I am saying things to you which I never talk about. And I say them feeling that it is no use saying them. And yet you're my sister, you know."

"Yes."

"I shall take you home now. I'm only dragging you through the mud and rain. The roads are soaked through. You'll be home in a minute or two."

He brought her home. She rang the bell. Truitje opened the door.

"Is Van der Welcke in, do you think?" Gerrit asked Constance.

"Yes, ma'am," Truitje answered, "the master's upstairs."

"I'll just go up and see him."

Gerrit ran up the stairs.

"I was forgetting, ma'am: there's a telegram come," said Truitje.

"A telegram?..."

She did not know what came over her, but she felt deadly afraid. The blood seemed to freeze round her heart. She took the telegram from Truitje, went into the drawing-room and closed the door before breaking it open....

Gerrit had only run up to say a word to Van der Welcke: he had to go back home, for it was twelve o'clock and getting on for lunch-time. Van der Welcke saw him down the stairs.

"Well, good-bye, old chap," said Gerrit, genially, shaking hands with Van der Welcke. "Constance!" he cried. "Constance!..."

She did not answer.

"Constance!" Gerrit called once more.

The kitchen-door was open.

"The mistress is in the drawing-room, sir," said the servant.

"Constance...."

He opened the door. But the door stuck, as though pushing against a body.

"What the devil!..." Gerrit began, in consternation.

They rushed in through the dining-room: Van der Welcke, Gerrit, the maid. Constance was lying against the door in a dead faint, with the telegram crumpled in her clenched hand:

"*Paris*....

"Henri dead. Am in despair.

"EMILIE"

CHAPTER XX

It was a dismal evening at Mrs. van Lowe's that Sunday. And yet Mamma knew nothing: together with Dorine, she had seen that the maids set out the card-tables, had seen, according to her custom, to the sandwiches, the cakes and the wine which were invariably put out in the boudoir, under the portrait of her husband, the late governor-general. But the old lady was different from usual; and Dorine, looking very pale and apprehensive, gave a start of amazement when she asked:

"Dorine, who's been moving Papa's portrait?"

The old woman asked the question testily and peremptorily.

"But, Mamma, it's been here for years. After Papa's death, you said you wouldn't have it always before your eyes in the drawing-room ... and it was moved in here...."

"Who, do you say, moved it?"

"Why, you yourself, Mamma!"

"I?"

"Yes, you...."

"Oh, yes!" said the old woman, remembering. "Yes, yes, I remember; I only asked because it looks so out of place here ... in the little room ... and it is such a fine portrait...."

Dorine said nothing more. Her legs shook beneath her; but she went on spreading out the cards.

Karel and Cateau arrived:

"How *aw-ful*!" said Cateau, pale in the face. "We thought we had bet-ter come ... for Mamma's sake ... didn't we, Ka-rel?"

"Mamma knows nothing," said Dorine. "But we can't possibly keep it from her.... Otto has gone to Baarn to break the news to Bertha."

The Van Saetzemas arrived:

"No details yet?" asked Adolphine.

"No," Dorine whispered, nervously, seeing Mamma approaching.

"How late you all are!" grumbled the old woman. "Why aren't Uncle Herman and Auntie Lot here? And why haven't Auntie Tine and Auntie Rine come yet?"

There was a moment's painful pause.

"But they haven't been coming for some time, Mamma," said Adolphine, gently.

"What do you say? Are they ill?"

"The old aunts haven't been for ev-er so long on Sunday even-ings," said Cateau, with a great deal of pitying emphasis.

Suddenly Mrs. van Lowe seemed to remember. Yes, it was true: the sisters had not come on Sunday evenings for a long time. She nodded her head in assent, with an air of knowing all about the sad things which happen in old age and which will happen also in the future that is still hidden from the children. But in her heart she thought:

"There's something."

And she seemed to be trying to gaze ahead. But she did not see it before her, did not see it before her vague eyes, as she had seen the death of Henri's mother, yonder, in a dark room at Driebergen, in a dark oak bedstead, behind dark green curtains. She felt that there was something that they had kept from her in order to spare her pain; but she did not see it as she had but lately seen other things which the children did not know. It was as though her sight were growing dim and uncertain, as though she only guessed, only suspected things. And she would not ask what it was. If there was something ... well, then her Sunday family-evening could not help being dreary and silent. Adolphine's children no longer sat round the big table in the conservatory: the old lady did not understand why, did not see that they were growing up, that the round games bored them. Only, as she looked at her empty room, she asked just one more question:

"Where's Bertha? And where's Constance?"

This time, Adolphine and Cateau did not even trouble to remind Mamma that Bertha was living at Baarn. As for Auntie Lot, how could they tell her that the good soul had had a nervous break-down after being told of Henri's sudden death, about which no one knew any details? Toetie arrived very late and said that Mamma had a little headache. As for Constance, not one of the children would have dared to say that she and Van der Welcke had gone to Paris by the night-mail at six o'clock, as soon as they could after Emilie's telegram. Gerrit wanted to go with them, but he was ill and had hardly said a word to Adeline about the telegram when he returned home from the Kerkhoflaan. He had got into bed shivering, thinking that he had a feverish attack, influenza or something. The daughters also thought it better not to tell Mamma that Gerrit was ill; and Mamma did not even ask after Gerrit, though she missed him and Adeline and thought that her rooms looked very empty.

Where could they be? the old woman wondered. None of Bertha's little tribe; the old sisters not there; Constance not there; Gerrit not there; Auntie Lot not there: where were they all? the old woman kept wondering. How big her rooms looked, what a shivery feeling the card-tables gave her, with the markers, with the cards spread out in an S! Well, if there were no children left, it was not worth while having the table put out for the round games in the conservatory, at least not until Gerrit's children were bigger, until a new warmth surrounded her, on her poor Sunday evenings! And what was the use of ordering such a lot of cakes, if there was nobody there to eat them?

And it was very strange, but this evening, now that her rooms were so empty, she grew very weary of those who were there—Adolphine, Cateau, Floortje and Dijkerhof—very tired. She felt her face becoming drawn and haggard, her drooping eyelids twitching over her dim eyes and her heavily-veined hands trembling in her lap with utter weariness. She did not speak, only nodded: the wise nod of old age, knowing that old age spells sadness. She only nodded, longing for them to go. They were uncomfortable: they whispered together, their faces were pale; they sat there staring in such a strange, spectral way ... as if something dreadful had happened or was going to happen.... Had the servants made up the fires so badly? Was it so bitterly cold, so creepily chilly in her rooms, that she felt shivers all down her old, bent back?... And, when the children at last, earlier than usual, took leave of her—still with that same spectral stare, as though they were looking at something dreadful that had happened or was going to happen—she felt inclined to say to them that she was getting too old now to keep up her Sunday evenings; she had it on her lips to say as much to Floortje, to Cateau, to Adolphine; but a pity for them all and especially for herself restrained her and she did not say it. On the contrary, she said, very wearily:

"Well, I hope that you will all be more particular about coming next Sunday ... all of you, all of you.... I want you all here.... I want to have you all around me."

Then they left her alone, earlier than usual, and the old woman did not ring at once for the servants to put out the lights, to go to bed, but first wandered for a little while longer through her large, empty, still brightly-lit rooms. How much had changed in the many, many years that very slowly accumulated about her and seemed to bury her under their grey mounds! Sometimes it seemed to her as if nothing had changed, as if the Sunday evenings always remained the same, even though this or that one might be absent for one reason or another. But sometimes, as to-day, it seemed to her as if everything, everything had changed, with hardly perceptible changes. Did she alone remain unchanged?...

She had now reached the little boudoir: hardly any of the cakes had been touched; above them hung the fine portrait of her husband, in the gold-laced uniform, with the orders. He was dead ... and with him all their grandeur, which she had learnt to love because of him, through him.... She wandered back to the other rooms: there were portraits on the walls, photographs in frames on the tables and mantelpieces. Dead was the old family-doctor; as good as dead her two old sisters; dead was Van Naghel; as good as dead Bertha, now so far away. Aunt Lot, she still remained, she still remained, bearing up bravely, in spite of financial disaster.... Then the children: they were all dying off, for surely it was tantamount to that, when they were becoming more and more remote from her: Karel; Adolphine; Ernst; even Paul; and Dorine, her youngest. There was only Constance ... and Gerrit, perhaps.... And the grandchildren: Frans, in Java; Emilie and Henri, in Paris: O God, what were they doing in Paris? O God, what was it, what was the matter with them? For she suddenly saw the boy ... white as a corpse ... with his clothes open ... and a deep, gaping wound above his heart, sending a stream of purple blood from his lung ... while he lay in the last agonies of death.... Why did she see it, this strange vision of a second or two? It couldn't be true, yet it filled her with anxiety.... And in sad understanding she nodded her old head, with the dim eyes which were suddenly seeing visions more clearly than reality ... until the time when they would see nothing, numbed by the years which were slowly accumulating about her.... Why did she see it?... And, amid the emptiness of her brightly-lit drawing-room, a sort of roar came to her from the distance, from the distance outside the room, the distance outside the house, the distance outside the night, the very distant distance of eternity, the eternity whence all the things of the future come: a roar so overwhelming that it seemed to come from a supernatural sea in which the poor, trembling old woman was drowned, drowned with all her vanity and all her unimportant, insignificant sorrow, a sea in which her very small, small soul was drowned, swallowed up like the veriest atom in the roaring, roaring waves; a roar whose voice told her that it was coming, that it was coming, the great sorrow, the thing before which she trembled with fear because she had long foreseen it and because it would be so heavy for her to bear ... now that she was too old and too weary to bear any more sorrow! And, with an unconscious gesture, she raised her trembling old hands and prayed, mechanically:

"O God, no more, no more!..."

Why must fate be like that, so heavy, so ruthless and crushing? Why had it not all come earlier, including the thing which advanced with such a threatening roar and under which she, too weary now, too weak and too old, would succumb when it passed over her, when it reached her at last out of the roaring, threatening, distant, distant eternity, wherein all the things of the future are born....

But the roar of that doom and her knowledge of it lasted no longer than a second. And, when that second was past, there was nothing around her but the empty, brightly-lit rooms. It was eleven o'clock, the children had all gone home and she rang for the servants, to put out the lights, to go to bed, duly observant of the small needs of her very small life, in spite of all those supernatural things which threatened from afar, out of eternity....

Leaving the maids occupied in the empty room, where they turned off the gas in the chandelier, the old woman slowly climbed the stairs, nodding her old head in bitter comprehension, knowing too well, alas, that the great sorrow would come ... even though, trembling with fear, she prayed:

"O God ... no more, *no more!*"

CHAPTER XXI

"Are you going out, Gerrit?" asked Adeline.

She was surprised to see him come down the stairs, dressed, in uniform. He had spent the morning in bed, but he felt better now; and a feverish excitement acted like a spur. He said, in answer to his wife's question, that he was better, played for a moment with Gerdy, took his lunch standing and then hurried out of the house and rushed through a parade at barracks, where he was not expected. The fever, which he still felt sending shivers through his great body, drove him out of barracks again; and he walked to the Kerkhoflaan and asked Truitje if there was any news of her master or mistress, if Master Addie had had a telegram from Paris; but Truitje didn't know. Then he tore off like one possessed, first to Otto and Frances' house, where he found Frances and Louise, both sick with waiting: Otto had gone to Baarn, to break the news to Bertha.

He could not stay with the two women: Frances wandering from room to room, crying helplessly; Louise, calmer, looking after the children, the entire care of whom she had taken on herself since she had come to live with Otto and since Frances had become such an invalid. Gerrit could not possibly stay: with long strides, he flew to the Alexanderstraat, to Mamma, who was glad to see him well again after his two days' illness. He found Dorine with her; Adolphine called, followed by Cateau, all obeying an impulse not to leave the old woman alone in these days, when at any moment Van der Welcke, Constance and Emilie might arrive from Paris, bringing home the body of Henri, of whose death no one had telegraphed any details, much to the indignation of Adolphine and Cateau.

But, when Auntie Lot came in, her small eyes red and swollen with weeping, and cried, "Oh dear!... *Kassian!*"—an exclamation at once hushed by the children, an exclamation which Mamma, staring dimly into space, failed to understand—Gerrit could no longer endure it among all those overwrought women; and, convinced that Mamma did not even yet know that Constance and Van der Welcke had gone to Paris, convinced that the sisters had not even paved the way by telling her that Henri was seriously ill, he cleared out suddenly, without saying good-bye, and rushed into the open air, down the street, into the Woods, gasping for breath.

What was it, what could it be, hanging in the air? The clouds seemed to be bending over the town in pity, an immense, yearning pity which turned into a desperate melancholy while Gerrit hurried along with his great strides; the wintry trees lifted their crowns of branches in melancholy despair; the rooks cawed and circled in swarms; the bells of the tram-cars tinkled as though muffled in black crape; the few pedestrians walked stiffly and unnaturally; he met ague-stricken, black-clad figures with sinister, spectral faces: they passed him like so many ghosts; and all around him, in the vistas of the Woods, rose a clammy mist, in which every outline of houses, trees and people was blurred into a shadowy unreality. And it seemed to Gerrit as if he alone were real and possessed a body; and he ran and rushed through the spectral landscape, through the hollow avenues of death.

What was it in the air? Nothing, nothing extraordinary: it was winter in Holland; and the people ... the people had nothing extraordinary about them: they walked in thick coats and cloaks, with their hands in their pockets, because it was cold; and, because the mist was cold and raw, their eyes looked fixed, their lips and noses drawn and pinched and they bore themselves rigidly and spectrally when they came towards him out of the fog and passed him with those shadowy and unreal figures. And, with all sorts of fever-born images whirling before his eyes, like shining will-o'-the-wisps in that morning mist, his thoughts touched hastily on every sort of subject: he saw the barracks before him; Pauline; the Paris train and Constance and Van der Welcke in a compartment with Henri's coffin between them; Auntie Lot and Mamma; Bertha at Baarn. He saw his boyhood at Buitenzorg; the foaming river; all his bright-haired children. He saw a worm, big as a dragon, with bristles like lances sticking straight out of its dragon's back....

He was still feverish and had been unwise to get up and go out. But he could not have stayed in bed, he couldn't have done it: his feverish excitement had driven him to the barracks, to his mother and to.... Where was he going? Was he going to Scheveningen? And why was he going through the Woods like that? What was it that constantly impelled him to keep to the right, to turn up the paths on the right, as though he were making for the Nieuwe Weg? What did he want on the right?...

Suddenly, as a counteragent to his fever, he turned to the left; but, on coming to a cross-road, he wandered off to the right again, helplessly, as if he had forgotten the way.... There was the Ornamental Water, with the Nieuwe Weg behind it. There lay the ponds, like two dull, weather-worn mirrors, under the sullen pity of the skies; and the rather tame landscape of the Woods, with its wreath of dunes, became cruel, a tragic pool surrounded by all that avenue of chill death, which seemed to be creeping through the wintry air....

But what was it in the air? Why, there was nothing, nothing but the Ornamental Water, in a misty haze; the few villas around it looming vaguely out of the fog; no pedestrians at all; nothing but the familiar, everyday, usual things.... Then what impelled him to wander so aimlessly past the Ornamental Water to the Nieuwe Weg? Why were those ponds like tragic pools? Was it not as though pale faces stared out of them, out of those tragic pools, pale, white faces of women, multiplied a hundredfold by strange reflections, eddies of white, faces, with dank, plastered hair and dying eyes, which gleamed?...

Yes, yes, he was in a fever. He had been unwise to go out, in that chill morning mist. But it was rotten to be ill ... and he was never ill. He had never said that he was ill. He was a fellow who could stand some knocking about. But for all that he was feverish. Otherwise he would not have seen the Ornamental Water as a tragic pool ... with the white faces of mermaids.... Lord, how cold and shivery the mermaids must feel down there in those chilly, silent pools ... their dying eyes just gleaming up with a single spark! Were they dead or alive, the chilly mermaids? Were their eyes dying or were they ogling? How strangely they were all reflected, until they became as a thousand mermaids, until their faces blossomed like white flowers of death above the light film of ice coating the pool! Whew! How chill and cold they were, the poor, dead, ogling mermaids!...

Dead: were they dead?... Were they ogling and laughing ... with eyes of gold?... He shivered as though ice-cold water were trickling down his spine; and he wrapped himself closely in his military great-coat. He felt something hard in his breast-pocket, a square piece of cardboard. Yes, he had been carrying that about for ever so long ... and yet ... and yet he couldn't do it. It was the photograph of his children, the latest group, taken for Mamma's last birthday. For weeks he had been carrying it about in his pocket, in an envelope with an address on it ... and yet, yet he couldn't send it or hand it in at her door. The portrait of all his children:

"I expect they're charming kiddies, Gerrit?"

Gad, how could she have asked it, how could she have asked it, as though to drive him mad?... Whew, how cold it was!... He looked fearsomely at the mermaids: no, no, there was nothing, nothing but the chilly pool. He was in a high fever, that's what he was ... Gad, how could she ask such a thing?

Still ... still, it was over. She was no longer the girl she was. She was finished with, done for; she had lain in his arms like a corpse, tired of her own kisses, broken by his embrace, white as a sheet, done for.... Lord, how rotten, to be done for and still so young, a young woman!... Done for ... like a defective machine: Lord, how rotten!... No, he couldn't give that photograph ... of all his children ... to a light-o'-love.... He couldn't do it.... If she had only asked for a necklace or some such gaud ... he would have managed somehow, out of his poverty, to buy her a nice keepsake.... Whew, how raw and cold it was!... The will-o'-the-wisps of all sorts of images shone in front of him; and, through them, through the flames, the flying Paris express ... with the compartment, the coffin, Van der Welcke, Constance, two motionless figures. And yet it was bitterly, clammily cold; he was chilled to his marrow; and a great hairy dragon split its beastly maw to lick that chilled marrow with a fiery tongue. How big the filthy brute had grown! It was no longer inside him, it was all around him now: it filled the air with its wriggling body; it lifted its tail among the wintry boughs; and its tongue of fire licked at Gerrit's marrow; and under that marrow—how strange!—he was simply freezing.... Brrr, brrr!... Lord, how he was shivering, what a fever he was in!... Home ... home ... to bed!... Oh, how good to get into bed ... nice and warm, nice and warm!... Still better to be nice and warm in women's arms ... no kissing ... just sleeping, nice and warm!... Brrr, brrr!... Lord, Lord, Lord, the water pouring down his back! Never in his life had he shivered like that!... How hard that photograph of his children was! He felt it on his heart like a plank. How long had he been carrying it about with him? Brrr, brrr! He might just as well have let her have it: it was the only thing that she had asked him for.... Money he had never given her: only fifteen guilders—brrr, brrr!— fif—brrr!—teen—brrr!—guilders.... Come, why not do it now?... Just hand it in, at her door—brrr!—and then—brrr!—and then—brrr!—home, to bed ... nice and warm in bed!...

The thought suddenly took definite shape and it drove him on along the Kanaal. Here also the mist hung like a haze over the water and the meadows on the other side; and, shivering and shuddering under the fiery lick of the dragon's tongue, Gerrit hurried to the Frederikstraat. That was where she lived, that was where he had been so often lately, until that last time when she had begged him not to come back again and to give her, as a keepsake, the portrait ... the portrait of his children. He would leave it now at the door. He had taken it in his hand, because it lay like a plank an his heart; and her name was on the envelope.... Brrr!... Hand it in quickly and then—brrr!—nice and warm in bed.

The landlady opened the door.

"Would you please give this to the young lady?"

He meant to shove the envelope into the woman's hand and then—brrr, brrr!—home ... to bed ... warm ... warm....

"Don't you know, then, where the young lady is, sir?"

"Where she is?"

"Where she's gone to?"

"Has she gone?"

"She didn't come home yesterday afternoon. I don't say I'm anxious; but still she always used to come home of an evening. She owes me some money, but she hasn't run away ... for everything has been left as it was, upstairs: her clothes, her bits of jewellery...."

"Perhaps she's out of town...."

"Perhaps ... only she's taken nothing with her."

"Perhaps, all the same...."

"Yes ... it's possible.... So I'm to give her the envelope ... when she comes?"

"Yes.... Or no, no, give it to me ... I'll see to it myself.... Or no, you'd better give it her when she comes back.... No, after all, I'll see to it...."

He stuffed the envelope into his pocket, went off. Brrr! It lay on his chest like a plank.... Where could she be gone to? Where was Pauline gone to? Had she gone out of town?... Why hadn't he simply left the envelope? Well, you never knew: *if* she didn't come back, it would be there, with the photograph of his children.... She'd probably cleared out.... Yes, she had probably cleared out ... with her rich young fellow.... Well, he, whoever he was, wouldn't remember her as *he* remembered her in the old days.... Brrrrrr!... Lord, Lord, how he was shivering!... Oh, to be in bed!... When could Constance and Van der Welcke be back?... Oh, the express!... Oh, the coffin!... Oh, the fiery lick of the dragon, whose great, hairy body filled the whole grey sky with its wriggling!...

He turned down the Javastraat: he wanted to hurry home; his teeth were chattering; he felt as if ice-cold water was dripping from him, while the confounded brute sucked his marrow with long, fiery licks of its tongue. Near the Schelpkade, he met a little group of four or five policemen: rough words sounded loud; their words sounded so loud through the unreality of the mist that they woke him out of a walking sleep, out of his dream of the dragon-beast with the stiff bristles:

"She was quite blue," he heard one of them say. They were striding along, talking loudly, as if something startling had happened. Gerrit suddenly stood rooted to the ground:

"Who was blue?" he asked, in a hoarse bellow.

The policeman saluted:

"Sir?"

"Who was blue?" bellowed Gerrit.

"A woman, sir.... A woman who drowned herself, last night, in the Kanaal...."

"A woman?"

"Yes, sir. My mate here was the first to see the body, when it was floating with the face out of the water. Then he came and told me; and we went and fetched the drag. It was a young woman...."

"And she was quite blue, you say?..."

"Yes, sir, and all bloated: she'd swallowed a lot of water.... We took the body to the cemetery near the Woods and we're on our way to the commissary."

"To the cemetery?..."

"Yes, sir...."

The men saluted:

"Sir."

"She was quite blue," Gerrit repeated to himself.

And he hurried on at a jog-trot. Brrr, brrr! Oh, to be in bed ... he wanted to get to bed! He was as cold as that woman must have been last night, floating in the water until her face blossomed up like a phantom flower of death.... Brrr! Icy cold water: wasn't he walking beside icy cold water twenty minutes ago? Hadn't it seemed to him that the whole tame landscape, in its wreath of dunes, had melted away into a hazy unreality, with those ghostly villas and trees ... and the ponds like tragic pools, in which were mirrored the motionless, low, grey skies, full of the wriggling of his giant worm ... until the faces of mermaids, with wet, plastered hair and gold-gleaming eyes had risen up like dead flowers, water-lilies of death, and ogled him with the last quiver of their dying eyes?... Oh, the Paris express!... Oh, what a fever he was in!... He must go quick to bed now ... but, before he went, he would just call in at the Kerkhoflaan and ask if there was no telegram from Van der Welcke and Constance.... But how cold he felt and how he was shivering: brrr, brrr!...

It was as though his legs moved independently of his will, propelled by alien instincts, by energies outside himself; for his legs moved healthily, sturdily and quickly, with the click-clack of his sword knocking against his thigh, while, above those sturdy legs, his body shivered in the clutch of the monster, which licked and licked with fiery dabs of its tongue. And, above his body, towered his head, colossally large, with vertigos whirling like tangible circles around the huge head in which he seemed to be carrying a heavy lump of brains. From it there shot forth the strangest dreams; and these dreams, together with the contortions of the monster, filled the whole grey sky until everything became one great dream: all that town of unknown streets; houses; people who bowed and nodded to him; a couple of hussars, who saluted; a couple of officers whom he knew and to whom he waved:

"*Bonjour!*"

"*Bonjour!*"

And, in this singular dreaming and waking and suffering and walking, he knew things which nobody had told him, knew them for certain: knew that a woman had drowned herself last night in Paris, in the lake in the Bois; knew that Van der Welcke and Constance had gone to fetch her body and were now bringing it back to him in a rushing express-train, but a train that came rushing through the sky on whirling aerial rails, cutting through the contortions of a huge snake-thing which wriggled round the clouds and filled the whole sky. Oh, how full the sky was! For round the snake wriggled like corkscrews the whirling rails, all aslant and askew, tangled into iron spirals; and the express, in which Van der Welcke and Constance sat with a coffin between them containing a woman's blue corpse, had to follow all those turns and came rushing and puffing along them, constantly curving round its own track and covering them a thousand times, as though that aerial express were climbing and descending endless wriggling corkscrews. Then the rails and the dragon-coils were all tangled together; and the rails became dragon-coils; and the express flew and flew along the twisting dragon-thing, flew along every curve of its tail. The train became a toy-train; the dragon was enormous and filled the firmament; the town underneath was a toy-town; and Gerrit walked and walked with hurrying legs; and his head towered colossally large; and his brains became like heavy clouds: he saw his lump of brains massing in curling clouds outside him. Nevertheless he was propelled by instincts and energies of assured consciousness, for, when he turned down the Kerkhoflaan and left the Kerkhof, the cemetery, behind him, on one side, he knew quite well that there lay in it a blue woman who had been dragged out of the Kanaal by policemen; but he also knew, with equal certainty, that, up in the sky above, the express flew and flew over the body of his dragon and along its every curve; and he also knew that he was now standing outside Van der Welcke's villa: so small a house, such a toy-house that Gerrit's head stuck out above the roof of it and that his own voice sounded to him like distant thunder as he asked the person who opened the door:

"Telegram? From your master and mistress? Telegram?"

He did not at once recognize who was at the door nor at once understand the reply:

"Telegram? Telegram?" he repeated.

And the thunder of his voice sounded distant and dull compared with the rattle of the express-train right through the sky.

"What do you say?" he now repeated. "What do you say?"

"Uncle, are you ill?" asked Addie.

"Ill? Ill? No, I'm not ill, my boy. But ... telegram? Telegram?"

"Papa and Mamma will be back to-morrow morning; they're bringing Henri's body with them, Uncle; and they're bringing Emilie; and I've been to the undertaker's ... to arrange to have the body fetched at the station at once.... I've seen to everything.... And I must go to all the uncles now: to Uncle Karel and Uncle Saetzema.... I've telegraphed to Otto; I don't know if Aunt Bertha will come or not.... It's very sad, Uncle, and it'll be very sad for Grandmamma when she knows everything: Henri ... Henri was murdered; he was drunk, it seems; and...."

"He drowned himself and he was quite blue?..."

"No, Uncle, he was murdered: stabbed with a dagger.... Mamma is bearing up, Papa writes, but she is terribly overwrought ... on Emilie's account also. Emilie is quite beside herself. Papa fortunately is keeping calm: he is doing all that has to be done; he has been to the legation.... But, Uncle, you're not at all well; you're shivering; you've caught a chill. Oughtn't you to go home and get into bed?..."

"Yes, yes, I'm going home."

"Then you'll be better in the morning...."

"Yes, of course, of course.... I shall be better...."

"Then will you come to the station too, early to-morrow morning, and meet the train from Paris?"

"To-morrow morning early ... yes, certainly, certainly...."

"You oughtn't to have gone out."

"No, no ... but I'm going home now ... going to bed.... Good-bye. To-morrow morning early."

"Good-bye, Uncle."

Gerrit went away.

Above the Woods, on one side, the low sky sank lower and lower, heavy with grey clouds, such heavy grey clouds that they did not seem light enough to continue hovering there, seemed bound to fall ... and to Gerrit they were, in the dim hues of his fevered vision, like purple pieces falling from the dragon's body, which was cut up by the express. The whole sky was full of purple dragon's blood; and it now streamed down like pouring rain. The blood streamed in a violent downpour and appeared intent upon drowning everything....

Gerrit had now turned in the direction of the cemetery; and, impelled by instincts and forces outside himself, he walked in and, vaguely, asked the porter some question, he did not know what. The man seemed to understand him, however, and led the way: Gerrit followed ... brrr, brrr!... Nevertheless, it was as though his fever abated; and, in that sudden cooling, he all at once felt and knew the truth. It must be so: it was *she*. The water, the policemen, *she*. Who else could it be?... He walked on, following the porter....

146

On either side, the silent graves, with their tombstones, the lettering blurred and melancholy in the rain.... Yonder, on the left, the family-grave. Gerrit recognized it in the purple rain of dragon's blood: a sombre mausoleum of brick, like a small house; and it looked larger to him than the toy-villa of just now. What a huge building it was, that family-tomb of theirs! It was like a great palace: it would be able to contain all their dead within its walls. For the present, Papa was living alone there, quietly; but he was waiting, waiting for all of them, waiting for all of them ... until the shadows had deepened into thick darkness around all of them and they came to him, in that huge sepulchral palace.... Lord, Lord, how small he was now: he was walking like a dwarf past the tomb, which stuck its steeple into the clouds, high as a cathedral....

What was that strangeness in the air?... How long had he been walking?... Was life no longer ordinary?... Were there not, as usual, houses, people, things: the barracks ... his children ... Adeline?... Who was that man who went before and led the way?... Was it a real man, that porter?... Or was it a dead man, walking?... Wasn't everything dead here?... Was it morning or was it evening?... Was it life or death?... Was he alive or was he dead?... Brrr, how cold he felt again!... Was that the cold of death?... What was this building which they now entered?... What a huge place!... Was it a church or was it only a tomb?... Where was he and why was he alone, alone with that dead man, that ghost showing him the way?... Where on earth was Constance and where was Van der Welcke?... Hadn't they brought it back from Paris, Pauline's blue body?... Was that Pauline?...

The coffin was open, covered only with a sheet; he lifted it, the sheet.... Brrr, brrr, how cold he was!... He remembered: Paris; yes, yes, he remembered: Paris; poor fellow; poor Henri!... But this, this wasn't Henri.... Who was it, who could it be?... Wasn't it Henri the policemen found?... What had become of those policemen?... When was it he met some policemen?... It was years since he met those policemen ... and her body had turned quite blue.... What was the matter now?... What was that porter saying, hovering round him like a ghost?...

Yes, everything was dead, for the shivering cold which he felt could only be the cold shiver of death....

Blue, was she blue?... The man lifted a corner of the sheet: Gerrit saw a face, pale as that of a mermaid whose features had blossomed up out of the icy stillness of a tragic pool.... The eyes were open.... What sad golden eyes those were!.... Had they not always laughed ... with golden gleams of mockery?... Then why did he now for the first time see them weeping ... in death ... see them mournfully staring ... in death?... Had they never laughed?... Had they always gazed mournfully ... even though they gleamed golden and mocked ... or seemed to ... seemed to?... Then what was real?... Was everything ... was everything dead then?... Did he ... dead ... want to bring her his gift ... what she had asked for so strangely ... the portrait ... the portrait of his children?... He had it here: he felt it lying on his chest ... hard and heavy ... like a plank, like a plank.... He had it here....

"Gerrit, dear, are you coming?"

Who was calling him from so very far away?... Wasn't it his sister?... His favourite sister?...

"Come along, Gerrit!"

Who were those calling him away from that woman?... What were those voices, which he vaguely recognized?... Was it not the voice of his favourite sister, was it not the voice of her husband, of the two of them, who had brought Pauline's body back from Paris?... Yes, he recognized them, it was....

"Come on, Gerrit, old man, you're not well.... What are you doing here, beside this woman, beside this corpse? She's all blue, drowned in the lake in the Bois de Boulogne.... Did you know the woman?..."

Yes, yes, he had known the woman....

"Come along, old chap!"

"Gerrit, dear, won't you come?"

"Constance," whispered Gerrit, "you brought her from Paris...."

"Beg pardon, sir?" asked the porter.

"Yes, there she lies, there she lies, dead...."

"Gerrit, come away!" cried the voices.

"Lay your flowers over her now!... Constance, lay your flowers over her.... She is lying so cold and all alone ... and it is all so big here ... big as a church ... she is lying ... as if in a cold, damp church.... Lay flowers beside her...."

"What do you say, sir?"

"Yes ... lay flowers beside her ... lay flowers beside her ... Constance...."

"Won't you come away now?"

"Yes, yes, I'm coming...."

There, there she lay ... covered all over, with the sheet. She was nothing but a blue, motionless woman's shape ... under a sheet. Now ... flowers lay over the sheet: all the white flowers of his imagination. Now his fingers tore into little pieces the plank which he carried on his heart and strewed them in between the flowers: into such little, little pieces that they were as the petals of flowers ... and nothing more ... over the woman....

The voices called him.

"Yes, yes, I'm coming ... I'm coming...."

The voices lured him home, to bed; and he jogged on through the streets raining with dragon's blood....

When he reached home, Adeline at once sent for the doctor.... It was typhoid fever.

CHAPTER XXII

Next morning, in a mist, a drizzly mist, the relations met at the railway-station: Otto van Naghel; Karel; Van Saetzema; Uncle Ruyvenaer, just back from India; Paul; Addie. They moved about, in the waiting-room, on the platform, with gloomy faces and upturned coat-collars, waiting for the train, which was late, which would not arrive for another quarter of an hour or twenty minutes.

"Does Grandmamma know about it yet?" Uncle Ruyvenaer asked Addie.

"No, Uncle. No one liked to tell her. I believe the uncles and aunts would really prefer to keep it from her altogether."

"That's impossible."

"I think it would be very difficult, Uncle. Grandmamma might hear it from an outsider.... She has friends who call to see her."

"Is Emilie coming?"

"Yes, Uncle. She'll stay with us."

"Is Uncle Gerrit very ill?"

"Yes, Uncle, very ill indeed."

"Does Grandmamma know he's ill?"

"No."

"The children are now all out of the house, aren't they? We've got Alex and Guy with us."

"And we have Adèletje, Gerdy and Constance. The three little ones are at Otto's: Louise came and fetched them. Marietje is with Aunt Adolphine."

"Has Aunt Adeline any one to help her?"

"There are two male nurses, Uncle. Uncle Gerrit is very violent in his delirium."

"Oughtn't the train to be here soon?"

"It's overdue now."

"It's a very sad affair. And how people will talk! Yes, how people will talk! Lord, Lord, how they're going to talk!"

"Here comes the train, Uncle."

The train steamed slowly into the station, like a grey ghost of a train through the ghostly, drizzling mist; and the waiting relations saw Constance, Van der Welcke and Emilie get out, Emilie leaning heavily upon Constance. Then came the dreary, dreary task of taking possession of the coffin. The hearse was waiting outside. And it all went as in a dream, in the ghostly, drizzling mist....

"How people will talk!" Uncle Ruyvenaer whispered to Karel and Van Saetzema, with whom he was sitting in the second coach.

"Yes, it's a damned rotten business."

"It's not over-respectable...."

"Having a nephew who becomes a clown...."

"And then, it seems, goes and gets murdered in Paris...."

"For a girl?"

"Yes ... some obscure story about a girl ... in Paris."

"I thought he had committed suicide?"

"We really don't know anything. Constance wrote no particulars."

"In any case, it's not over-respectable."

"I call it a damned rotten business."

"Constance has gone on ahead with Emilie."

"Yes. What a sight Emilie looked!"

"Very odd, that sister and brother."

"Yes, it was because of *him* that she left her husband. And now—no doubt through his own imprudence—stabbed, I suppose...?"

"Unless he committed suicide."

"Van Raven, after all, was a decent fellow."

"Van Raven? I believe you! Van Raven was a *very* decent fellow."

"Those young Van Naghels never had a sensible bringing-up...."

"No, I bring my boys up very differently."

"Ah, but then they're fine boys!"

"Is Van der Welcke in the first coach?"

"Yes, with Otto, Paul and Addie."

"Then why did they put us in the second coach?"

"Perhaps it was a mistake."

"I daresay, but it's not the thing. Uncle ought to be in the first coach."

"Yes; and you too, Karel."

"Yes; and you too, Saetzema, of course."

"Well ... I daresay it's a mistake. The thing wasn't arranged...."

"No; but when Van der Welcke has to arrange a thing...!"

"It was that young bounder who arranged things."

"Addie?"

"Of course."

"Oh, so that young bounder arranged things!"

"Look here, what are we to say to Mamma?"

"Well, I don't intend to mention it. For that matter, I know nothing."

"Nor I. The women had better do it."

"But they're too much upset."

"The best thing will be not to say anything."

"Yes, it's best not to say anything to Mamma."

"Lord, what a day!... And to have to ride for an hour in this weather at a foot's pace ... behind the body of an undergraduate who has been sent down from Leiden and must needs run away to Paris with his sister and become a circus-clown...."

"And go getting murdered into the bargain! But we mustn't tell anybody that. No, no, we won't speak about it. We'll merely say that he was taken ill. After all, it's a rotten incident ... for us."

"Yes, it's very rotten for us."

"Lord, Lord, how people will jabber!"

"Of course they will."

"Of course they will."

"If things con-tin-ue like *this* ... *I* shall leave the *Hague*," said Karel. "Ca-teau said so *too*."

He copied his wife's voice: he always copied her voice, unconsciously, when he talked about her.

"Are we nearly there?"

"No such luck!"

"Lord, what a day!..."

"How people will talk!..."

The carriage containing Constance had driven on ahead of the procession. Emilie leant against her, feebly and listlessly, without speaking or hearing. When they approached the Kerkhoflaan, Emilie said:

"Auntie ... it's just stupid chance...."

"What, dear?"

"Is this life? My life has never been anything but stupid chance! The little pleasure I had ... and the sorrow ... was all stupid chance! I am now so miserable; and it's all ... all stupid chance!... Oh, Auntie, I shall never be able to live ... not now, when Henri's death will always ... will always haunt me like an accusing ghost!... Auntie ... do other people have so much stupid chance in their lives?... If I hadn't gone to Paris!... If Henri had not ... oh, I can't say it, I can't say it! Auntie, we shall never know! It's *too* awful, what happened! I can never tell you ... what I think!"

"My darling, I suspect it!"

"Oh, it's awful, awful! Uncle suspects it too ... so they do at the legation.... It's awful, awful!... He's disappeared: Eduard, I mean.... It was a mere accident: we were walking together, Henri and I, when we ... when we met Eduard.... They looked at each other.... They hated each other.... Then he walked on ... but we met him again later.... Then, in the evening, when I came home ... and found Henri ... lying in his blood...!"

She flung herself back with a scream.

"Auntie, Auntie, we know nothing!... But the suspicion will *always* be with me! I shall always see it like that! Oh, Auntie, Auntie, help me ... and keep me with you always, always!..."

She closed her eyes in Constance' arms, too weak to face her life, which had changed from fantastic humour into tragedy.... The carriage suddenly, stopped, in the Kerkhoflaan; Truitje opened the door; Constance made a sign to her to ask no questions. She herself, on the other hand, asked:

"How is Mr. Gerrit doing?"

"Not at all well, ma'am."

"Where are the children?"

"They're in the dining-room, ma'am, playing: it's easier there for me to keep an eye on them."

Constance opened the door of the dining-room, with her arm round Emilie. She saw Gerdy and Constant; but, just as in the drawing-room at home, they had hidden behind a sofa standing aslant, where they were quietly playing at father and mother, worshipping each other like a little husband and wife, two small birds in a little nest.

"Peek-a-boo!" said Constance, mechanically.

They were quiet at first and then burst into chuckles, crept out, kissed Auntie and Emilie:

"Auntie," asked Gerdy, "is Papa ill?"

"Yes, darling."

"Will Papa get better *very* soon?"

"Oh, yes, dear!"

"Are we staying with you long?"

"No, not very long, darling."

And Constance did not know why, but she suddenly saw the children staying on; and this vision was mingled with a vague impression of the gloomy house at Driebergen. She thought that her brain must be very tired in her head, that she was sleeping while awake, dreaming as she moved about. Everything before her was confused: that terrible day in Paris; Henri's body; the mystery about the whole affair, with the dark, half-uttered suspicions; the formalities; the legation; the journey back: oh, she was dead-tired, dead-tired!... Oh, that coffin, that coffin!... And in the middle of it all a letter from Addie: Uncle Gerrit seriously ill; the children ordered out of the house; he was taking Gerdy and Constant and giving them his room: he was sure Mamma would approve.... Oh, how dead-tired, how dead-tired she was!...

"Auntie," said Constant, "Truitje has been so kind: she made us a lovely rice-pudding...."

"But we'd rather be at home!" said Gerdy.

And the children suddenly began to cry. Constance took them in her arms, pressed them to her:

"You would be just a little in Mamma's way," she said, with a dead voice. "Mamma must look after Papa...."

And she dropped almost fainting into a chair.

"Aunt Constance!" Emilie sobbed: "Aunt Constance, let me ... let me ... stay with you!... Let me stay with you!... Where ... where could I go?"

She sobbed wildly, huddled on the floor against Constance' knees. The children were also crying. Constance had put one arm round Emilie and held the children in the other. It was very gloomy out of doors. Indoors, life's tragedy lay heavy upon them.

CHAPTER XXIII

The gigantic beast wriggled through the sky, from end to end of the vast sky. The beast wobbled the point of its tail slowly up and down over the earth: in the room, above the bed, which had become a narrow coffin; and, commencing with that wobbling tail, the beast's body wound up and up, filling the room and the house with one mighty contortion of monstrous dragon's scales and sweeping away with its tangible reality all the dreamy unreality of the room and the house, the ceilings and roofs. With thousands of legs the beast humped its sinuous body over the chimney-stacks and church-steeples, slung itself wriggling round the church-steeples and chimney-stacks like a festoon of scales, which then turned into a long, dense chain of clouds, filling the sky with great cloud-eddies, which whirled and whirled over the town and through the sky, from end to end of the vast sky. And the monstrous beast now lifted its long crocodile's jaws out of its own winding clouds; and its eyes belched forth fire like volcanoes; and shafts of flame shot like lightning-flashes from its darting tongue: shafts darting to such a length from the very high expanse, right up there, up there, from the sky above the clouds, that they shot through the man in one second and retreated and hid themselves again in the abyss of the dragon's mouth, from such a height indeed that they shot quicker than lightning right down to his marrow, licking it until it dried up; and, after each burning lick, after each dab of fire, the lightning-quick, darting flame, the miles-long shaft withdrew to its own source and birthplace in the deep funnel of the fiery jaws. And the martyred man shivered under the dabbing lick; and in his shivering he raised himself high as though upon waves of trembling, as though his fever were a stormy sea that bore him away from his bed high above the clouds, the clouds that were the windings of the beast's body.... And, as he rose, as the man rose, the beast set up all its stiff bristles, which stuck out between its scales like trees, stuck them up and drew them in again, until the whole sky, the whole vast stretch of sky, was all the time growing full of tree-trunks, straight forests of dragon's bristles which swarmed and vanished, swarmed and vanished as the beast put them out or drew them in.... And the point of the beast's bristly, scaly tail flicked with such oppressive weight upon the chest of the man who lay in the bed which was a coffin that the man moaned and groaned and tried with both hands to lift that heavy, flicking tail from his crushed heart.... But the beast grinned with its cavernous jaws, shot fire from the volcanoes of its eyes, darted swiftly up and down the miles-long fiery trail of its all-penetrating tongue, split into myriad needles of fire, and with long voluptuous licks sucked away the man's marrow, until the man, all shivering and shaking, was scorched and roasted and shrivelled within.... The beast left him no blood, licked up his marrow and blood and poured fire into him instead. When the beast smacked its lips voluptuously, when it greedily swallowed the blood and the marrow, when the man thought that he was dying, then the beast pricked him with a needle of its fiery tongue and goaded him to shivering-point; and the man shivered and raised himself high upon the waves with his shivering, as though his fever were a stormy sea....

Thus the man lay twisting and tossing, till he put out his hands towards the demon and tried to fight the beast with human hands.... And it seemed to him as if he were flinging his hands, the hands of a brave man and a martyr and a hero, around the beast; and, while the stormy sea, the sky, which was churned into billows by the contortions of the beast, bore him up and up and up, he fought and wrestled with the ever more violently writhing and coiling beast; and the beast humped its way through the sombre universe of clouds, shooting out its thousands of feet; its head was now here, now there; its tail flicked now high, now low; the beast lashed earth and sky; the beast became one vast, dizzying whirl, with town, spires, roofs and chimney-stacks all whirling in it; the bed which was a coffin was now here, now there, now high, now low; and he fought and wrestled and twisted round the beast and the beast round him; and he would not let himself be conquered by the beast. Until the beast from out of the volcano of its eyes and the abyss of its jaws belched so much fire that the sky was a sea of blood-fire wherein a hell of faces flamed—faces of women and children: naked women with eyes of gold; bright children with flaxen hair—like a sudden flowering of tortured affections, of tortured passions, all blossoming up in the blood-fire into faces of laughing and crying children and ogling siren-mermaids; and through it all and through them all the man writhed and wrestled with the wrestling, writhing beast, which could not free itself from him, even as he could not free himself from the beast....

"Gerrit, dear Gerrit," voices sounded, soft-murmuring, earthly voices, voices from far below,

"Gerrit, dear, are you coming?"

And he answered:

"Yes ... yes ... I'm coming...."

And he, the man heaving up and down, down and up, on the mighty swaying of the storm, down and up, up and down, he, this heaving, wrestling man, one with the beast and the beast one with him, saw a woman, between the faces of children and women, saw two women, two women belonging to him: his wife and his sister. But in between them crept a third woman; and her eyes mocked like golden eyes of mockery ... until suddenly they ceased to mock and died away in sadness, in unutterable sadness, as though really they had always been sad and had never mocked or laughed.

"Gerrit ... dear Gerrit ... are you coming?"

"Yes ... yes ... I'm coming...."

"He's delirious," whispered Constance.

The room around the sick man had now become as glass, but not transparent glass. For he no longer, through the walls of the room, saw the universe and the beast: he saw nothing now save the room; but so brittle was that room, so brittle all the things which it contained that it seemed to be all of glass—the room, the bed and he—all glass, all brittle glass, which a single incautious movement might shiver into dust. Yes, now that the beast had sucked up all his marrow with that voluptuous licking, it had let him go, left him lying exhausted on his bed; and he lay, his glass body lay powerless to move; and, now that, after a long time, he had laboriously opened his eyes and saw his room around him as glass and felt himself as glass, he knew that the beast would no longer dart the fiery shafts of his tongue, because it had eaten the whole of him up. His body lay lifeless, like a glass husk; and he asked himself if he wasn't dead. He did not know for certain that he was alive. He saw that the room was very quiet; beside him, in the glass atmosphere of his room, sat a man, who also seemed made of brittle glass; and the man sat motionless: he seemed to be sitting with a book in his hand, reading in the glassy twilight that filtered through the close-drawn window-curtains....

The sick man laboriously closed his eyes again; and it seemed to him that he sank away very slowly, into a great, downy abyss, lower and lower, a very depth of down, into which he sank and went on sinking, sank and went on sinking....

"There's less fever now," said the military doctor. "He's asleep."

"Is he out of danger?" asked the pale little wife, who sat with Constance' arms around her.

"Yes.... You would be wise to take a rest, mevrouw."

"I can't ... I can't...."

"Go and get some sleep, Adeline," said Constance. "I'll stay in the room with Gerrit; and the nurse will keep a good watch."

"He looked round for a moment very peacefully, before he fell asleep," said the male nurse by Gerrit's bedside.

"Go and get some sleep, Adeline...."

How long the sick man sank and sank and sank in the downy abyss no one knew.... At last he opened his eyes again and looked into the room and saw the quiet attendant sitting on a chair at the foot of his bed, where he also saw a woman standing:

"Constance," the sick man murmured.

He tried to smile because he knew her, but he felt too weak to smile.

Another woman appeared beside the first: he knew her too, but it was as though she were dead....

"Line," murmured the sick man.

"He knows us," whispered Constance.

CHAPTER XXIV

Gerrit made progress every day. He was now so much better that he sat in a big chair, sat dozing until he sank away in the downy abyss and fell asleep in his chair. He was now so much better that he was able to speak a few words to the two women and the doctor and the nurse; and his first question was:

"The children...?"

He had understood that they were not there and that he would not see them just yet.

He was now so much better that he remembered his recent life and asked:

"Pauline...?"

And he saw that they did not understand. Why they did not understand he failed to see, for, when he asked after the children or Mamma, they always understood and answered kindly, telling him that Mamma and the children were well.

Then he asked:

"Your husband, Constance...? Your boy...?"

And Constance answered that they were well.

Then he asked:

"Pauline...?"

And she gave a gentle, smiling nod.

Yes, of course, she understood now, told him that Pauline was well.

Yes, yes, he remembered: Mamma, the children, Pauline.... They were as ghosts in his empty memory, looming up and making him ask questions of the women around him. But, apart from that, his memory was one vast emptiness, like an empty universe, now that the beast had vanished into space ... into nothingness ... into nothingness....

He had no marrow left: the beast would not eat him up any more. There was no centipede rooting at his carcase now. Lord, Lord, how done he felt, how utterly done for!...

He now recognized his doctor:

"Ah, is that you, Alsma?"

"Well, Van Lowe, do you recognize me?"

"Yes, yes.... Didn't I recognize you before?"

"No ... once or twice you didn't know who I was.... Well, you'll soon be all right again now. You're getting better every day...."

"Yes, yes ... but...."

"What?"

"I feel very queer ... damned queer...."

"Yes, you're a bit weak still...."

"A bit weak?..."

He gave a grin. He felt his arm, thought it odd that he couldn't find his biceps:

"Where's the thing got to?" he asked. "Is it gone?..."

"No, you'll get your strength back all right.... It doesn't take long, once you're well again."

"Oh, it doesn't take long?"

"No, you'd be surprised...."

"I say, Alsma, can't I see my children ... just for once?..."

"No, it would tire you a bit.... Later on, later on...."

"I say, do you know what's so rotten? I don't know ... all sorts of things ... whether I've been dreaming ... or not...."

"Don't worry about it. That'll all come right ... bit by bit, bit by bit...."

"A lake full of white-faced mermaids: that's rot, eh?... An express-train: was I away, shortly before my illness? I wasn't, was I?... The body ... of a girl: did I see that?... A snake-thing, a great wriggling snake-thing: yes, that snake-thing was there all right; I fought the thing.... I believe it was all rot ... except the great snake-thing, which licked me up ... with its tongue...."

"You mustn't talk so much."

"... Because I always used to feel that snake-thing inside me ... always...."

"Come, Van Lowe ... keep very quiet now ... and rest ... rest...."

The sick man sank away, sank away in the downy abyss....

Gerrit made progress every day. He was now so much better that he had walked across the room, on Constance' arm, and just seen his two boys, only for a moment, because he longed for them so:

"The others too," he said.

The next day they brought Marietje and Gerdy and Constant to him; the day after that, the four others.... He had now seen them all:

"But for such a short time!" he said.

He recovered slowly. He had seen Van der Welcke and Addie; and, one pale, wintry, sunny day, he had been out for a little while, but the outside world made him giddy. Still he couldn't deny it: he was getting better. He saw his mother; and, when she saw him, she forgot that he had been ill:

"Where have you been, Gerrit?..."

"Laid up, Mamma."

"Laid up?..." The old woman nodded wisely. "You haven't been ill, have you?"

"Just a little, Mamma. It wasn't very bad...."

And he got better, he made progress. He went out walking, with his wife, with Constance, with Van der Welcke. He went out with his nephew Addie; the outside world no longer made him giddy. On his walks, he recognized brother-officers; one day, he met the hussars:

"Oh, damn it all!" he swore, without knowing why.

It was as though he suddenly saw that he would never again ride, straight-backed, clear-eyed, at the head of his squadron. But it was all rot, seeing that....

Still he was unable to resume his service. He lazed and loafed, as he said. In the evenings, always very early, he sank away into a downy abyss, dropped asleep, heavily....

And he no longer remembered things:

"I say, Constance."

"What is it, Gerrit?"

"When I saw that girl ... in the cemetery ... were you there too and did you call me?..."

"No, Gerrit. You've been dreaming."

"Oh, did I dream that?"

"Yes."

"No, no."

"Yes, Gerrit, you dreamt it."

Another time, he said to Van der Welcke:

"I say, Van der Welcke."

"What is it, Gerrit?"

"You don't know ... but I was carrying on with a girl ... one I knew in the old days.... Find out what's become of her, will you?"

"What's her name and where does she hang out?"

He reflected:

"Her name ... her name's Pauline."

"And where does she live?"

"In ... in the Frederikstraat."

Van der Welcke made enquiries, but said nothing, next time he came. The sick man remembered, however:

"I say, Van der Welcke."

"Yes, Gerrit?"

"Did you ask about that for me?"

"Yes," Van der Welcke answered, hesitatingly.

"Well?"

"The girl's dead, old chap."

"Did she drown herself?"

"Yes."

"They took the body to the cemetery?"

"Yes."

"Oh, then I wasn't dreaming! You see for yourself.... And your wife came and fetched me there...."

"No, no."

"Yes, she did."

"No, no, old chap."

The sick man reflected:

"I no longer know," he said, "what I've lived and what I've dreamed. The confounded snake-thing: that ... that was real. It had been eating me up ... eating me up since I was a boy...."

He grew very gloomy and sat for hours and hours, silently, in his chair ... until he sank into the downy abyss.

CHAPTER XXV

It was time that he became the old Gerrit again, bit by bit, you know, bit by bit. The weeks dragged past and the weeks became months and it was time that he became the old Gerrit again, bit by bit, you know, bit by bit. His doctor wouldn't hear yet of his resuming his service; but he saw his pals daily: the officers looked him up, fetched him for a walk; and in their company he tried to go back to his breezy, jovial tone, his rather broad jokes, all the noisy geniality which had characterized the great, yellow-haired giant that he had been. And it was all no use. He had grown thin, his cheeks were hollow, his flesh hung loosely on his bones and he was soon tired and, above all, soon giddy....

But the rottenest part of it was that he didn't remember things. No doubt he felt that, by degrees, with the diet prescribed for him, which Adeline observed so conscientiously, he would be able to strengthen his carcase a bit; he even took up his dumb-bells once, in his grief at the disappearance of those grand muscles of his; but he very soon put the heavy weights down again. Then he smacked his emaciated thighs and, despite his inner conviction, yielded to a feeling of optimism:

"Oh, well!" he thought. "That'll get right again in time!"

But the rottenest part of it was that he no longer remembered things—he was ashamed of that above all, he did not want it noticed—and that everybody noticed it. Then he would sit in a chair by the fire—it was a raw, damp January, cold without frost—and his thoughts stared out idly before him, with a thousand roaming eyes, his idle thoughts. They hung heavily in his brain, filling it, like clouds in a sky.... He would sit like that for hours, with a newspaper or an illustrated weekly: French comic picture-papers, which Van der Welcke brought him to amuse him. He hardly laughed at the jokes, only half understood them, sat reading them stupidly. And, in his turgid brain full of clouds, full of those idle thoughts, an immense, world-wide melancholy descended, a leaden twilight. The twilight descended from the sky outside and it descended from his own brain.... Then everything became chilly around him and within him; and, above all, memory was lost. Since the beast no longer held him in its clutching dragon's claws, since the thousand-legged crawling thing had devoured all his marrow with voluptuous licks, since it had perhaps sucked up his very blood: since then it had left him like an empty house, with soft muscles and flabby flesh; and he almost longed to have the beastly thing back, because the beast had given him the energy to fight against the beast: for himself, in order to conquer; for others, in order to hide himself. The beast had conquered, the beast had eaten him up. It wanted no more of him; the great dragon-worm had disappeared. It no longer wound through the skies; and nothing more hung in the skies but twilight-distilling clouds.... Oh, the creepy, chilly twilight! Oh, the all-pervading mist, dank and clammy all round him! He shivered; and the fire no longer warmed him. He crept up to it, he could have crept into it; and the glowing, open fire no longer warmed him.

"Line, ring for some wood: I want to see flames; this coke's no use to me."

Then he heaped up the logs until Adeline feared that he would set the chimney on fire.

Or else Constance would come to fetch him, wanted him to go for a walk.

"No, dear, it's too chilly for me outside."

He remained sitting in what to the others was the unendurable heat of the blazing fire. He shivered. He shivered to such an extent that he asked:

"Line, send in the children."

"But, Gerrit, they'll only tire you."

"No, no ... I'm longing to see them."

They would come in; and, when the others came home from school, he would gather them round him and try to play with them, teasing and tickling them now and again. It tired him, but they were something warm around him: more warmth radiated from a single one of them than from his glowing log-fire.

"How many have I?" he reflected, groping in his memory, which fled in front of him with winged irony.

And he counted on his fingers. He was not quite certain. Until he saw them all gathered round him and had counted them on his fingers, silently—Marie, Adèletje, Alex, Guy—he did not always remember that he had nine. The children were very sweet: Marie saw to his oatmeal, which he had to take at five in the afternoon; the cheeky boys were very attractive. But he suffered because little Gerdy, the child with such a passion for caresses, had become afraid of him. She shrank back timidly from him, thinking him strange, that thin, emaciated father whom she used to embrace in her little childish arms as a strong father, a great, big father who tossed her up in the air and caught her again and romped with her and kissed her. She had become frightened of his long, lean fingers and looked in dismay at the hands that gripped her with the fingers of a skeleton. He noticed it and no longer asked her to come to his room, now that he saw that she shuddered when she sat on his thin legs and that she disliked the big fire, which made her frown angrily and draw in her little lips. But it hurt him, though he said nothing.

But what hurt him most was ... that he did not remember things. It was as though daily the twilight deepened around him, around his soul, which shuddered in his chilly, shuddering body. One day, Constance said:

"We have good news from Nunspeet...."

But Gerrit remembered nothing about Nunspeet; still he did not wish to show it:

"Really?" he said.

Nevertheless she saw it in his blank look.

"Yes," she continued, "Ernst is a great deal better. I shall go and see him again to-morrow."

He now remembered all about Ernst and Nunspeet, but yet he was ashamed of his recent lack of memory and his hollow cheeks almost flushed....

A week later, Ernst came to see him, with Constance. He was so much improved that the doctor himself had advised him to go to the Hague for a few days; he was staying with the Van der Welckes. His hallucinations had almost vanished; and, when Gerrit saw him, it struck Gerrit that Ernst was looking better, his complexion healthier, probably through the outdoor life, his hair and beard trimmed; and his eyes were not so restless, while he himself was neatly dressed, under his sister's care.

"Well, old chap," said Gerrit, "so you've come to look me up?... That's nice of you.... I'm a bit off colour. And you...?"

"I'm much better, Gerrit."

"I'm glad of that. And those queer notions of yours: what about them?"

Ernst gave an embarrassed laugh:

"Yes," he confessed, shyly. "I did have queer notions sometimes. I don't think I have any now. But I am staying on at the doctor's. I've only come up for a day or two.... I've seen my rooms again."

"You have, have you?... And your vases?"

"Yes, my vases," said Ernst, greatly embarrassed.

"And all the voices that you used to hear, Ernst ... all the souls that used to throng round you, old chap: you don't feel them thronging now, you don't hear them any longer?"

Gerrit tried to put on his genial bellow and to poke fun at Ernst about the vases and the souls, as he used to; but it was no good. He lay back in his chair, by the big fire; and his idle thoughts stared before him.

"No," Ernst answered, quietly. "I only hear the voices now and again; and I no longer feel them thronging so much, Gerrit.... And you've been very ill, haven't you?" he added, quietly.

"Yes, old chap."

"You're getting better, eh?"

"Yes, I'm getting better now. My carcase can stand some knocking about. I'm glad you're better too...."

Constance made a sign to Ernst: he got up, good and obedient as a child. And they left Gerrit alone.

Adeline was sitting in the other room, with both doors open, because Gerrit's big fire was too much for her and also because she didn't want the children to be running in and worrying him.

"Ernst is looking well," she said, glancing up at him.

Then her hands felt for Constance' hands and she began to cry, sobbing very quietly lest Gerrit should hear.

"Hush, Adeline, hush!"

"*He* won't get better!"

"Yes, he will, he'll get quite well. Ernst is better too."

"But *he* ... he's lost all his strength ... he's so weak!..."

"He'll get well and strong again...."

"What day of the week is it, Constance?..."

"It's Sunday, Adeline.... I'm going with Ernst to Mamma's for a minute or two. How glad Mamma will be to see him!... Are you coming to Mamma's this evening, Sissy?"

Adeline shook her head:

"No," she said, "I can't. I daren't leave Gerrit alone yet...."

CHAPTER XXVI

Oh, how the twilight was gathering, oh, how it was gathering around him! It was dark now, quite dark; and the fire on the hearth was dying out in the dark, shadowy room. But what was the use of making it blaze up: did the room not always remain shiveringly cold, however much the fire might glow? What was the use of lighting lamps: was the twilight not deeper and gloomier day by day, whether it were morning or evening? Did not the pale gold of the dawn shimmer more and more vaguely through the dense mist of twilight?... A dull, apathetic, feeble man.... Had he kept his secret all his life, concealed the real condition of his body and his soul, to become like that? And yet was he not Ernst's brother? Had he not always been Ernst's brother ... though it had always seemed otherwise? Were they not of the same blood and had not they, the brothers, the same soul, the same darkened soul? Was the darkness not gathering around all of them now, the sombre twilight of their small lives?... Would the darkness one day close in upon his own pale-golden dawn: his children, who also shared the same soul?... It might be the darkness of old age as it closed in upon Mamma—he could see her as she sat—or it might be the darkness of sorrow and weariness and loneliness, as yonder, round Bertha. Were the shadows not deepening round Paul and Dorine, for all their youth?... Had it not been as a night round Ernst, even though he was now stepping out of the dark ... back into the twilight that surrounded them all?... Was it their fault or the fault of their life: the small life of small souls?... Did the twilight come from their blood, which grew poorer, or from their life, which grew smaller?... Would they never behold through the twilight—the vistas, far-reaching as the dawn, where life, when all was said, must be spacious ... and would they never strive for that? Would his children never strive for that? Would they never send forth the rays of their golden sunlight towards the greater life and would they not grow into great souls?... Would the twilight, afterwards, deepen ... and deepen ... and deepen ... around them too ... until perhaps the very great things of life came thundering and lightening unexpectedly before them, crushing them and blinding them ... because they had not learnt to see the light?...

He tried to remember thoughts of former days ... but they shot ahead, like winged ironies. He knew only that night was falling, one vast night around all the family, under the grey skies of their winter. He knew only that the light was growing dimmer and dimmer around them, until it became unillumined dusk: the dusk of age; the dusk of sorrow; the dusk of cynical selfishness; the dusk of life without living; all the heavy, sombre twilight that gathered around small souls ... until with Ernst the dusk had grown into night and the dark dream from which he was now emerging.... They called that recovering.... They thought that he would recover.... Oh, how dark and gloomy were the shadows of the twilight and how heavy was the fate that hung over their small souls, hung over them like a leaden sky, an immensity of leaden skies!...

He, yes, he would get better. It might take months yet; and then he would resume his service as a dull, decrepit old man, diseased through and through, from his childhood, under the semblance of muscular strength, until one serious illness was enough to break him and make him dull and old for all the rest of his life.... Yes, he would get better. But it would no longer be necessary to raise his voice to a roar, to make his movements rough and blunt, to make a show of strength and force and roughness; for they would now all see through the sad pretence. He would jog along through his small, shadowed life, until the shadows gathered around him ... as they were now gathering, around his mother; and ... and ... and his children would never again recognize in him their father of the old days, who used to romp with them and fill the whole house with all the rush of his healthy vitality.... It was over, over for the rest of his life....

It was over. In the room which had grown chill and dark, the black thought haunted him, that it was over. It almost made him calm, to know that it was over, that for his children, his nine—did he not remember their golden number correctly?—he could never be other than the shadow of their father of the old days.... Oh, would he never again be able to love them, to be a father to them? Could he never do that again? Must he, when cured, remain for all the rest of his life the man conquered by the beast, the man eaten up by the beast, the man broken in the contest with the dragon-beast? Was it so? Was it so?...

Why did they leave him in the cold and the dark? Shivers ran down his back—his marrowless back, his bloodless body—like a stream of ice-cold water? Why didn't they make up his fire and why didn't they light his lamp?... Did they know that nothing could give him warmth and light?

"Adeline!"

His voice sounded faint and weak. In the next room, which was now dark, nothing stirred. He rose out of his deep chair with difficulty, like an old man, groped round for the door of the other room. A feeble light still entered from outside.... There she sat, there she lay, his wife: she had fallen asleep with weariness and anxiety for him, her arms on the table, her face on her arms.... Was it his imagination, or had she really changed? He had not noticed her for weeks, since his illness, had not looked at her, though she had nursed him all the time.... Certainly he was very fond of her; but she was doing her duty as his wife. She had borne him his children and she was nursing him now that he was ill. Had he been wrong in thinking like that? Yes, perhaps it had not been right of him.... Gad, how she had changed! How different from the young, fresh face that she used to have, the little mother-girl, the little child-mother! Was it the ghostly effect of the faint light or *was* it so? Was she so pale and thin and tired ... with anxiety about him, with nursing and looking after him?... He felt his heart swelling. He had never loved her as he did now! He bent down and kissed her ... with a fonder kiss than he had ever given her. She just quivered in her sleep: she was sound asleep.... Lord, how tired she was! How pale she was, how thin! She lay broken with worry and weariness, her head in her arms....

"Adeline...."

She did not answer, she slept.... He would not wake her; he would ring for the fire and the lamp himself.... But what was the good? Lamp and fire would make things no brighter around him, now that the great twilight was descending.... Oh, the great inexorable, pitiless twilight! Would it fall around him as it had fallen around Ernst ... around whom it was now slowly clearing? Did the twilight clear again? Or would the shadows around him gradually deepen into darkness, the darkness that was now gathering around his mother? Or would it just remain dim around him, with the same wan light that glimmered around Paul and Dorine? What, what would their twilight be?...

The house was very cold and he felt chilly. Was there no fire anywhere? Where were the children? Were Marietje and Adèletje and the two boys not back from school yet?... He now heard Gerdy and Constant playing in the room downstairs—the nursery and dining-room—heard them talking together with their dear little voices.... Oh, his two sunny-haired darlings!... But Gerdy was afraid of him.... He was becoming afraid of himself.... He was no longer the man he used to be.... People now saw him as he was.... He could no longer put on that air of brute strength.... His voice had lost its blustering force....

He did not know why, but he roamed through the house.... It struck him as lonely, dreary and quiet, though the children were playing below.... He stood on the stairs and listened. What was that rushing noise in the distance? No, there was no rushing.... Yes, there was: something came rushing, from outside, to where he stood; something came rushing: a melancholy wind, like a wind out of eternity.... An immense eternity; and immense the wind that rushed out of it; and chilly and small and dreary the house; everything so small; he himself so small!... He did not know what was coming over him, but he felt frightened ... frightened, as he had sometimes felt when a child.... He was so afraid of that rushing sound that he called out:

"Adeline!... Line!..."

He waited for her to hear and answer. But she did not hear, she slept.... Then he roamed on, shuddering ... upstairs ... to his own little room.... And it was all so dreary and chill and lonely and the sound of rushing from the immense eternity outside the house was so melancholy that he sank helplessly into a chair and began to sob.... He was done for now.... He sobbed.... His great, emaciated body jolted up and down with his sobs; his lungs panted with his sobs; and, in his great, lean hands, his head sobbed, in despair....

He was done for now.... He knew now that he would not get well.... He knew now that he ought really to have died ... and that he had gone on living only because his life had gone on hanging to a thread that had not broken. Would that last thread soon break? Or would his darkened life go on for a long time—he always ill—hanging to that last thread? Would he yet be able to be a father to his children ... or would he ... on the contrary ... become ... a burden to his dear ones? Was it growing dark, was it growing dark? Was not that eternity rushing along?...

He heaved a deep sigh, amid his sobs. His eyes sought along the wall, where a rack of swords and Malay krises hung between prints of race-horses and pretty women. He had a whole collection of those weapons. Some of them had belonged to his father. At Papa's death they had been divided between him and Ernst.... Among the krises and swords were two revolvers....

He stared past the swords and krises ... and his eyes fastened on the revolvers.... In among the swords and krises, in among the race-horses and the pretty women whirled all the heads of his children—he did not know if they were portraits or spectres—as they had been, children's heads of six months, one year old, two years old: growing older and bigger, radiating more and more sunlight, his golden dawn of nine bright-haired children?... Would he be able to be a father to them, or would he on the contrary become a burden?...

It was as if his imagination were digging in a deep pit. In a deep pit his imagination, with hurrying hands, dug up sand. What was it seeking, his rooting imagination? What was it seeking in the deep pit, why was it flinging the sand around him ... just as Addie once told him that Ernst had dug and flung up sand ... in the dunes ... in the dunes at Nunspeet?... What!... What!... Was he going mad too!... Was he going mad ... like Ernst? Was he going mad ... like Ernst?... A cold sweat broke out over his chilly, shivering body. Was he going mad?...

"Gerrit!... Gerrit!"

A voice sounded very far away through the house, which had suddenly become very deep, very wide, very big.

"Gerrit!... Gerrit!"

He could hear the hurrying footsteps on the creaking stairs, but he was powerless to answer.

"Gerrit!... Gerrit!... Where are you?"

The door opened. It was Adeline, looking for him ... in the dark:

"Gerrit!... Are you here?..."

Even yet he did not answer.

"Where are you, Gerrit?"

"Here."

"Are you here?"

"Yes."

"Why are you sitting in the dark ... in the cold?... What are you doing here, Gerrit?..."

"I ... I was looking for something."

"For what?..."

"I've forgotten."

"Why didn't you ask me?"

She had lit the gas.

"You were asleep."

"Don't be angry, Gerrit. I was tired."

"I'm not angry, dear. I didn't like to disturb you."

"Why didn't you wake me?"

"You were asleep."

"You ought to have waked me."

He put out his arms to her:

"Come here, dear."

She came; he drew her to his knees.

"What is it, Gerrit?"

"Darling ... Line ... I believe I'm very ... very ill."

"You've been ill, Gerrit. You're ... you're getting better now...."

"Do you think so?..."

"Oh yes!"

"Line, I believe.... I'm very ... very ... ill."

"Why, do you feel worse?... It's so cold in here. Come downstairs. We'll make up the fire."

"No, stay here.... Tell me, Line: if I died, would you...."

"No, no, Gerrit, I can't bear it!"

"Hush, dear: if I died, would you believe ... after I am dead...."

"Oh, Gerrit, Gerrit!"

"That I have always been very fond of you...."

"Gerrit, don't!"

"That I have always been kind to you ... that I have not neglected you?..."

"Oh, you're not going to die, Gerrit!... You will get better ... and you have always, always been kind!..."

"Line ... and all our children...."

"Don't, Gerrit!"

"Won't they think ... if I die ... that I had no business to die ... because I ought to have lived and been a father to them?..."

"But, Gerrit, you're not going to die!"

"I should like to go on living, Line ... for you, dear, and for the children. But I fear I'm very ill...."

"Will you see the doctor, Gerrit?..."

"No, no.... Stay like this, quietly, for a minute, on your husband's knees.... Line, Gerdy has become frightened of me. Tell me, Line, are you also frightened of your skeleton of a husband?"

"Gerrit, Gerrit, no! Gerdy isn't frightened ... and I ... I'm not frightened...."

"Put your arms round me."

She put her arms right round him. She hugged him, warmed him against herself, while she sat upon his knees:

"I'm not frightened, Gerrit. Why should I be frightened of you? Because you've been ill, because you've grown thin? Aren't you still my husband, whom I love, whom I have always loved? Sha'n't I nurse you till you are yourself again, till you're quite well ... and strong?... Oh, Gerrit, even if it should take weeks ... months ... a year! Gerrit, what is a year? In a year's time, you will be yourself again and well ... and strong ... and then we shall be happy once more ... and then our children will grow up...."

"Yes, dear ... if only it doesn't get dark...."

"Gerrit...."

"If only it doesn't get so dark!... Do you know that it got very dark around Ernst? It's getting lighter around him now ... but there's some twilight around him still ... even now. ... Do you know that it is getting dark around Mamma ... and that it will get darker and darker?... Do you know that the twilight is closing around Bertha ... and that there's twilight around the others?... Line, darling, I'm frightened. I'm frightened ... when it gets dark. As a child, I remember, I used to be frightened ... when it grew dark.... You've lit the gas now, you see, Line.... Is there only one light burning? The flame of a gas-jet ... and yet ... and yet it's getting dark...."

"Gerrit, my Gerrit, is the fever returning? Would you like to go to bed?"

"Yes, Line, I want to go to bed.... Put your baby to bed, Line ... it's tired, it's not well. Put it to bed, Line, and tuck the nice, warm clothes round its cold back ... and promise to stay and sit with it ... till it's asleep ... till it's asleep.... Put it to bed, Line.... And, Line, if your baby ... if your baby dies ... if it dies ... will you promise never ... to think ... that it did not love you ... as much as it ought to?..."

She had gently forced him to rise from his chair and she opened the partition-door. He stood in the middle of the little room while she busied herself in the bedroom and lit the gas and then came back for him and helped him undress.

"It's getting dark ... it's getting dark," he muttered, shivering, while his teeth chattered with the cold.

And he felt that it was not the cold of fever, but a cold in his veins and his spine, because the beast had sucked all his blood and marrow with its voluptuous licks, had eaten him up from the days of his childhood, had devoured him until now, in the twilight, his soul shrank and withered in his body, which had no more sap to feed it....

"It's getting dark," he muttered.

CHAPTER XXVII

It was snowing heavily. For days the great snowflakes had been falling over the small town out of an infinite sky-land, out of infinite sky-plains of infinite snow. And, after all the gloom of the dark days that had been, the days under the grey skies of storm and rain, it was now snowing whiter and whiter out of a denser greyness of sky-plains and sky-land, flakes falling upon flakes in a soft white shroud of oblivion that enveloped houses and people. And, in that ever-falling snow from the great, grey infinity above the small town and the small people, the town seemed still smaller, with the outline of its houses now scarcely defined against the all-effacing oblivion, which fell and fell without ceasing, and the people also seemed still smaller, as they moved about the town or looked through the windows of their small houses at the white flakes descending from the grey infinity overhead.

For old Mrs. van Lowe the white days dragged on monotonously from Sunday to Sunday: only the Sunday gave her a glimpse of light; but the other days had become so white and blank, so white and blank in their twilight emptiness. Even though the children called to see her regularly, she no longer knew that they had been. It was only on Sundays that she missed them: when she did not see all of those whom she still carried in her mind gathered in her large rooms, rooms which not the largest fires now seemed able to warm, a mournful reproach swelled up in her heart; and her head nodded in sad understanding and protest against the sorrows of old age....

"But here is Ernst, Mamma, coming again as he used to," said Constance, leading Ernst by the hand to her mother.

He now came up once a week from Nunspeet, for the day, in order to reaccustom himself to all the familiar things at the Hague, to the houses and the people; and, though still a little shy, as usual, he had lost all his nervous restlessness and become quite calm.

"Ernst?" asked Mamma.

"Yes, Mamma, he is coming again as he used to."

"Has he been long away?"

"Yes, Mamma."

Light seemed to break upon the old woman and she smiled, becoming younger in her smile, now that she remembered. She took her son's hands and looked at Constance with unclouded eyes:

"Is he better now?"

"Yes, Mamma," said Constance.

"Are you better now, Ernst?"

"Yes, Mamma, I am much better."

She looked very glad, as though a flood of light were shining around her:

"Don't you hear ... any of those ... of those strange things?"

"No, Mamma," he answered, smiling gently.

"And don't you see ... don't you see any ... of those strange things?"

"No, Mamma."

"That's good."

She said it with grateful, shining eyes, the flood of light making everything very clear.

"I have been very strange, I believe," Ernst admitted, softly and shyly.

"That's all cured now, Ernst," said Constance.

"But Aunt Lot?" asked Mamma. "What's become of her ... and the girls?"

"They've gone to Java, Mamma."

"To Java?..."

"Yes, don't you remember? They came and said good-bye last week. They'll be back in twelve months.... Don't you remember? They thought they could live more cheaply in India...."

"Yes, yes, I remember," said the old woman.

"India ... I wish I could go there myself...."

She felt as if she must go there to have warmth in and around her. And yet ... Ernst was back; and at the card-tables were Karel and Cateau; Adolphine and her little tribe; Otto and Frances were there; Van der Welcke, Dorine and Paul, Addie....

"There are a good many, after all," she said to Constance. "There are a great many.... But I miss ... I miss...."

"Whom, Mamma?"

"I miss my big lad ... I miss Gerrit. Where is Gerrit?"

"He hasn't been very well lately, Mamma. I don't think he'll come."

"He's ill again...."

"Not ill, but...."

"Yes, he is, he's ill.... He's very seriously ill.... Constance...."

"What is it, Mamma?"

"You're the only one to whom I dare say it.... Constance, Gerrit is very ... very ill.... Hush ... he's ... he's dead!..."

"No, Mamma, he's not dead."

"He is dead."

"No, Mamma."

"Yes, child.... Look, don't you see, in the other room?..."

"What, Mamma?"

"That he's dead."

"No."

"What do you see in the other room then?"

"Nothing, Mamma. I see the two card-tables and Karel and Adolphine and Adolphine's two girls playing cards."

"And that light...."

"What light?"

"*All* that light: don't you see it?"

"No, Mamma."

"He's lying there ... on the floor."

"No, no, Mamma."

"Be quiet, child ... I can see it plainly!... There, now it's gone!..."

"Mamma darling!"

"Constance...."

"Yes, Mamma?..."

"Go ... go to Gerrit's house...."

"Do you want me to go to him?"

"No, no, stay here.... Constance...."

"Yes, Mamma?..."

"Send your husband ... or your son."

"Are you feeling anxious?"

"Anxious?... No. But send your husband ... or your son.... Send Addie.... If you send Addie ... that'll be best."

"Would you like him just to go ... and find out for you how Gerrit is?"

"Yes, yes."

"What's the matter with Mamma?" asked Van der Welcke.

"Isn't Mamma well?" asked Adolphine, at the card-table.

"Mamma is very restless and excited," said Van Saetzema. "Hadn't we better send for the doctor?..."

"The doctor?" they repeated, irresolutely.

"Addie," asked Dorine, "are you going to the doctor's?"

"No, I'm going to Uncle Gerrit's. Granny is uneasy. She wants to know how he is."

"Constance," whispered the old woman, with strangely luminous eyes, "it's better that you should go too."

"Addie's gone now, Mamma."

"You go too ... with your husband. You and your husband go too.... Tell the others that I am tired. Let them go away ... now ... soon. Tell the others that I am tired, dear. And tell them ... tell them...."

"Tell them what, Mamma?"

"That I am *too tired* to...."

"Yes?"

"On Sundays...."

"To have us here on Sundays, Mamma?"

"No, dear, no, don't say it.... Don't say that!... But tell them that this evening...."

"This evening?"

"Is the last time...."

"The last evening?"

"No, dear, no, not the last.... Just tell them to go away, dear ... and you go with your husband.... Has Addie gone? But you go now ... you go also ... to Gerrit's house.... And then come back here again.... I want to see you ... all three of you ... here again.... Do you understand?... All three of you ... do you understand?"

"Yes, Mamma."

"Go now ... go...."

They went; and the children took their leave.

Outside, it was snowing great flakes. The snowflakes had been falling all through the night over the small town out of an infinite land of death, out of infinite sky-plains of infinite death. And, after all the gloom of the dark nights that had been, the nights under the grey skies of storm and rain, it had snowed whiter and whiter out of the dense greyness of sky-plains and skyland, flakes falling upon flakes in a soft white shroud of oblivion that enveloped houses and people....

CHAPTER XXVIII

Outside, the snow was falling in great flakes. The parlour-maid had opened the door:

"But your cab isn't here yet, ma'am...."

"It doesn't matter. We'll walk."

"I must say, it's a little absurd of Mamma," said Van der Welcke, on the doorstep. "Must we go to Gerrit's ... in this weather? And has Addie gone too?... Was Mamma as anxious as all that?... It's snowing hard, Constance: it's enough to give one one's death, to go out in this weather...."

"Well, then you stay, Henri."

"Do you mean to go in any case?"

"Yes, Mamma wants me to."

"But it's absurd!"

"Perhaps so ... but she would like it.... And we mayn't be able to do things to please her much longer!"

"Then send the cab on to the Bankastraat, when it comes...."

"Very well, sir."

They went....

"Didn't Addie go just now?"

"Yes, a minute or two before we did."

"I don't see him."

"He walks very fast."

"Was Mamma so uneasy?"

"Yes.... She was very restless and anxious."

"Have the others gone away as well?"

"Yes, Mamma was tired.... All the same, she relies upon us ... to come back presently for a moment."

"Mamma is becoming a little exacting...."

"She's growing so old.... We may as well give her that pleasure ... of just going."

How much gentler her tone had become!...

Once, ah, once she would have flared out at him violently for less than this little difference!... Now, ah, now, how much gentler everything about her had become!...

She stumbled through the snow.

"Take care, Constance.... The pavements are slippery.... Take my arm."

"No, I can manage."

"Take my arm."

She took his arm. She slipped again; he held her up. He felt that she was trembling.

"Are you cold?"

"No."

"You've got a thick cloak on."

"I'm not cold."

"What are you so nervous about?"

"I don't know...."

"Your nerves have been all wrong for some time.... You often cry ... about nothing."

"Yes. I don't know why.... It's nothing.... It's the weather...."

"Yes ... our Dutch climate.... Now at last it's something like winter. It's freezing like anything. The snow is crisp underfoot."

She slipped again. He held her up and they walked close together, in the driving snow, which blinded them....

"I must say, it's absurd of Mamma ... to send us out in this weather...."

She did not answer: she understood that he thought it absurd. The cold took her breath away; and it seemed to her, as she kept on slipping, that they would never reach the Bankastraat.... At last they turned the corner of the Nassauplein. And she calculated: not quite ten minutes more; then a moment with Gerrit and Adeline; the cab would fetch them there; then back to Mamma's with Addie ... to set Mamma's mind at ease. And, as she reckoned it out, she grew calmer and thought, with Henri, that it was certainly rather absurd of Mamma. She planted her feet more firmly; she was now walking more briskly, still holding her husband's arm.... Was it the cold or what, that made her keep on trembling with an icy shiver?... Now, at last, they were nearing the Bankastraat and Gerrit's house; and it seemed to her as if she had been walking the whole evening through the thick, crisp snow. Suddenly, she stopped:

"Henri," she stammered.

"What?"

"I ... I daren't...."

"What daren't you?"

"I daren't ring."

"Why not?"

"I daren't go in."

"But what's the matter with you?"

"Nothing.... I'm frightened. I daren't."

"But, Constance...."

"Henri, I'm trembling all over!..."

"Are you feeling ill?"

"No ... I'm frightened...."

"Come, Constance, what are you frightened of? Now that we're there, we may as well ring. What else would you do?... Here's the house."

He rang the bell.... They waited; no one came to the door; and the snow beat in their faces.

"But there's a light," he said. "They haven't gone to bed."

"And Addie...."

"Yes, Addie must be there."

"Ring again," she said.

He rang the bell.... They waited.... The house remained silent in the driving snow; but there was a light in nearly every window.

"Oh!... Henri!"

He rang the bell.

"Oh!... Henri!" she began to sob. "I'm frightened! I'm frightened!..."

She felt as if she were sinking into the snow, into a fleecy, bottomless abyss. Her knees knocked together and he saw that she was giving way. He held her up and she fell against him almost swooning.... He rang the bell....

The door was opened. It was Addie who opened the door. They entered; Constance staggered as she went. And, in her half-swooning giddiness, she seemed to see the house full of whirling snowflakes, coming through the roof, filling the passage and the rooms; and, amid this strange snow, her son's face appeared to her as the face of a ghost, very white, with the blue flame of his big eyes....

At that moment there came from upstairs a wailing cry, a long-drawn-out shriek, uttered in an agony of despair; and that cry seemed to call to Constance out of Adeline's body through all that night of snow indoors and out.

"Mamma, Papa, hush!... Uncle Gerrit ... Uncle Gerrit is ... dead.... Uncle Gerrit has...."

It was snowing, before Constance' giddy eyes, as she went up the stairs, with her husband and her son; it was snowing wildly, a whirl of all-obliterating white; it was snowing all around her. And through it, for the second time, Adeline's long wail of despair rang out loud and shrill....

The rooms upstairs were open.... The maids ... and Marietje in her little nightgown ... were peeping round the doors, trembling.... Gerrit's little room was open ... and on the floor lay the big body, looking bigger still, stretched out like that ... and, beside it, beside the big body, on her knees, the wife ... the small, fair-haired wife.... And her wail of despair rang out for the third time.

"Adeline!"

She now looked round, flung up her arms, felt her sister's arms, Constance' arms, around her:

"He's dead! He's dead!"

"No, Adeline ... perhaps he's fainted."

"He's dead! He's dead!... He's cold ... wet ... blood ... feel!..."

She uttered a scream of horror, the small, fair-haired wife. And suddenly, drawing herself up, she looked at the sword-rack.... Yes, the missing revolver ... was clutched in his stiff hand.

Van der Welcke and Addie closed the doors. The maids were sobbing outside. But the sound of little voices came; and small fists banged at the closed door:

"Mamma! Mamma! Mamma!... Aunt Constance!"

Constance rose, giddy and fainting, not knowing whether to go or stay....

"Constance! Constance!" cried Adeline, calling her back, holding her in her arms.

"Mamma! Mamma!... Aunt Constance! Aunt Constance!"

Constance rose to her feet, made a vast effort to overcome that dizzy faintness ... and, now that the body of the small, fair-haired woman lay moaning upon the body of the dead man, she opened the door.... Was every light in the house full on? Why were the maids sobbing like that? Was it real then, was it real?... Was this Marietje, clasping her so convulsively, trembling in her little nightgown?... Were these Guy and Alex, sleepy still their gentle eyes, cheeky their little mouths?... Were these Gerdy—oh, so frightened!—and little Constant?...

"Aunt Constance, Aunt Constance!"

She overcame her dizziness, she did not faint:

"Darlings, my darlings, hush!... Hush!..."

And she led them back to their bedroom.... What could she do but embrace them, but press them to her?...

"Darlings, my darlings!..."

The wail of despair rang out once more.... Oh, she must go back to that poor woman! Oh, she had not arms enough, not lives enough!... Oh, she must multiply her life tenfold!...

"Mamma." It was Addie speaking. "The cab is here.... I'm going for Dr. Alsma. One of the maids has gone to another doctor, close by."

"Yes, dear; and then ... and then go to ... oh, go to Grandmamma's! She's expecting us! I know for certain that she's expecting us!... Stay in here, darlings, don't leave the room, promise me!... And, Addie, don't tell her ... don't tell her anything yet ... tell her ... tell her that...."

The wail of despair rang out. And there were only two of them, now that Addie was gone, there were only two of them, helpless, she and Henri, in that night of death and snow—as though death were snowing outside, as though death were snowing into the brightly-lit house, with its all-obliterating whiteness, dazzlingly light, dazzlingly white—there were only two of them....

CHAPTER XXIX

The twilight had passed away in the dazzling white light.

But yonder, in the big, dark, chilly house, the old woman sat waiting. She had sent the maids to bed and told them to put out all the lights, but she herself did not go to bed; she waited. She sat in her big, dark room, with just a candle flickering on the table beside her.

It seemed to her that she was waiting a long time. She felt very cold, though she had put her little black shawl round her shoulders. And she peered into the frowning shadow, which quivered with dancing black ghosts and with the flickering of the candle. It was a dance of ghosts, hovering silently round the room, and they seemed to have come from the distant past to haunt her, to have come out of the things of long ago, of very long ago: far-off, forgotten years of childhood and girlhood; the young man whom she had married; their long life together; their children, young around them.... Then the rise of their greatness; the rise of the white palaces in tropical climes; the glitter around them and their children of all the glittering vanity of the world.... Then the children growing up and moving farther and farther away from her.... And she saw it all looming so darkly and so menacingly in the long, dark rooms, while she sat waiting and watching by the flickering flame of the candle.

Then her old head nodded very slowly up and down, as if to say that she recognized all the things of long ago which loomed so darkly and threateningly, that there was not a ghost which she did not recognize, but that she did not understand why they all thronged round her to-night, like a vision of menace, a dance of death.... And, while she sat and wondered, it was as if each dancing phantom blacked out something of the room and the present that she still saw faintly gleaming, blacked out one outline after the other with dancing phantom after dancing phantom, until at last all was black around her ... and not only the room and the present had become black, but also the pale visions of the past: the years of childhood and girlhood; the young man whom she had married; and the children; and all the life, yonder, in the white palaces amid the tropical scenery: black, everything became black, until everything was blotted out, until the dance of all those phantoms was obliterated in shadow and the old woman, nodding her head, still sat peering into the dark, with the flickering candle beside her.

Thus she sat and waited; and, with the darkness before her, it was as if she did not see the candle, now that everything had become black. Thus she sat and waited and wondered whether many and many nights would still drag their blackness over her: how many black hours, how many black nights could the black future still drag along?... Until at last she heard a bell, clanging like a shrill alarm through the livid darkness. And mechanically—because she was waiting—she rose painfully and took her candle. Through the dark room and the dim passage she went; and the faint light went with her, so faint that she did not see it, that she just groped her way painfully through the passage and down the stairs, still holding high the candle.... The stairs seemed steep to her and she went cautiously, waiting on each step; at each step the faint light of the candle descended with her; and behind her the night accumulated with each step that she left behind her.... She had now reached the foot of the stairs; and, slowly and painfully, with the dragging tread of age, she went through the hall to the front door, whence the alarm had rung.

And her trembling hand opened the door. Addie entered:

"Granny, is that you yourself?..."

"Yes, child."

"I came, Granny dear, because Mamma said that you expected us."

"Yes."

"Were you waiting up for us, Granny?"

"Yes."

9 781406 896916